Because of
DYLAN

ERICA ALEXANDER

A NOTE FROM THE AUTHOR

It took me two years to write this book. It had not been my original intention to tell Becca's story just yet. But she hunted me down and cornered until I sat at my desk and allowed her to tell her truth.

This was not an easy book to write. I shed many tears over it and had to walk away to deal with the mounting anxiety unaccountable times.

But writing her story was also cathartic and freeing. I could not have told Becca's story without the help of dozens of mental health professionals. I owe all of you my gratitude. During these two years, I spoke with, and interviewed psychologists, therapists, social workers, psychology professors, and real life people who lived through the same hardships that Becca did. I'll forever be grateful for their candor, for letting me into their lives and talk about something that's never easy.

I also want to thank the ladies at RAINN for taking my calls and answering my many questions. I will donate a portion of the sales of this book to RAINN.ORG.

I've read many books in my search for information. I'll list them at the end as I believe that they may benefit many people.

Finally, in name of plot, I took some liberties with this story. This is fiction after all, even if I based it on some very real events. It takes time and courage to face one's fears and overcome them. I hope that in sharing Becca's story we all can learn something that moves us forward.

"Healing doesn't mean the damage never existed.
It means the damage no longer controls our life."

— Akshay Dubey

To the little kid inside all of us.
To the little kid who dared dream and make wishes
on stars, dandelions and eyelashes.

The dreams you dreamed, the wishes you made,
they were not in vain.

Find your way back.
That little kid—heart and soul full of dreams,
awaits you.

CHAPTER ONE

BECCA

ANGER PRICKS AT MY SKIN LIKE BITING ANTS, AND IT burns hotter with each bite. Anger at him and myself for not being able to say no. For the turbulence that has taken residence inside me because of him. I want to scratch myself until I get rid of this feeling of uncertainty. Of not knowing.

I push the heel of my hand into my chest, willing the gesture to dislodge my building unease. I haven't been able to think of anything else since I received the text message yesterday.

"Earth to Becca." River pokes me on the side to get my attention.

"What?" I can't hide the annoyance in my voice even though it's not her fault I'm a mess.

River gives me a look.

"I asked you the same question three times. You're ignoring me."

"Well, as much as you'd like to believe it, the world doesn't revolve around you, Miss Look-at-Me." That's not fair, and it's untrue. River never seeks attention. She just always gets it.

"Someone is in a mood today." She nudges me, making me lose my balance. I step to the side and hike my backpack up on my shoulder.

"Dude!" Irritation gets the best of me.

River gives me a sideways glance and takes a step forward in line.

She lured me here with the promise of buying me a coffee. I have one class in the Maslow building, but I find myself here often because of River. It's a good place to escape the cold weather and people-watch. The entire front of the building is made of glass windows facing the Green, where there are always people around. And because it's mirrored glass, I can watch them without being seen myself. I love this building.

Only two more people ahead of us now. I nudge her back. "Sorry. I'm grumpy. What did you ask me?"

She dismisses the apology with a wave of her hand. "About the party this Friday. Can you pick me up?"

"Yeah, sure."

"And not leave me hanging this time so you can hook up with some freshman?"

The guy in front of us tilts his head a bit, turning an ear our way. By the look of his clothes, a deep navy-blue suit, he's a professor or some other staff. I glare at River and nod my head at the guy. We stay in place when he walks up to order his coffee.

"What?" River looks at me like I have five heads. As always, she's oblivious to her surroundings and what she says around people. River has no filter. Everything that crosses her mind spills out of her mouth. Had it been anyone else, I'd think she does it on purpose.

But she doesn't. She's just that honest. She doesn't say things to hurt or embarrass. Nothing fazes her, and she thinks everyone else should be the same. But I have too many skeletons in too many closets. And there are always too many ears and eyes around for my taste.

The guy ahead of us orders his coffee, then turns and looks directly at us.

"Fuck me," I whisper under my breath. River hears me.

"You and me both. He's yummy," she whispers back. Thank goodness, this time she said it low enough he doesn't seem to catch it.

Yeah, that's hot-as-fuck Professor Dick. Tall, tanned, and beautiful—with the body of an Olympic swimmer. And my nemesis.

He walks away but not before giving me one more disapproving glance as we walk up to the counter.

"Two coffees, please." River turns to me. "Want anything to eat?"

My stomach growls, but I shake my head.

"Two coffees and two blueberry muffins. Separate bags, please." She ignores my denial and orders me food.

We watch Professor Dick's retreating form while the guy behind the Coffee Heaven kiosk gets our order ready.

I push at my chest again. A different kind of unease jabbing at me now. "He hates me."

"Who? Professor Beckett?"

"Professor Beckett for you. For me, he's Professor Dick."

She laughs.

The barista calls River's name, and I grab our coffees while she grabs the muffins. My stomach grumbles again.

River sips her coffee. "Why do you call him that? Wait! Have you seen the goods?"

"What? No! I call him Dick because his first name starts with a D, and he's a dick."

"I don't know. Everyone says he's an amazing teacher."

"Not everyone." I glare at his back, sending imaginary daggers his way. He always looks at me like I'm a bug he wants to step on.

"There's always a waitlist for his classes. I finally got in. I'm taking his class in the spring."

"Ugh."

"What makes you think he hates you?"

I've never told River this story. "He caught me making out with a guy in his classroom," I mumble behind the coffee cup.

"What? He caught you having sex in his classroom!" She leans into me, her face inches away. Thank God she whispered the words.

"No! Just kissing. But we were really into it, and apparently it took Beckett a while to get our attention."

"He had to yell at you?"

"Technically, he had to tap our shoulders and pull us apart." I cringe.

"Damn."

"Yeah …"

"Holy crap." Her eyes widen.

"I know."

"I'm jealous." She says this with a sigh.

"Jealous? Of one of the most embarrassing moments of my life?"

"Well … I want mind-bending-reality-forgetting kisses too."

I stop at that. My mouth open while I stare at my best friend.

"Dude. You can have anyone you want. Every guy on campus has the hots for you. And I dare guess about a quarter of the female population too." At first, I thought being friends with the most beautiful girl on campus would be detrimental to me. But when I'm with River, I become invisible. And that's exactly how I like it.

She points at me with her coffee-holding hand. "And look at you. You're beautiful, but you don't let anyone in. Guys look at you, but you can be as prickly as a porcupine, and you never ever have a problem finding someone to take home."

She points at herself. "They don't want me. They want this." She waves a hand. "All they see is the shell. No guy ever tries to get to know me. And the girls, well, they get catty and see me as competition. Being beautiful"—she makes air quotes with her fingers when she says beautiful, coffee sloshing a little over the side—"isn't all it's cracked up to be."

A touch of hurt tinges her words. Is River as lonely as I am? Despite having her family's love and support? I guess we're both cursed in a way. River by her looks and me by my past.

Beauty fades. But the past? The past never goes away.

CHAPTER TWO

DYLAN

THAT FAMILIAR TINGLE HITS ME FIRST. THEN HER NAME, spoken out loud, confirms what I already know.

Becca.

Thousands of students.

Hundreds of employees.

A dozen different spots to get coffee, and yet she stands behind me.

I don't have to look. I always know when she's near. It starts with a shiver on the back of my head.

That awareness that shouldn't be.

CHAPTER THREE

BECCA

Perhaps meeting in a public place wasn't my best idea. I want to get up, flip the table and run. The urge to rage, scream, and throw things, burns into my chest like a wildfire begging to turn the world into ashes. Instead, my fingers tightly grip the coffee mug until my knuckles turn white. My gaze zeros in on the cracked, black nail polish on my thumb. I can't evade this any longer. I chose to meet him and hear what he has to say. Avoiding looking into the eyes of the man sitting across from me, into a face so much like my own, won't make meeting my father for the first time any easier.

I school my face, drag in a breath, inhaling the ever-present scent of coffee and sugar at Pat's Café, and glance at him. He doesn't look much older than me—in the right clothes, he could easily pass for a grad student. I take in the cut of his gray suit jacket. Not designer, but not cheap, either.

His hands wrap around his coffee mug. A few calluses and a scratch or two. The hands of someone who's not afraid of manual labor.

I drag my gaze upward and finally meet his eyes. His eyes

are my eyes—the same amber-green color. Do they change colors with his moods like mine do?

"Why now?" The question has been needling me since he first texted three days ago.

"Because it took me this long to grow some balls." He laughs, but there's no humor behind it. He covers his mouth as if regretting the ill-timed laugh, then runs a hand through his hair. The same honey-blond as mine. His stare is intense, as if trying to encompass all the missing years at the same time.

"I have regretted not being in your life a thousand times over. I know that nothing can make up for twenty years of lost time—"

"Twenty-two years. It's been twenty-two fricking years!" The words spill out of me uninvited, and I bite my tongue to keep the rage in. I swallow a lifetime of anger. It burns going down.

He flinches, his gaze drops to the table as he gives a small nod.

"I deserve that. I'm sorry. I can't go back, I can't change what happened—"

"What do you want from me?"

His mouth opens and closes again, as if looking for the right words to say. "I want to get to know you. I want you to know me too."

He waits for an answer, like I waited for him my entire life. I say nothing. The seconds stretch into a full minute of silence. I rejoice in his discomfort. His shoulders sag a little more with each moment until he finally recognizes I'm not going to make this easy for him, and he speaks again.

"I know I'm too late, and you don't need me in your life, but I hope you'll make room for me. Please?"

I almost get up and leave. Now? Now he wants to be a father?

"You're right. I don't need you. I don't need anyone."

Expect nothing and you'll never be disappointed. But a small, quiet voice inside my head reminds me of all the times I hoped my dad would come and take me away from the messy house and the empty fridge. I'm not a little girl anymore. So, why do I still carry that kid's hope inside me?

Because you never stopped hoping.

The voice whispers, a neutral outside observer who watches all but never judges. It shakes me to my core.

My lips press together, resentment tasting bitter on my tongue.

And yet, I hope.

I hate hope. I hate how hopeless hope makes me feel. Like the proverbial dangling carrot. Always out of reach. Fuck hope. And fuck him for awakening the glimmer again. He waits for an answer that will not come.

His chest expands under a heavy breath, then pauses. His eyes never waver from mine. "Becca—there have been too many secrets and lies, and I don't want to hide behind secrets and lies anymore. You deserve better."

He takes another breath as if buying time before bearing unpleasant news. "I loved your mother, but not enough to stay." His cheeks redden, and he won't look at me now.

What about me? Couldn't he have stayed for me?

"Your mother was seventeen, and I had just turned eighteen. We were dirt poor, and I was fresh out of high school. I enlisted in the military as soon as I graduated. It was my ticket out. I didn't know she was pregnant until after I left. And she said—" He runs a hand over his face. "She said she wasn't keeping the baby. As soon as I got my first paycheck, I sent her some money to help with the abortion."

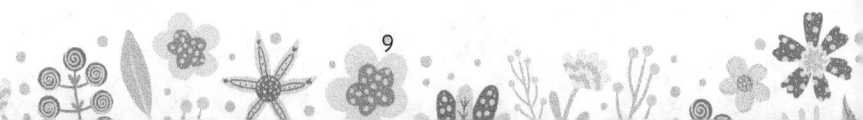

He flinches. "I'm sorry. I didn't mean to say it like that." His voice rises and cracks a little.

I dismiss his apology with a shrug as if the hurtful words don't matter. But his words sting like salt on a never-healed wound. Echoes from the past reach out to me with cold bony fingers, scratching at my chest and squeezing my heart, and I'm hit with every backhanded blow, every push and shove, every unwelcome touch, every hurtful word all at once. The weight of it all pushes into my shoulders and makes me want to fold in half again and again until I disappear.

"It's nothing I haven't heard before." I make a "go on" gesture, but it doesn't hide my defensive tone.

I've lost count of the many times my mother told me she should have aborted me or tossed me in the trash. Or the times she kicked me out of the house, only to beg my forgiveness hours later. Her rejection was branded on my skin just as much as the physical blows. But none of it hurt as much as when she turned her back on me when I needed her protection most. That pain rushes back in now, pushing aside my anger. I'm choking on the bitter taste of it all over again. It sours in my stomach, knots my throat, coats my lips.

"When did you find out about me?" My voice trembles, matching the erratic cadence of my heart. I hate myself for this small display of weakness.

I hook both feet under the chair legs, anchor myself to it, square my shoulders and push down the knot in my throat. Allow the anger in again. Rekindle the flames. Anger is a far better companion than self-pity. I'm a mess of conflicting emotions, forced out of balance as if the ground is shaking underneath my feet.

He takes a sip of coffee, and I remember the cup I hold in a death grip. I will my fingers to relax, but my body rebels, tensing with the effort to stay grounded.

"About seven years later. I ran into an old high school friend, and he mentioned your mother and her kid. I realized then that she had kept you. I looked her up and called her." He shakes his head, then looks around the room. I follow his gaze. His eyes fix on a man sitting with a young child. The man is cutting pancakes into bite-sizes for his kid. Another reminder of what I never had.

His gaze cuts away from them. He looks down. Does the image of that father and his child hurt him as much as it hurts me?

"Your mother said she had a boyfriend and didn't want me coming around." His fingers draw invisible lines on the table. "I asked to meet you, but she refused." He glances back at me, blinks a few times. His voice lowers. "She said she told you I was dead and seeing me would mess with your head."

I look into my cup. "She lied."

"What?" He leans into the table and tilts his head to the side. I didn't intend to say the words out loud. They were no more than a whisper, but looking into his face I know he heard me.

"She never said you were dead. She said you didn't care, that you didn't love me." I say this casually, as if the words don't add fuel to the flames.

"Becca—"

"Go on." I dismiss the coming excuse with a wave. "It's not like you cared enough to even try."

He sighs as if the weight of the world rests on his shoulders. "I was not in a good place when I came home. I didn't think I had the right to come into your life and mess it up, so I agreed to stay away. I had recently left the army and was trying to adjust to civilian life. But eventually I got a great job and grew with the company. I sent her a check every month. Still do. I know money is a poor substitute for a real father, but I did what I thought was best. I regret that decision." He speaks quietly, but his leg bounces under the table, betraying his calm speech.

"I hope." His voice shakes. He looks away and back at me. "I hope you can forgive me."

My heart speeds up with each word that spills out of his mouth until I'm lightheaded. I take a sip of my now lukewarm coffee, and it sours on my tongue. I push the mug away but snatch it back so I have something to hold on to.

I never saw a cent of that money. It certainly wasn't used to put food on the table or clothes on my back. My mother drank it away, or it was taken by one of the losers she called her boyfriend.

How different my life could have been if he'd been around. The thought rips at my chest and claws inside of me. But I left that life behind and vowed to never look back. I created an alternative version of myself. A new school, a new state, new friends, a perfect GPA—and yet none of it is enough of a barrier. The past catches up with me again and again. I'm so tired of running, of lying to myself, and everyone I know. I'm a farce. A lie. A parody of a carefree girl.

I'm hurting. Broken. This is eating me alive. I have no place to go, nowhere left to hide, and the one person who could have made a difference sits across from me asking for forgiveness.

I laugh and stuff the pain under a thick coat of fuck-yous and I-don't-cares.

I stand up and push away from the table, the chair dragging on the floor with a metallic screech. The sound sharp in my years.

"My forgiveness won't change the past." I turn away from

his pleading gaze. I can feel it burning holes in my back and trying to reach my heart, but no such luck. I killed the little bastard years ago.

I take three steps before he calls my name.

"Becca?"

I hesitate, stop, glance over my shoulder.

He's standing now. "No, you're right. Forgiveness can't change the past. But it could change the future."

His words hold my feet captive under the weight of their truth. I swallow hard, force my body to turn and walk away. But I can still feel the weight of his hopeful gaze on me all the way back to the dorm.

CHAPTER FOUR

BECCA

"W E'RE STICKING TOGETHER TONIGHT, RIGHT?" R IVER leans down to speak into my ear. She's a few inches taller than me, and that's without the boots she's wearing right now.

I nod and salute her with my red cup.

"Be right back." She walks away toward the bathroom at the back of the house.

I don't want to be here. My mind can't stop racing and playing the meeting with my father again and again. It's been three days, and I thought of little else. I promised River we would stick together tonight, but the pressure building inside me needs an escape. I need a distraction. My usual distraction comes in the form of either a hookup or alcohol. I take a sip of beer. Ugh. Warm. I stare at the red cup in my hand. I don't really want a beer. Alcohol clearly isn't going to cut it tonight.

I drag in a deep breath. Colossal mistake. The air is stale and heavy as it fills my lungs. The walls are closing in on me. I need to get out.

I try to move around the dancing and mingling people. Familiar faces litter the crowded space. I don't want to see them.

I'm in search of fresh faces, and I'm bound to find a few freshmen in any of the campus parties. It's the first Friday of classes, which means a party at every frat and sorority house on campus. It's a Riggins tradition.

I push the heel of my hand into my chest as if I could dislodge the increasing anxiety with the rubbing motion. I don't want to think about my father and the life I left behind. I need to get out of here. I head down the hall. Where is River? I can't find her, but I find something better. This is what I need. A distraction.

A blue-eyed freshman leans on the wall and takes turns between looking around and staring at his phone. He's trying to act cool and fit in, but his darting eyes and stiff shoulders betray him. He's nervous. He wants out of here as much as I do.

The weight in my chest gets lighter with each step I take to him. The rush of taking charge, of being the one to choose, gives me the control I crave. It pushes aside the pressure in my solar plexus. I'm a thousand pounds lighter by the time I'm close enough to touch him.

I lean into him and speak loudly enough for him to hear me over the music and the chatter of dozens of people crammed into the frat house living room.

"Hi. You look a little lost. Freshman?"

He's quick to smile. "That obvious, huh?"

"You seem a bit out of place." I tap my red cup to his in salute. "Welcome to Riggins University."

He's beautiful, in a boyish Captain America-minus-all-the-muscles way.

"I'm Becca." I hold my hand out to him.

"Tommy." He hurries to move his cup to the left hand, and fumbles, spilling some liquid over his fingers. "Sorry." He wipes his hand on his jeans before shaking mine.

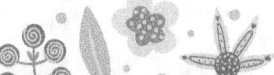

I like him. He's sweet. Perhaps too nice. I don't want to hurt him or string him along. I just need to get lost for a while. A part of me wants to retreat and let this boy go. But the other part, the part that needs a distraction, wants this. My hands are sweaty, and I cross my arms, drying a hand against the fabric of my sleeve. I hold on to the red cup tighter as not to drop it.

"Do I make you nervous?" I'm unsettled—like I'm on the verge of something big. My heart beats erratically.

"No." He shakes his head. "I don't like crowds." He blushes, his cheeks turning pink, and he clears his throat before taking a sip of his drink.

I almost change my mind, but he gave me a perfect opening.

"Want to get out of here?" I throw the overused line at him.

"Sure." He nods, hair falls over his eyes, making him look even younger.

I set my cup on the nearest flat surface, already littered with empty and half-full cups. He follows suit and trails behind me. I grab my phone to text River.

I look at him over my shoulder. "Anyone you have to say goodbye to?"

"Nope, came alone. Don't really know anyone here."

I text as we pick our way out of the crowded space, the loud thumping of an obnoxious Kanye West song gradually getting softer as we move away from the speakers and make our way to the door.

Becca: Bailing.

River: Dude!

Becca: Sorry.

> River: You said you wouldn't hook up with anyone tonight. I left you alone for five minutes!

> Becca: I know I suck. But Skye can pick you up, right?

> River: You do suck. Yes. I'll call her. Be careful.

> Becca: Always am.

> River: Ha! I call BS on that.

> Becca: I'm the worst best friend ever.

I add a sad face emoji and a heart. River replies with two emojis.

A kissing face and a peach. *Kiss my ass.*

Laughter bubbles up. And guilt. I promised River I'd stay with her. It weighs on my chest, but nowhere near as much as how I felt before.

I'm so relieved to be leaving the party, I can't make it out of the house fast enough. I need this. I need to numb the pain. And this beautiful boy next to me is my drug of choice.

He follows me out of the house and down the sidewalk.

"My car is over there." I point to the ten-year-old Toyota across the street. I shiver. It's too early in the season to be this cold. Heck, it's not even fall yet.

Tommy notices. His jacket is off and over my shoulders in seconds.

"Your momma taught you right." I nudge him with my elbow.

His face drops a little, he smiles, but it doesn't reach his eyes. He shrugs and follows me to the car.

"You okay to drive?"

"Yeah, I didn't really drink."

We don't talk during the few minutes it takes to get to my dorm. Despite the chilly night, the streets are busy.

"Lots of people out tonight." Tommy watches out the window.

"Yeah, it's tradition for every Greek house to host a party the first Friday back on campus for the fall semester. They have an unspoken competition for who's hosting the best back-to-school party. And tomorrow all of them will claim to be the winner. A lot of people party-hop from one place to another. It's easier to walk than drive for most of them."

I park in the lot behind my building and hesitate in the car for a second. Do I really want to do this? Tommy looks at me and smiles. A genuine smile this time. It eases me.

"Ready?"

He nods, and we get out of the car. I make a beeline to the door and the heat inside. Tommy trails behind me.

"I'm on the third floor," I say as we get into the elevator. We're silent on the way up and as we walk in the hall. The dorm is eerily quiet. I guess everyone is out and partying. My heart skips a beat when I get to my room. He looks so sweet and innocent. I don't know if I'm doing the right thing. Do I really want this? Another guy I don't care about? A temporary fix to my emptiness?

I unlock my door with the keycard and push it open, gesturing for him to go in first. I follow him in, close the door and lean on it with my hands behind my back. Tommy looks around. There's not much. I haven't troubled to make the room mine. Why bother? It's all temporary.

I try to see what he sees. The faded blue walls and windows facing the campus Green. There's a twin bed tucked against one wall with a gray comforter and an extra blanket on the foot of the bed. A small black and gray area rug takes up most of the free floor space. On the opposite wall there's a desk, my four-year-old laptop, a lamp. The door to the small closet which holds all my possessions. The only personal touch is a poster of a sunny beach with sugar-white sand in stark contrast with the turquoise water and clear blue sky and the words *Turks and Caicos* written in white across the top. I found it in the trash outside a travel agency.

"It's cool you have a single. I'm sharing a dorm room with two guys. They snore so loud I have to wear earplugs to bed every night, which means I don't hear the alarm on my phone. I was late to class twice already, and it's only the first week of school." His face pinks.

If he notices the bare setup, he doesn't show it.

"Yeah, seniors and juniors have the option for singles. They say the room assignment is done through a lottery. But I have my suspicions. Every person I know in a single room has a perfect or near perfect GPA. I think it's more of a reward system."

"That must mean you're smart, then."

I shrug. I work hard for my grades. If I were really that smart, though, I would have figured my shit out already. But I'm the same mess now that I was nearly four years ago when I left home and never looked back.

His eyes are intent on me, and suddenly, he looks much older than I imagine him to be. There's too much knowing in his eyes. As if he's lived more years than indicated on his birth certificate.

Tommy tilts his head, his eyes locked on mine. "Why me?" Hands in his jeans pockets, he waits for me to answer.

My heart speeds up with each second his eyes stay on mine.

I don't have the power to look away. He's so honest in the way he gazes at me, so completely open and the opposite of everything I am.

"What do you mean?" I feign ignorance, but the lie heats my cheeks. I know exactly what he's asking me.

"Of all the guys at that party checking you out, older and more experienced, why did you pick me?"

No one has ever asked me that before. I always make the first move, and they follow along. For a moment, I'm at a loss for words. It's not like I can tell him the truth.

"How old are you?"

"Eighteen. You?"

"Older than you," I hedge. I don't know why I don't tell him the truth. I never lied about my age before. Well … that's not true either. Damn it!

He takes a step closer to me, hands in pockets still. "You haven't answered my question yet."

I don't want to lie to him.

"You're cute and sweet. I liked you as soon as I saw you." And there's something familiar about him. Something I'm drawn to.

The words don't have the effect I expected. Flattery usually wins them over and feeds the ego well enough that the guy stops thinking about me and ponders his own greatness.

He doesn't smile or puff up with pride like every other guy I've been with and paid a compliment.

He runs a hand through his hair. "No, that's not it. I mean, I know I'm easy on the eyes, but there were a dozen other guys at that party much better looking than me. I'm not complaining, I didn't expect to leave that party with someone."

I'm surprised again by his response. Even as he says he knows he's good looking, he's not cocky. He watches me as if trying to read me. I cross my arms, my defenses coming up. I'm about to tell him to leave, but he stops me with a gesture of his hand.

"I like you too." He waves his hand between us. "But this liking each other—it feels like the beginning of a beautiful friendship. And I'd hate to mess it up with a meaningless hookup."

For the third time in as many minutes he surprises me. And I surprise myself as well. I expected to feel rejection, but instead I'm relieved. I smile, and for the first time in a long time, there's a flutter of lightness inside me. Before I can say anything else, he speaks again.

"I could use a friend more than a hookup. In case you didn't notice, I'm a little on the introvert side, and it would be cool to have a friend who can help me find my way around campus."

I like that. I like that a lot. This may not be the distraction I set out to get, but maybe, just maybe, this is even better. His friendship offer cracks a tiny fissure in my armor, but instead of scaring me, it gives me a little more room to breathe.

He gives me his hand to shake. "Let's start over. I'm Tommy. Do you want to watch a movie and eat junk food?"

I laugh. A real laugh. "All right, Tommy. Friends it is. I'm Becca. Nice to meet you." I shake his hand as I introduce myself to him for the second time tonight.

A smile lights up his face. "Now that we got that out of the way, what kind of chips do you have?"

I reach under my bed for the large plastic box where I keep my junk food and snacks handy. Open the container and survey my bounty. Tommy peers into the plastic tote and points at the salt and vinegar potato chips bag. My favorite. I knew I liked him.

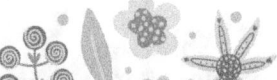

A bag of chips, two cans of soda, a whole sleeve of chocolate chip cookies, and two hours later, we finish watching *The Breakfast Club*. That's another first. I have never had a guy pick that movie to watch with me. It's usually some mindless action movie, or they ask if I'm into porn.

That would be a negative.

"Okay, Tommy, I hate to kick you out, but I need to catch some Z's. Which dorm you at?"

"The building next door. Room 203."

A new neighbor and friend, and all in the space of a few hours. My senior year may be starting on a different track.

"Can we exchange numbers?" His blue eyes widen, hopeful and eager, like a puppy in a shelter hoping this will be his chance. His tone hints at loneliness and a fear of rejection. And even if I don't want to admit it, the same thing hammers inside my chest.

"Yeah, sure." I unlock my phone and give it to him. He does the same and hands me his phone.

I have a new friend. And it feels good.

CHAPTER FIVE

BECCA

"Make a wish."

I stop and look at the dandelion puff Tommy is holding inches away from my face. I can't help the smile or the flood of memories that come with the simple gesture.

As a kid, I had only one wish. For my father to come and find me. I wished on anything and everything a kid could wish on—dandelions, stars, eyelashes. I even made up a few of my own. Any time I saw the same three numbers lined up in a row, be it on the clock or a license plate, I made a wish. And it finally came true. It's here. I should have set a time limit. Given the universe a deadline. Fucking universe and its loopholes. My eyes shoot to the sky, and I send out a *fuck you, fuck you very much* note of thanks.

"Where did you find it?" I look around the concrete sidewalk. Tommy points to a crack on the curb where a dandelion grows.

"Come on, make a wish." He smiles at me. I have the urge to ruffle his hair and give him a hug. If I had a younger brother, this is what it might have been like. Having a sibling would have eased some of my loneliness growing up, but I'm glad I was an only child. I'd hate to have anyone else live through the hell my life had been until I left for college. Having siblings would have meant leaving them behind, and I don't know if I would have been able to do that.

"I don't know what to wish for." I tuck a lock of hair behind my ear.

"Close your eyes and clear your mind. It will come to you." He nods at me. "Come on. You can do it."

I do as he says. Close my eyes, breathe in, clear my mind. I wish … and then it comes to me. What I truly have been wishing for all along. I want to be loved. I want someone to know me—all of me—and love me anyway.

I open my eyes, look at the dandelion, and blow. The tiny seeds swirl between us for a few seconds before catching in the breeze and floating away.

Tommy smiles, takes a step closer to the curb and gently puts the dandelion stem next to the plant he picked it from, his lips moving silently as he does so. Most people would probably drop the stem to the ground.

"What did you just do? Did you say something to the dandelion?" I point at the weed growing through the crack on the curb.

His cheeks pink a little. "When I was little, I felt bad for picking dandelions. I thought it would hurt them. I know they're weeds and a nuisance for most people. But I loved the bright yellow flowers." He puts his hands in his pockets, and we continue walking.

He speaks again. "My mom used to say that dandelions trade wishes for the chance to fly away and create new life. So when I picked a dandelion, I was helping it fulfill its destiny."

I have to stop moving to completely absorb what Tommy said. *Dandelions trade wishes for the chance to fly away and create new life.* "That's beautiful. I love that. Your mom is a wise woman."

His smile fades.

He shrugs. "So, to get back to your question, I was saying thank you, for the wishes, and for the trade."

I look back in the direction we came from. The dandelion puff is long gone in the wind, but I send it a silent thank-you anyway.

We walk without speaking the rest of the way to Pat's Café where we order two coffees and a doughnut for Tommy. I introduced Tommy to Pat a couple of days ago, and she's already taken him under her wing. I'm grateful for that. Like always, her gaze stays on me a little too long when I walk in, but she never looks at me with disapproval or judgment or makes me feel bad. I know she wants to say something, but she respects my walls. I'd hate to have to find another place to hang out when I need to feel welcome.

We take a seat. "You're on your own tonight. I won't be home."

Tommy's hung out with me in my dorm room nearly every night this week, and I'm growing used to having him around. Being with Tommy helps me keep any thoughts of my father at bay. Dad texted a few times, but I have yet to respond. A small, vengeful part of me rejoices in his attempts and my rejection, but the shallow joy is short-lived. Part of growing up and being in control of my life is also having the courage to confront the things I don't want to.

"You're going to a party?" He takes a huge bite of his doughnut.

"Kind of. It's my friend River's twenty-first birthday, we're having a girls' night out."

"Sounds fun. Where are you going?"

I hesitate. "We're going to Skins."

He stops mid-bite. "Isn't that a strip club?"

"Yes. They're having a *Magic Mike* night. And no, I don't make a habit of frequenting strip clubs, but tonight they're hosting an all-male show, and I thought it would be something different to do." I got tickets for River and her sister, but River said Skye is on an actual date with a hot cop. Good for her. Skye could use a little spice in her life.

He grins. "I have a few dollar bills if you want to borrow some money."

I ball up my napkin and throw it at him. He ducks and laughs.

I catch Pat looking at me. I know she notices my hair. I'll need to touch up my roots soon since the honey-blond roots are showing. I've been dyeing it darker since I was sixteen. Even if it's a temporary color, the brown makes me feel less like myself, and the less I am me, the better I feel.

I walk into Skins, and my stomach rolls. The stink of stale beer and cigarette smoke mingles with the scent of whatever cleaner they use on the floors, and it suffocates me. It smells like broken dreams and hopelessness, forcing old memories to come to mind and creating a time machine of misery I have to remind myself I'm no longer that girl at the mercy of a drunk man who always smelled of alcohol and cigarettes. My chest tightens. I should have known better than to come to a seedy place like this.

I'll need a drink if I'm to stay here for another couple of hours.

I make my way to the bar and get a shot of José Cuervo. José is an old friend that I was first introduced to at the tender age of twelve by one of my mother's many boyfriends. I lift the glass and silently toast the now-dead loser my mother brought home to live with us. One of many, but the worst by far. I hope he's rotting in hell.

River finds me as I finish downing my first shot. I slam the glass down.

She raises an eyebrow. "Starting early?"

"Never too early for José." I smile big and slip into my well-crafted happy-girl persona. I wear it like a shield. No one questions happy people. River sits on the stool next to mine. Her eyes linger on me, and I know she has more to say.

"Happy birthday, best friend. Welcome to the age of legal drinking!" I hug River, and whatever she was about to say is lost in the moment. I don't give her a chance to try again. "Let's find the girls." I grab her hand and pull her along behind me until we find the table I reserved for tonight where two of our friends are already sitting.

Our tiny table, not meant for holding more than a few drinks, is front and center, acting as a poor barrier between us and the stage. River takes a seat, and I follow, sitting across from Sabrina and Juliana. They're a couple, but it's not widely known. They surprised me by wanting to come along when I mentioned my plans for River's birthday. They said they liked dick, just not the men attached to it.

That cracked me up. I can totally understand what they mean even if we don't play for the same team.

A waitress arrives right after we're settled with the pitcher of sangria I ordered at the bar.

River uses the wooden spoon and plucks out an apple chunk. "Yummy, but I'm not drinking tonight. I have to drive. I'm adulting." She shouts to be heard over the music pumping through dozens of speakers and the voices of a hundred other excited women.

River rolls her shoulders as if trying to shake something off. She looks around the semi-darkened room. I follow her gaze. She's spotting all the EXIT signs. She seems as uncomfortable as I feel. I want to escape too, already regretting tonight's choice of entertainment.

I'm about to suggest we go somewhere else when the lights blink and dim even more. The women around us whoop and scream louder. A single spotlight illuminates the stage, revealing a guy wearing very low-cut jeans and no shirt. He's huge and muscular. My stomach clenches, but not in the way one might expect when faced with such a beautifully sculpted body. All I see when I look at him is someone who could easily overpower me. I see *his* face. Theodore. My mother's boyfriend. The thought of him sends pangs of revulsion through me. One of my legs begins bouncing incessantly. I gnash my teeth, breathing in and choking on the heavy air. I close my eyes and grip my knees. Squeeze until my fingernails bite into my skin through my jeans' fabric. The small pain grounds me, gives me something else to focus on.

The guy on the stage is still talking. Listing all the rules of what we can and can't do. No worries there. I have no intention of getting any closer to these guys. This Magic Mike thing looked way more fun in the movies.

I want another shot, but I won't. I need to keep my wits about me. I reach for the sangria pitcher and fill my glass with mostly fruit. It looks full, but it's probably less than a third of actual liquid. I sip and try to look like I'm enjoying myself. River looks at me and reaches out to squeeze my hand. The lights go out completely, and the music grows louder. The sound of *Pony* by Ginuwine reverberates off the walls and thumps inside my chest.

The screams, the excitement, the loud music, the smells, the lights—it's all too much. I squeeze my eyes shut and swallow down the bile rising in my throat. My heart runs miles inside my chest as if it could replace my feet and escape on its own. Too late now.

The room is closing in on me. I find a spot on the floor and try to concentrate on it, blocking everything else out. It's not working.

I can't do this. I have to get out of here. This was a stupid idea. I'll excuse myself and hide in the bathroom until it's over. Like old times. Like when I locked myself in the bathroom and hid from *him*.

But I don't have a chance to escape.

Eight men fill the stage. Eight huge men. They're all dressed in very low-hanging jeans and white T-shirts. Muscles bulging everywhere. Skin glistening under the spotlights. I swallow again. Take a deep breath, but instead of clean, calming air, all I get is a stronger dose of the cigarettes, sweat, and alcohol, even more nauseating as it mingles with the perfume and heat of over a hundred overly excited women.

The men continue to dance in a choreography of simulated sex. In sync, they rip all their shirts off and fall to the ground. Their movements pick up with the beat of the song. The screams get louder. The pants go next. Easily ripped and dropped to the ground. Golden strips of fabric barely cover their groins. A nervous twitch breaks through my panicked, frozen state. I try to distract myself by thinking about those pants and what are they made of that they can so easily be ripped away. My face heats up, and sweat breaks out on my brow. I probably look like all the other desperate, lonely, and under-sexed women in here.

I'm having a panic attack and on the verge of hysteria—run, run, run, hide, hide, hide—the words play on repeat in my mind like a mantra. But I'm frozen in place. I can't move a muscle except for the small gasps of air I force myself to suck in through my mouth.

Amid all the excitement, no one can tell. No one but River, that is. Her brows furrow, and she reaches out to me, a tentative hand on my shoulder. I squeeze my eyes shut to hold in the tears. Force more air into my lungs. Hold my breath. Count to ten. Release. Do it again. And again. I open my eyes, and River is watching me, not the men dancing a few yards away. The men who begin to jump off the stage and walk up to the screaming women who grab at them eagerly.

Dizziness overcomes me. I'm so sickened by the entire thing that I don't notice when one of them approaches me until I feel the presence of a body inches away from me. The smell of sweat and weed slaps me in the face.

I flashback to a scene I'd give anything to erase from my mind—*the hot breath on my face, the stink of cigarettes and cheap alcohol. His weight pressing down on me, stealing my childhood*—my entire body shudders in rejection of the memory, streaming across my mind like a reel of film. My stomach rebels and turns inside out. The nausea and bile can no longer be contained. It rises up my throat, ready to purge the memories along with the contents of my stomach. I bend forward, into the gyrating hips of the dancer in front of me, and I puke all over him.

He jumps back with a curse and steps away from me,

disappearing into the dark hall next to the stage. I stay in place, paralyzed under the weight of the past and what just happened. My face burns, sweat beads on my hairline. River grabs me by the shoulders and gently pulls me up. We step around the mess, and she walks me toward the back where the bathrooms are located. The dimmed lights hide our exit. If Sabrina and Juliana noticed anything wrong, they don't say. I don't dare look at them.

We walk into the bathroom and I blink at the too bright lights. My heartbeat is steadier now that we left the noise and men behind. River's holding me still. She stops halfway into the bathroom. "Stall or sink?"

"Sink. I think I'm done puking."

We veer right, and she turns the faucet and holds my long hair back so it doesn't get wet.

I cup my hands under the water and rinse my mouth until the taste of regret fades away.

River hands me a few paper towels.

"How much did you have to drink?"

"Five shots," I lie. The falsehood easily slips out. Lies and secrets have been my companions for far too long. They're second nature now.

She narrows her eyes at me, arms crossed over her chest, and I notice a purple silk scarf I've never seen her wear before. It must be new. My mind locks on that minor detail. It's a trick I learned long ago. Pay attention to something else, focus your entire being on it. For a few seconds or even minutes. However long it takes me to ground myself again.

River is about to say something else when the bathroom door opens, and a woman walks in and into a stall. We're no

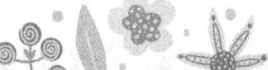

31

longer alone, and the silence between us is like a thick fog as we wait and stare at each other.

The woman leaves the bathroom without washing her hands. Nasty.

River opens her clutch and out comes a package of Tic-Tacs. The cinnamon kind. I empty half of them into my palm and put them all in my mouth. There's an explosion of flavor as it burns my tongue.

"I'm sorry. I fucked up your birthday."

She dismisses my apology with a headshake. "I worry about you, Becca. What's going on?"

"Boy trouble," I lie again. There are no boys. My mind flashes to Tommy, but he's no trouble. Tommy is a little spot of sunshine in my life. He's kind and uncomplicated. And unlike every other guy, he's not trying to use me or get anything from me. Other than my salt and vinegar potato chips.

Her shoulders drop, and she uncrosses her arms. I know her well enough to know this is River letting go of the inquisition she wants to unleash on me. For now, at least.

"What do you want to do?" Her voice is low, even though we're alone now.

"I don't want to go back out there again," I gesture at the door. "You can go back. But I'm going home."

She scoffs at me. "As if."

River does her best imitation of Cher in Clueless. We watched the movie a few nights ago. I laugh. A genuine laugh this time.

"Leave your car here. I'll drive you and tuck you in."

"Yes, Mom." I try for sarcasm, but my voice cracks a little when I say Mom.

River squeezes my arm. "I love you, you know that, right?

And I don't know what's going on with you, but whatever it is, I'd never judge you because of it. You can tell me anything."

She has been more insistent with her questions lately.

"It's a two-way street, River. Feel free to open up about what's eating at you any time."

That shuts her up.

CHAPTER SIX

BECCA

"I don't know why you put up with me. I'm not a good friend." I squeeze the phone between my ear and shoulder and grab a rag to clean the already clean bar top.

"This again? Yes, you are. I don't need someone to hold my hand, Becca. I need someone who gives me space but is always there when I need them. That's you."

I sigh. River is a much better friend than I'll ever be. "I'm sorry about ruining your birthday."

"Pfffff. That was ages ago. And you didn't ruin it. I'm still here. Still twenty-one, and we can go out again any time we want."

"It was three days ago, and instead of celebrating your birthday, you dragged my ass to my dorm and watched over me all night. So no, that was not a good birthday celebration at all. I owe you a proper celebration."

"It's my turn to do laundry at home. Come over and do the laundry, and we'll call it even." She chuckles. River is not really the domestic type.

"In your dreams. Hold on." I put the phone down and take an order before grabbing the phone again.

"Sorry. Had a customer."

"You're at work? Sorry. You should have said something. I won't bother you."

"No bother. The place is dead. There's like five people here. It's never busy on Tuesday nights."

"So … what's going on with your new boy-toy? You've been together for what? Ten days now? Is this one going to stick?"

I roll my eyes. "Tommy is just a friend. I told you that already."

"Yeah, but you two spend so much time together. I thought he was working his way into your pants."

"Nothing to work on. I like the kid. He's nice."

"You don't do nice."

I pause. True. She's right. I don't do nice. So what?

"He's different."

"In my experience guys always, always want something. They're never in it just to be nice or friends," River says, and I can almost see her twirling a long strand of hair in her fingers.

"That's because you look like a freaking supermodel. Can't blame them for going stupid every time they see you."

"Ugh." River rejects all mentions of her good looks like I reject any notions of nice guys and love. Except for Tommy.

"I'll let you get back to work. Don't want you to get in trouble."

"Nah, you can't get me in trouble in this hole-in-the-wall. Gus doesn't have anyone else to take over the bar. I call the shots, and he doesn't care."

"Okay, boss lady, if you say so. But I'm tired. Going to bed. See you tomorrow?"

"Sure. Meet you for coffee in the morning."

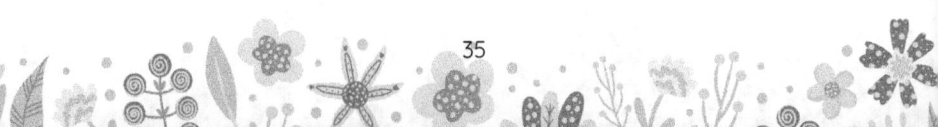

"Bye." She hangs up with a yawn, and I pocket my phone.

River may not believe Tommy is just a friend and not a future boy-toy, but that's okay. I like the kid. It feels like having a younger brother. I know it's crazy, but I feel somewhat responsible for him. I enjoy having someone to talk to who doesn't try to get into either my brain or my pants. I can let my guard down around him.

I snatch a dirty shot glass from the bar and put it upside down in the dishwasher tray before going back to wiping the counters. When was the last time I had a drink? River's birthday? And I haven't hooked up with anyone since … meeting Tommy.

Wow. I didn't even miss it. Being around Tommy calms the constant churning in my chest. I don't feel the need to always be on the move or to be a step ahead of everything I left behind. Why? I don't have any romantic feelings for him. Is this because he's a break in my routine?

No. It's more than that. I care about him, and I care about what he thinks—what he thinks about me. The idea of disappointing him disturbs me.

My phone buzzes in the back pocket of my jeans. I toss the rag I'm using to clean the counter into a bucket filled with cleaning solution, and wash and dry my hands before picking up my phone.

Tommy: Hey, you working tonight?

It's like Tommy knows I'm thinking of him.

Becca: Yep. Till midnight.

Tommy: Mind if I stop by?

Becca: It's a free country.

Tommy: I was thinking of bringing my brother with me.

Becca: You have a brother?

That's what I get for not asking personal questions. How much does Tommy know about me? Less than I know about him for sure. When you ask those kinds of questions you open up the floor for them to ask them back. Then the lies and evasion start, and Tommy deserves better than that. But even thinking about opening up to him, or anyone else, puts a vise around my chest that makes it hard to breathe.

Tommy: Yes. I never told you about him?

Becca: Duh, no. If you had, I wouldn't be asking, would I?

Tommy: LOL. We'll stop by. I think you'll like him. He's a nice guy.

My somewhat rude words never faze him.

Becca: Whatever you say, Tommy boy.

Tommy: See you in a few.

I look at the time on my phone. Eleven PM.

Three locals sit at one end of the long and scarred dark, wood bar top. They're here nearly every night, always in the same spot. I swear those stools are the exact reverse shape of their asses. They're in their late forties or early fifties, and based on their conversations and bitching about their wives, they come here to escape the nagging they get at home.

They try to pull me into their conversations, asking for my opinion on this or that or to settle an argument, and I play my part well. Smile, serve their beers ice cold, replenish the bowls of stale pretzels with more stale pretzels, but for the most part I try to stay out of their conversations. They're harmless. But this is my job, I'm not here to socialize.

It's only me tending the bar right now. The owner, Gus, is out back. He keeps out of the way most of the time, which works just fine for me. The lights around the aged room are dimmed, not for ambience, but to hide the dirt and neglect that has accumulated over decades of not updating the space or not caring enough about it. And because Gus is a cheap bastard who likes to cut corners everywhere he can. But he doesn't get on my back or demand much of me, and I don't have to share the tips with anyone. Also, he doesn't expect me to be warm and fuzzy to the customers.

The only thing Gus really asks of me is to wear a black T-shirt with the bar name and logo. The word Players, with two dice hanging from the letter Y. I have no idea why. The only game in the place is darts. The board sits on the back wall, and every time someone goes to the bathroom, they risk getting hit by a flying dart. The whole setup is a lawsuit waiting to happen.

"Becca?" One of the regulars calls me, and I step up to their corner. Their glasses are half full still, so this is not a call for a refill.

"You're a woman. We're trying to understand. Our wives are always so cranky. Why do women get like that?"

It's his fourth beer of the night, and Joe is the smallest of them, no more than one hundred thirty-five pounds on his skinny frame. The alcohol makes his words slur a bit.

I lean into my side of the counter, like I'm about to share a secret. All three of them lean closer to me. Their attention is on my face, expectant, hopeful even. As if I alone hold the Holy Grail answer they're looking for.

"Let me ask you a question first, Joe."

He nods, eager.

"When was the last time you gave your wife an orgasm?"

His mouth opens and closes in a perfect imitation of a fish. No sounds come out, but I half expect air bubbles to float out of it. The other men snicker.

"And the same question goes for both of you." I point at his two friends. "You want to know why your wives are cranky all the time? Maybe it's because they haven't gotten laid properly in years."

The snickers stop, and all three of them avert their gazes.

"If you spent half of the time you waste here every night bullshitting and complaining about your women on actually paying attention to them, I guarantee they would not be cranky."

I lower my voice, lean in a few inches more. Their eyes are back on me.

"You want a happy woman at home? Fuck her. Fuck her often, and fuck her well."

"Now, it's not as easy as you say. What if she doesn't want to be fu"—his words stumble—"made love to?" This question comes from Arnold, the more outspoken of the three.

"Would you want to make love to yourself?" I ask, making quotes motions with my fingers when I say make love. "Switch places with your wife for a second. Would you be receptive and eager if the roles were reversed?"

He says nothing.

"Go home and think back to the time when you first met. What did you do? How did you win her over? You already know what to do. You did it before. The problem is not that she's cranky or that you're too tired. The problem is that you're taking your wives for granted. And start appreciating them as women and individuals. Stop seeing them as extensions of you or your kids. Win them over again."

The three of them look at each other and, as if by mutual agreement, push their unfinished beers away and stand up. Bills drop on the counter. More than enough to cover their bar tab three times over.

"Keep the change," they say.

They leave the bar with brighter eyes than when they walked in, and they stand a little taller as they walk across the room. I know it won't be as simple as that, but's it's a start. I smile to myself while closing their tab and pocketing the very generous tip. The extra money will go straight into my savings. Every penny I save adds more distance between me and my old life. I'll never be that hungry or scared again.

"Move over, Doctor Phil. Here comes Doctor Becca."

I glance up, a smile already on my face as I recognize Tommy's voice. I grab a glass and fill it with ice and Coke and place it in front of him.

Then I notice the man sitting next to Tommy. He's judging me. Even though his handsome face is schooled into a neutral expression, I can pick up the clues. I have lived my entire life under the judgment and scrutiny of others. There's always a tell. They always think they're so good at hiding how they feel. But I'm better at reading them.

His eyes narrow on me, his jaw tenses. He casually drapes an arm over his brother's shoulders as if protecting him from me and pulls him a little closer.

Professor Dick.

Tommy's brother is Professor Dick.

His gaze is like a slap in the face. A sucker punch you can't anticipate.

The universe has a sick sense of humor. Just when I met someone I like and want to be friends with, I get a reminder I'm not good enough.

The professor's eyes are fixed on me—ice and fire. He wants to freeze me out and burn me alive at the same time. It hits me in the chest. The coldness and the burn. Professor Dick's dislike and disdain slithers across the space between us like an invisible snake ready to pounce.

I take a minuscule step back and stop myself. I will not allow this judgmental asshole to make me feel like less than I am. I put on my imaginary armor, forcing myself to raise an eyebrow in defiance, step closer to the bar top and lean in. I look at Tommy with a real smile on my lips.

Now that I see the two side by side, the similarities are undeniable. Tommy's brother is taller, bigger, with wider shoulders and more muscles. His hair is shorter, and he's sporting a scruff I know won't be there in the morning. Every time I run into him on campus, he's clean-shaven. His attire is also different from what I'm used to seeing. He's wearing jeans and a Henley instead of the slacks and button-down shirts he usually wears at Riggins. Also gone are the glasses, and without them his eyes are brighter, the color more vivid. That's one thing he doesn't have in common with Tommy. No baby blues for the professor. His eyes are whiskey colored, and I'm a little drunk gazing into them.

"Becca, this is my brother, Dylan. Dylan, this is my new friend, Becca Jones."

Dylan … well, that puts an end to the mystery. I know him as Professor Beckett. The nameplate on his office door says D.

Beckett, and in my head I've always called him Professor Dick. A little snicker escapes my lips at the thought.

As if he can read my mind, his eyes narrow further, hiding the beautiful amber color under a slash of dark eyebrows.

"You know each other?" Tommy asks. His curious glance bouncing between the professor and me.

"Yes."

"No," I say at the same time.

Tommy laughs. "Which is it? Yes or no?"

"I have run into Miss Jones a few times."

"But, we have never been formally introduced, and I'm not in any of his classes," I clarify.

"Yes, I guess ethics is not something you're interested in."

His dig hurts, but it goes unnoticed by Tommy. I know he's not referring to his class. This is a reminder of the time he caught me making out with Lucas in his then-empty classroom. It's not like we were naked. It was just kissing. But after that, every time I ran into him, he gave me a dirty look. And I run into him often because River's in a classroom next to his, and I often meet her there after class.

"What can I get you, professor?"

He takes his sweet time answering. His gaze takes me in, staying on my breasts an extra second. He's discreet, but I caught him. I guess Professor Dick has some not-so-ethical issues of his own.

"I'll take a Dos Equis."

"Lime?"

"Please."

It's all so polite and aloof, but underneath the surface, in the two feet of space between us, there's a silent war waging.

I slam the beer bottle on the bar top harder than I intend, and, even with the lime on top, some of it slushes over. A few drops fall on the back of my hand, and, on instinct, I lick it. Professor Dick's eyes track the movement like a heat-seeking missile.

I curl my lip. He's too big. Too tall. Too beautiful. Too much of an ass. And yet my stomach doesn't revolt, my throat doesn't clench. The need to run and hide is not there. I want to dig into this revelation, analyze and understand it, dissect it like a bug under a microscope, cut it down into tiny bits until there's nothing left. Doesn't matter ... as attractive as he is, he's still Professor Dick.

I tend to what few customers I have and go around the bar, cleaning tables. The night is winding down. Another thirty minutes and I can leave. Gus always comes back exactly five minutes before midnight and shoos away whatever stragglers are still around. He pays me in cash for the night, plus the tips I have already pocketed. It's not exactly legal, but I prefer it this way. Cash can't be tracked the way paychecks can. He gives me extra when we don't have a busboy to clean the tables. Lucky for me, tonight is one of those nights. Every dollar counts.

I make my way back to the brothers as Tommy gets up and walks toward the restroom.

I look at the nearly empty bottle sitting in front of Dylan. "Last call. Want another one? If so, you gotta get it now, we're closing soon."

He shakes his head. "I'm driving. One is enough."

I'm sure he can handle more than one beer, but who am I to question him?

"What are you doing with my brother?" His fingers play with the etched label on the bottle. If it were a paper label, it would clearly be in shreds by now.

"Nothing, he's a friend." For once, I can say that about a guy I picked up at a party and be truthful. It's been a few weeks since that night, and nothing has happened between Tommy and me.

"I know all too well how friendly you can get." His voice is disdainful. Sharp.

Jesus! Asshole much? He saw me kissing one guy. How dare he make a judgment about me like that?

Heat flares in my chest. "You're a dick." The words are out before I can stop myself. I don't care if he's a professor and can get me in trouble. It's the truth. He's being a dick. I call it like I see it.

"That shouldn't be a problem for you, then."

I tilt my head, still staring at him. Did he imply I like dick? For real? The urge to throw something at him is so overwhelming I fist my hands until I feel my nails dig painfully into my palms.

His fingers tap the scarred wood top. "I want you to leave my brother alone. Do I make myself clear?"

"You talk like I'm some kind of predator."

"Aren't you?"

The question is a spear through my heart. I'm not a predator. I'm not a pervert. I have never been with anyone under eighteen. Not even when I was under eighteen myself. I'm the furthest thing from it. I hate anyone who preys on kids with an intensity that scares me. I don't prey on kids. I'd kick anyone's ass who tried the crap that was done to me.

"You don't know me. We've never even had a conversation before—"

His voice lowers. "I know enough. I've seen enough. I've heard enough. Tommy is a sweet kid. Sweet and naïve."

I grip the edge of the counter. Fingernails digging into the wood. "We're both adults, and Tommy can make his own decisions."

He leans into the bar top, eliminating the space between us to mere inches. "I don't want him to get hurt or catch an STI. Stay away from my brother."

The fuck? He just about called me a whore. I know Tommy is sweet. That's exactly why I like him. That and the fact that he's one of a few guys who treats me with respect. Who talks to me like he cares. I'm not giving up on him. Not that easily. I ignore the not so veiled insult.

"And if I don't?"

He stretches to his full height and looms over me, puffing his chest out, causing his shirt to strain over his shoulders. He shoves his barstool aside, and its legs screech across the linoleum. He leans across the bar top, hands holding his weight, and stops like he's loath to get too close to me.

"I wouldn't try me if I were you." His gaze is so cold I have to hold back a shiver.

I don't have a chance to respond as Tommy comes back then.

"What's going on? You're leaving now?" Tommy asks, oblivious to the tension.

Professor Dick's demeanor does a one-eighty. He leans against the wood, smiles and wraps an arm around his brother, tucking him into his chest. The smile transforms his face and illuminates the entire space around me.

I'm unsettled by the warmth and love in that smile. It tugs at something in my heart I thought was long dead. And for the briefest of moments, I'm filled with envy and jealousy that anyone could be loved that much when I never was. But as quick as the feeling comes over me, I kick it to the curb.

Self-pity never helped anyone. I have never allowed myself to feel sorry for the life I had, and I'm not about to start now. Especially not because of him. Professor Dick can kiss my ass. I will not be intimidated into losing one of the few good things in my life.

The professor squeezes Tommy's shoulder. "Ready to go? They're about to close. I'll drop you off at your dorm."

Tommy looks at his brother. "You sure? That's out of your way."

Before either of them can say anything, I speak up. "I can drive Tommy. His dorm is right next to mine."

Tommy smiles. The professor glares at me.

"That's okay. I wouldn't want to impose." Professor Dick tries to gain the upper hand.

"Oh, it's no trouble at all, professor. I've taken Tommy home many times before. It won't be the first time." I give him my sweetest smile. "Or the last." I blink twice, feigning complete innocence.

Tommy laughs, still unaware of the silent battle he's in between. God bless his naïve little heart.

"You can call him Dylan. Professor makes him sound like an old guy, and he's only twenty-eight."

Dylan stiffens, as if even that bit of information about him is something he prefers to keep a secret.

"Twenty-eight? Isn't that young to be a professor?" He looks his age. I don't even know why I'm asking this.

"Right?" Tommy socks his brother on the arm. "Overachiever. He took college classes all through high school, graduated college at twenty, started his PhD while working as a TA, and then became Assistant Professor. He's done with the PhD now and got his tenure in record time. He's the youngest Associate Professor at Riggins."

Professor Dick looks down, color tints his cheeks. "Tommy." The single word an admonition. "She's not interested in my bio."

I am. I'm very interested in his bio. "Impressive, professor. Or should I say … Dylan?" His name sounds strange on my lips.

He stares and says nothing.

"I promise to take excellent care of Tommy. He'll be in expert hands." I show him my hands and wiggle my fingers at him.

Gus comes in then and calls out his five-minute warning. The last couple of people sitting around get up to settle their tab, and Dylan has no other option but to relent. Either that or make an ass of himself. Which I bet he's not in the habit of doing.

The way the professor looks at me tells me there will be hell to pay for my little stunt. Of that, I'm sure. I'm kind of looking forward to it. What does that say about me?

CHAPTER SEVEN

DYLAN

I'm an asshole. What the fuck is wrong with me?

CHAPTER EIGHT

BECCA

I SHOULD BE HAPPY RIGHT NOW. HALLOWEEN IS MY favorite holiday. But here I am at this party. Sans Tommy. Bet his brother said something to him. Fuck the professor and his ethics bullshit. Where's the ethics in judging someone you don't even know?

Asshole.

Dick.

Of all the people on campus, why did Tommy have to be related to him?

Last night's meeting with Professor Dick was still fanning the flames of anger in my chest. I want to hit something. Preferably the Dick himself. Punch him right in the face. Or the dick. Yes, punch Professor Dick in the dick. I do a little stepping and punching like Rocky and get a *"you're weird"* glare from a group of girls. Screw them too.

I make my way to the kitchen in the back of the house and find the line for the keg. Some random dude offers me a beer. I decline. "Thanks. But I always get my beer straight from the

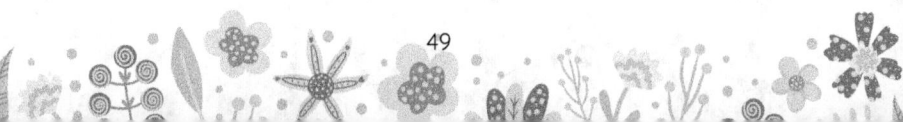

keg." It's the safest way to get a drink. He shrugs and walks away, drinking from the cup he tried to give me.

I get in line for the keg and check my costume while I wait, making sure to align my dollar store cat ears, confirm the tail is still attached to the back of my black leggings and tug down at my black crop shirt. Everything is in place.

When it's my turn, the guy manning the keg looks me up and down with a lascivious smile on his face.

"Helloooo, pussycat," he slurs, putting emphasis on pussy.

I ignore his attempts to get my attention and help myself to the beer.

"Ah, don't play hard to get. Come here, pussycat. I got some catnip for you."

I make the mistake of glancing over my shoulder at him.

"Right here," he says, grabbing his crotch before nearly falling over laughing at his own stupid joke.

I make my way back to the living room, looking for a familiar and friendly face. I see many familiar faces, but friendly, not so much.

My own fault for mistrusting everyone and keeping them at bay.

I miss Tommy.

> Becca: Happy Halloween! You're missing a great party.

Nothing. When I texted him earlier and asked if he wanted to come to this party with me, he said he couldn't. He was busy. No other explanation.

> Becca: What are you up to?

Usually Tommy texts me nonstop.

"Becca!" My name is barely audible over the loud music. *Closer* by The Chainsmokers plays in the background. I turn around looking for whoever is calling me and see River across the room. She's sauntering my way, dressed like a sexy cheerleader and holding a red cup high above her head. People part for her, like Moses at the Red Sea. River draws both envious glares and lusty gazes, but she's oblivious to all of it.

"Hey, beauty." I tap her cup with mine once she's next to me.

She rolls her eyes at me and pinches my arm.

"Ouch!" I complain, but she didn't really hurt me. She hates when I call her that.

"That's aversion therapy for you. Every time you say something like that, I'm going to pinch you. I'll be your human rubber band."

I rub the spot. "You're alone?"

"Nope. Skye and her boyfriend are here. They're hanging out back by the fire pit."

"Wow, who managed that small miracle? Skye at a party? Was it you or her new guy?"

"It was a joint effort." She takes a sip of her drink, glancing around. This is something I have noticed River doing a lot lately whenever we're at a party. She's checking out faces, like she's looking for someone.

"Who are you looking for?"

"No one." Her eyes are back on me. "Just looking. Some new faces today."

"Yeah …"

"You look distracted." River fixes a quizzical gaze on me. Tommy's absence in getting to me. "There are always new faces in the beginning of the school year, transfers and freshmen." I wave my hand around, stating the obvious, and some of my beer spills over.

River takes the cup from me and puts both our drinks on a window ledge. She's going to rip me a new one about excessive drinking. I know it.

I'm rescued by a tap on my shoulder, and when I turn, my friend Lucas is there with a big smile on his handsome face. He picks me up and squeezes me in a bear hug before setting me back on my feet with a loud kiss on my cheek.

I can't help but smile when I see him. Lucas is the kind of guy everyone loves.

"Hey, you. How was your summer?" I ask him.

"It was awesome. Went on vacation with the family, had a lot of fun with my sisters. You?"

"Same old. Worked some, took a summer class, slept a lot."

Lucas, my sweet boy. He's the only hookup I'm friends with.

River narrows her eyes at the way his hand grips my hip and slides up to my waist to tug me into another hug, kissing my temple this time.

He extends a hand to River. "Hey, I'm Lucas, nice to meet you."

"Ugh. Sorry, I have no manners. This is my BFF River. River, this is Lucas, an … old friend. It's odd you guys never met before."

They shake hands, and River has a million questions flashing in her eyes. It won't be long before they all come spilling out. She thinks I'm dating Tommy. She met him a few times when he's joined us for lunch. The familiarity with which Lucas holds me close to him and touches me signals the intimate way we know each other. And right now River has a WTF look on her face. She knows I don't cheat. I may have had a lot of hookups, but two-timing has never been my thing.

River has met a few of the guys I've dated. Most of the time, I'm over them and moving on before she meets them, but Lucas lasted the longest, and he's a good friend. Now that I think about it, it's odd that River and Lucas never crossed paths.

"How's everything?" I ask him.

He knows what I mean. When we met last year, it was right after his high school girlfriend dumped him, saying they both needed to have the chance to meet other people. It hurt Lucas badly, and it's taken him a long time to get over her. For months, he hoped she'd come back to him, but she didn't. And, since she also attends Riggins, Lucas has been forced to see her hooking up with different guys at parties. She really took the whole meeting-new-people idea to the extreme.

Lucas gives me a huge smile and raises a hand for a high five. "One hundred percent. I'm cured."

"For reals?" I ask as my hand meets his.

"For reals."

It took him almost a year to get over his ex. And I know he went through a lot of girls to do it. He literally had to fuck her out of his system by fucking everyone else.

"Oh, fuck!" River ducks as if hiding.

"What's the matter?"

"Just saw someone I never expected to see at Riggins. I gotta talk to my sister. Be right back."

She disappears into the crowd. I turn back to Lucas, and his eyes are on a girl coming down the stairs on the opposite side of the room.

"Someone you know?" I bump into his shoulder.

"Yes. That, right there," he says waving to the girl. "Is the reason I know I'm one hundred percent cured."

My eyebrows rise. "Tell me more."

"Meet for lunch next week?"

"Yes, call me?"

"Sure thing," he calls out, his back to me as he makes his way to the girl at the bottom of the stairs.

I'm alone again. I lean against the wall. My phone is burning a hole in my pocket with the need to text Tommy. I don't fight it.

> Becca: Are you mad at me?

> Tommy: …

Dots appear and disappear. The screen goes black, and I tap it. This goes on for minutes until there are no dots and no response. He saw my text. He thought about a reply, but he chose not to.

My chest aches, and the back of my eyes burn.

River is back. She nudges me with her elbow, and I drop the phone. "Oops. Sorry." She picks it up before I can react. She gives me the phone, the screen facing up. "Hey, what's with the texting? Tommy ghost you?"

Tears fill my eyes, and I suck in a deep breath. It hurts more than I imagined possible.

I. Will. Not. Cry.

River steps in front of me and bends to look me in the eye. "You're upset. Sorry. It was a joke. What's happened?"

And in this moment, I hate Professor Dick with all the fury I've harbored for years. It doesn't matter that Tommy's brother is not guilty of any of the things that happened to me. I blame him for all of it.

"This is all Professor Dick's fault. He's the reason Tommy's not here. He's the reason Tommy won't respond to my texts. It's all his fault!"

The people closest to us turn and stare, a few more move away and whisper to one another.

River's brows shoot up, and she touches my arm. "Wow. Back up a bit. Start from the beginning."

I pocket my phone and grab my cup from the ledge. Drink it. Then grab River's beer and drink that too before she can stop me. I stare at the empty cup. It won't be empty much longer. "I need something stronger."

I walk to the kitchen with River at my heels. The same asshole is manning the keg. I veer around the douchebag and make my way to the hard liquor sitting behind him. Never mind beer. This day calls for something stronger. I grab the first thing my hand lands on and tilt it into my cup, filling it halfway before River grabs the bottle from me. I walk away, clutching the cup to my chest like a lifesaver. River shadows me.

I didn't even see what the label on the bottle said, but the liquid in my cup is amber colored, like Professor Dick's eyes. I take a gulp and welcome the unfamiliar taste. It burns going down. Hits the spot in seconds. Soothing. Numbing. I enjoy this … this welcoming nothingness.

"Dude, slow down. What's going on?" River tries to take the cup away from me, but I pull back.

"I haven't gotten drunk in two months. I'm celebrating!" I lift my arms in salute.

River's shoulders drop. She presses her lips together.

"Don't look at me like that. I'm not even drunk yet. Not completely." I drain the cup. It burns going down.

I turn back to the kitchen, going for a refill on whatever that was.

River latches on to my arm. "I don't think so. Give me your keys."

I glare at her.

She says nothing, just puts her hand out. I fish into my pocket and give her my car keys. She pushes me toward a loveseat and gives the guy occupying it a killer smile. His face lights up at the attention. Poor sucker. He won't get lucky tonight. Not with River anyway. She's on a men-strike.

"Hi. Can you let my friend sit there for five minutes? I'll be right back."

The dude trips over himself, trying to make room for me.

Then she whisper-shouts, "Don't let her leave, please?"

"Sure," he answers with hearts in his eyes.

Dude stands there, watching over me like I'm a lost puppy, and he's eager for the reward he'll get when my owner comes back. River is back in less than five minutes.

"Can I get your number?" He leans in, tapping his phone.

She touches his arm and pouts. "Sorry, but I'm not really dating right now. Thank you so much for monitoring my friend, though. I have to take her home now."

She kisses him on the cheek. He smiles, not even mad. Bet he'll be jerking off to that innocent kiss for years to come.

CHAPTER NINE

BECCA

I PEER THROUGH THE WINDOW AND SMILE. BEING HERE, surrounded by these babies, always calms me down. I find Baby Jay in his incubator and wave even though I know he can't see or hear me from the other side of the NICU glass.

"Be right back, sweetheart."

I walk to the cleaning station to wash my hands and get a gown. My phone buzzes in my pocket. River.

"Hey," I whisper.

"Hi. Are you all recovered from Halloween?"

"I sure hope so. It's been two days, and I wasn't that drunk. You cut me off before I could do any real damage."

She snorts. "Why are you whispering?"

"I'm at the hospital."

"What?" Her voice is alarmed.

"With the babies." If sound could have an eye roll, my tone would have it.

"Oh, yes. It's Friday. I always forget about that. How's the cuddling today?"

"Haven't started yet. Need to prep before I go in."

"You still have baby Rose?"

"No, she went home with her parents three weeks ago."

"I don't know how I could do what you do. I'd fall in love with every baby and try to take them all home."

"I know, it was harder in the beginning, but you learn to let go. Having the babies go home is the goal. Plus, they're not stray puppies. They have families who love them …" I hesitate, thinking of Baby Jay. "For the most part anyway."

"What do you mean?" River asks.

"I have this new NAS baby."

"NAS baby?"

"Yeah, NAS stands for neonatal abstinence syndrome."

"Like a crack baby?"

Ugh. "I hate that term." These babies didn't choose to be born with an addition. "Yes. He was born addicted to heroin."

"Oh my God. That's horrible. How do they know? The mother said something?"

"The mom abandoned him in a firehouse. We don't know who she is."

"I can't imagine doing such a thing."

"He is lucky the mother left him in a safe place. Many don't get that chance."

"What's his name? How old is he? Do you have a picture?" River rapid-fires the questions, one after the other.

"He came in as baby John Doe. I can't stand calling him that, so I've been calling him Baby Jay. He's three weeks old, but he shouldn't be born yet. He's a preemie. They figured he was under thirty weeks when he was born. And no pictures. It's not allowed."

"Aw," she coos. "Again, I have no idea how you do that."

"I don't know. I can't say you get used to it because you don't. I've been coming here for three years every single Friday, and it both breaks my heart and heals my soul every single time." The truth of what I said weighs into my chest. I swallow.

"You amaze me."

I laugh. "I love being a baby cuddler."

"I know you do. Call me when you're done. Maybe we can do something this weekend."

"Sure. I'll be in touch. Bye."

I turn my phone off, put my things in the locker, then wash my hands before putting on a disposable gown, cap, and shoe coverings. I can't wait to hold Baby Jay. When I get to his incubator, sleepy eyes blink at me, tiny fists raised, skin so thin and pink, I can see the veins beneath. He's shaking. His little mouth opening and closing without making a sound. It's a terrifying thing to watch. I pick him up and cuddle him to my chest, and the shakes from his heroin withdrawal subside. His little body relaxes against mine.

"Hey there, sweetheart. How are you today?"

Baby Jay mewls in response.

I look around for a free rocking chair to sit in. Nancy, the senior NICU nurse, waves at me. I move Baby Jay from my shoulder to the cradle of my arm and settle in a rocking chair.

"Oh, look. Nancy has a bottle all ready for you. Are you hungry?"

"You're his favorite, you know?" Nancy hands me the bottle.

I smile. "He's my favorite too, aren't you, Baby Jay?" I touch his little mouth with the bottle, and he latches on.

Nancy smiles at me. "We'll miss you when you graduate and move away."

What? I'm shocked into silence for a moment. Graduation

is six months away, and I haven't thought much about what I'll do when the time comes. Stay on campus for a grad program or try to find my own place while I work and go to school. I didn't think of having to give up my volunteer time at the hospital. Nancy waits for a response.

"I don't know what I'll do. I hope to stay close enough to still come by."

"You're not going back home, then?"

Home. I know what the word means. I know its definition. But I don't experience the warm and fuzzies most people do when they think of home.

"No. Not planning on leaving. This is my home." I know she thinks I'm referencing the state or the town, but I'm not. This hospital, my dorm room, spending time with River, that's my home. I don't want to leave any of it behind.

"I hope you can still come by then. God knows these babies need all the love and help they can get."

"I love them."

"I know." She touches my shoulder. "And they love you back."

I feel a connection to these babies. A part of my soul speaks to them, and they speak back to me. From the outside it may look like these babies are the ones getting all the help and love. But that's not true. Not for me. I get so much more than I put in. I'm in debt to them. These babies don't judge me. They make me feel clean and worthy of love too.

Nancy walks away to tend to the other babies, and I'm left with Baby Jay and my thoughts.

I can let my guard down inside the NICU. No one here is trying to hurt me or use me. Watching the babies thrive and get stronger reminds me I can do the same. If such tiny creatures, so completely dependent on the care and kindness of others, can learn to heal and grow and overcome all the odds stacked against them, so can I. One day I will learn to do it as well.

The bottle is empty in a matter of minutes. I put Jay on my shoulder and pat his back. The strength of his belch betrays his size and makes me giggle.

I pace the open area and sing, quietly at first, but Baby Jay likes when I sing louder, and he demands I raise my voice with a series of squeals and gurgles that make me laugh.

"Okay, little boss. I'll sing louder for you. What would you like to listen to today?"

The first few notes of Parson James, *Only You*, rise in a hum, and I sway with Baby Jay. Words take form in song as I interject Baby Jay into the lyrics.

I dance with my little partner and sing, my eyes closed, my heart open, pouring all my love into the tiny being in my arms. A song turns into two, three and many more until a light tap on my shoulder gets my attention.

"Your time is up, Becca." Before I'm ready for it to end, my two hours of volunteer work for this week are over. The nurse smiles at me in a way I imagine a loving mother would. I inhale Jay's sweet baby scent, nuzzle his downy head. The nurse takes the sleeping baby out of my arms. He makes a sound of protest, but stays asleep.

I leave the NICU and the hospital and drive away in silence, trying to hold on to the feel of Baby Jay on my chest. But it dissipates with each mile I put between us until there's nothing but the sweet ache of the memory.

I turn my phone on when I return to Riggins and find a text message from my father. I haven't named his contact on my

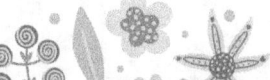

phone, so it still shows *unknown*. But I know it's him. I tap my passcode and open Messenger.

> Unknown: Hi. Can we meet? Have lunch, maybe?
>
> Unknown: Please.

I tap the number and add his name to my contacts. A name I have known for years but never even spoke out loud before. It's surreal.

"Robert Anderson," I whisper to myself.

> Becca: Okay. Tomorrow, at noon. Pick a place, I'll meet you there.

His reply is immediate.

> Robert: Thank you. Is The Griller, okay?

He names a burger place ten minutes away from campus.

> Becca: Yes. See you tomorrow.

> Robert: Thank you, Becca.

I stare at my phone until the screen goes dark, then find my way to class. It will be a long day. I have a shift at the bar tonight and still have to finish a paper for my Monday class.

My thoughts drift to Tommy again. And his evil brother, Professor Dick, who has occupied a ridiculous amount of time in my mind since that night at the bar. There's an empty spot in my chest, and it aches. I miss Tommy.

I'm lost in thought as I follow the throng of students walking down the hall in the Maslow building.

"Miss Jones."

My name, softly spoken near my ear, startles me. I trip on my own feet and drop my backpack to the floor. I'm halfway to a face-plant when an arm snakes around my waist and stops my fall. A few snickers and a mumbled "klutz" make my face flush. A hand at my hip steadies me, I follow it to thank my savior and find Professor Dick staring down at me. I stumble backward, to get his hands off me, and my heel catches my backpack. Now, I'm halfway to falling on my ass.

My arms reach for him, and he yanks me up. I crash into his chest.

We freeze.

He lets go of me like I've burned him and jumps back. He clears his throat.

My face heats.

Kill me now.

The exposed skin on my wrist, the very place he touched, tingles. Not with pain. He didn't hurt me. But he makes me feel … something. I rub my wrist on my jeans, trying to get the sensation off my skin.

I bend and pick up my backup, killing a few precious seconds until I have to face him.

He tilts his head a smidge as he looks me over—I look down at myself and what I'm wearing. Nothing special. Jeans, sneakers, and a Riggins hoodie. But his eyes linger, like he's looking for something or trying to solve a puzzle.

I adjust the backpack on my shoulders, pulling out a lock of hair that got caught under a strap. His eyes fall to the top of my head and narrow, and again I can see questions in his expression. I know what he sees. My real hair color peeking at the top of my head. The honey-blond hair contrasts with the brown dyed hair. I have to put a stop to his observation and gather my thoughts. It's only us and a couple of late arrivals to classes left in the wide corridor of the bottom floor. Light shines in from the expanse of windows that face the main part of campus. There's a riot of colors outside the windows. Oranges, yellows, reds, all a confirmation that fall is here, and winter is not far behind.

I drag in a breath, bite my lip, and finally speak. "I guess I should thank you for keeping me from falling. Twice. But then again, if you had not creeped behind me, none of it would have happened."

"I did not creep behind you. I simply said your name when you walked past me."

He always sounds so cold and controlled. Like a freaking robot.

"Why?" *Walk away, Becca. Just walk away.*

"Why did I say your name? Isn't that what polite people do when they meet someone they know?" One corner of his mouth quivers in almost a smile.

"Yeah, but we don't really know each other, do we? We met once."

His right eyebrow rises in challenge.

"Or twice." I correct myself since I know he's thinking of the time he caught me with Lucas in his classroom. "Neither time was pleasant nor memorable. It was pretty fucked up as far as meeting people goes."

His eyes narrow at my free use of the F-bomb. But I don't have to make nice to him. I know he's the reason Tommy stopped talking to me. And it pisses me off.

He tilts his head again. "You look like you want to … hit me."

"Well … if all you have is a hammer, everything looks like a nail." I hate that he's so tall, forcing me to look up.

His eyes widen. "Interesting choice of words."

"Why is that? Because I quoted Abraham Maslow, the very guy they named this building after?"

"You surprise me, Miss Jones." And with those parting words, he leaves. I track him until he turns up the stairs and disappears from view.

What's that supposed to mean? I surprise him? How?

CHAPTER TEN

BECCA

I GET TO THE GRILLER FIRST AND ASK FOR A TABLE IN THE back. I want the extra time to find a spot out of prying eyes and ears and to prepare myself. I need to get into the right headspace to talk to my father. There's a tug-of-war going on— my mind and my heart at opposite ends with me trapped in the middle. My heart says, "listen to him. Give him a chance." But my mind says, "fuck him and the horse he rode in on. You don't need him. You don't need anyone."

But I know that's not true. No matter how often I tell myself I need no one, no matter how much I fill my time with classes, volunteering, work, my internship, and meaningless hookups, at the end of the day there's an emptiness that can't be filled. There's a void I cannot name, and my quick friendship with Tommy only serves to make it even more real. Tommy may be asking for help and looking for a friend in a place where he doesn't know anyone, but it's me who's lost.

This time, I'll try something different. This time, I'll listen to my heart and give my father the second chance he's asking for. And maybe, just maybe, I can give myself a second chance too.

"Becca? You're here." He looks surprised and relieved at the same time. "Can I?" He points to the chair across from me on the other side of the table and waits for my permission.

I gesture to the chair. "Yes, please." It comes out more formal than I intended.

My heart speeds up as the silence stretches between us, second by second, until it's unbearable, and I have to break eye contact. I reach over and grab the icy water glass the waitress placed in front of me ten minutes ago. Moisture condensing on the outside makes it slippery, and I nearly drop it when my trembling fingers make a grab for it. I'm turning into a klutz. At this rate, I won't survive the weekend.

"I'm sorry," he says. "I know I'm staring. I can't help it. It's all so very surreal still. You look like my mother at your age. I brought pictures. I thought it might be a good way to start." His words come fast and clipped, all in one breath, as if he needed to push them out in a rush before he lost the courage to say them. "Do you want to see the pictures now?"

The irony is not lost on me. I can't find my words, and he can't hold his in.

"You ready to order?" The waitress is back, giving us a much-needed break. I suck in a deep breath and hold the air in my lungs, expanding under the conscious effort to keep it in. A trick I learned years ago.

Inhale as I count to five, hold to a count of ten and exhale until my lungs are empty again, and I can feel my chest concave. Repeat until my heart rate slows down to a normal pace. I do this now, deferring to him so he can order first. I take the time to look at him while he looks over the menu and asks for a cheeseburger, fries, and a Coke. He's wearing a gray T-shirt under a zip hoodie and dark jeans. A thick manila envelope sits on the table next to him. I'm staring at it. At the hidden pictures it must contain—a part of my history which I know nothing of.

"And you?" The question has me blinking a few times. Yes. Lunch. What do I want? My stomach recoils at the idea of eating, but I force myself to smile at the waitress. It's not her fault I'm a head case. "Yeah, I'll have a veggie burger and fries. And water is fine. Thanks." She takes our menus and disappears between the tables, leaving me without a shield again.

"Are you a vegetarian?"

"No, not really. But I figure it's an easy way to get my veggies in, and their veggie burger is delicious."

"Hmm, I'll have to try that next time."

Another stretch of silence. My eyes drift to the envelope. "Are those the pictures?"

"Yes, do you want to look at them now?"

"Sure."

"May I?" He points to the chair next to mine.

My shoulders shrug in response, and he takes that as a yes and sits next to me, bringing the envelope with him. I move my glass to the side to make room as he pulls out what must be dozens of pictures from the envelope—in all sizes and different states of wear and age. Some are black and white, some faded color, some are torn on the corners and others look newer, shiny and unmarred by time or touch.

"I figured I could show you these, and then you can ask any questions you may have about me or anything else."

My eyes dart everywhere, taking in snippets of images as he sets the pictures in a neat pile right in front of him.

The first picture he shows me is black and white and torn at one corner.

"They are your grandparents." He flips the picture and shows me the back—1969 is written in faded black ink on the yellowing paper. "They were fifteen here and high school sweethearts."

He gives me the picture, and I hold it with no small amount of veneration. I'm holding history in my hands and something flutters in my chest. A sense of belonging I've never experienced before.

"Are they still alive?"

"Yes, together and sickly in love still. It would be cute if I wasn't so disturbed by the amount of handholding and kissing I saw my entire life." He laughs, and I join in, the carefree sound escaping my lips almost alien to my own ears.

I do the math in my head. They've been together for over fifty years. I can't imagine such an enduring love. My eyes sting and I reach for the water glass, more careful this time, and take a sip to push down the knot forming in my throat.

The next picture is in color, albeit faded, and shows his parents again. On their wedding day. His mom—my grandmother is wearing a simple white dress, fitted to her torso and loose from the waist down. A short veil on her hair, and curls framing a beautiful face. I can see a bit of myself in her.

"She's beautiful."

"You look like her."

I nod in agreement, but I don't think myself beautiful. I never did. But looking into my grandmother's face makes me wonder how harshly I've judged myself.

"How old was she?"

"Twenty-two."

"My age … and she already had her life figured out."

"I don't think anyone has their life figured out at any age."

He heard me. I didn't intend to speak my thoughts out loud.

He rubs his chin. "I think everyone is bumbling around, but some people make it look easy, while others are still trying to figure how to make amends, apologize and figure out where to go from here."

His eyes are fixed on mine, an array of emotions skate through them until they mist, and my father blinks several times. He clears his throat and pulls the next picture out of the pile in front of him. "Ah, this is two years after they got married. And that fat baby is me."

His father holds a fat baby dressed in blue as his mother gazes at them. My heart constricts. I bite the inside of my cheek. Something dark and ugly washes over me. *This should be me.* I should have had loving parents who cared about me and took pictures. As fast as it comes, I push it away. The green monster has never helped anyone, least of all me.

I spent a lot of years angry and jealous of other kids when I was younger. But by the time I started high school, I realized that a lot of the happy faces were masks, and under the fake smiles and mean words they were no different from me. They might have had parents that cared, and food on the table, but all of them were trying to fit in or make believe they did. I knew I never would fit in and didn't bother to try. I was and would always be an odd piece. Unmatched. And unwanted.

The waitress comes back with our food and again saves me from my thoughts. If I had any extra money lying around, I'd hire her to interrupt me every so often with her timely, if annoying, presence. I pick a fry and take a bite. To my surprise, find I'm hungry. We eat, my father and I, as he shares picture after picture. Telling me little stories here and there, the colors in the pictures getting more vivid with each passing year.

He gestures as he speaks. "They were poor, yes. My father worked as a day laborer, and jobs weren't always available. Mom cleaned houses two towns over and had to take a bus to work. My grandma helped and watched me when they were both at work. Despite everything, we were happy."

He picks up another picture. One of him in uniform. "I had a plan. Join the military as soon as I graduated high school. It would be one less mouth to feed at home, and I could make money and help my parents."

He takes a drink of water. "Your mother and I, we were the same. We didn't have to pretend to have more than we did. But where I had loving and caring parents, your mother didn't." His eyes drift to the pictures between us, and he picks one up and places it in front of me. Our plates were cleared a while ago, and the bill was paid. He insisted on paying. I didn't fight him.

The picture shows both of them, my mother and father. It had to be summer as they were wearing T-shirts and cutoff jeans. My mother was even skinnier then. The line of her mouth challenged anyone to judge her, but the haunted eyes betrayed her true feelings. There was hopelessness in them, but even that was better than what showed in her eyes the last time I saw her. There was nothing left in the dark irises. She was an empty shell, and I left before she and the men in her life turned me into one of them.

He taps the picture. "Her father was a mean man, given to bouts of violence when he was sober and much worse when drunk. I don't think he ever hurt her, but the same can't be said about your grandma. No one knew we were together. We were both terrified of your grandfather. This picture is the only one of us together—my mother took it on the last day of school."

His gaze is lost in memory. "She took so many photos ... someone she worked for was a photographer, and he gave her an old camera and developed the films for her for free. Otherwise, I don't think we would have this many pictures."

"And my mother's parents?" Are they alive now, or did my mother also lie about it when she said they were both dead?

"I left before I found out your mother was pregnant with you, and I didn't keep in touch with her or anyone other than my parents. What I know, I heard from others years later."

"Okay …"

"The day your grandfather found out your mother was pregnant, he went ballistic. He wanted to know who the father was, and your mother refused to tell him. He beat her, and when your grandma tried to intervene, he beat her too. Someone called the police, and they arrested him."

"Good."

"Yeah, but they didn't keep him long enough. Five months later he was out and right back where he left off. But this time he didn't beat them. This time he kicked your mother out."

"While she was pregnant with me?" My heart tightens.

"Yes." He looks away from me.

I lean into the table. "She had to be seven or eight months pregnant by then."

He squeezes the back of his neck. "And remember, I had no idea any of this was happening. By then, I was away in boot camp and then deployed."

"What did she do?"

"I heard she rotated between friends, and eventually stayed with a guy who owned a liquor store. She worked for him, and he gave her room and board in exchange. She stayed with him for a couple years after you were born, but she started drinking as much liquor as she was selling, and he kicked her out. She went back to friends' couches with you in tow, but that only lasted a year. Until her father died. Cirrhosis, I heard."

"At least that part is true. My grandfather is dead." Bastard.

"When she found out he was dead, she went back home and stayed. Your grandma passed away a few years later. You were only four or five, I doubt you'd have any memories of it."

"I don't. I remember nothing about my grandparents or the other places I lived." And that's a relief.

"The house you grew up in is the same house they raised your mother."

"Right back where it all started …" I laugh without humor. The cycle of misery goes on unending. But I can change that, can't I?

More pictures and more stories follow. This time about him. He shows me pictures of his parents, my grandparents. Pictures of him in uniform. He was—is a good-looking man. I can see myself in him. How strange this is to recognize myself in a stranger and for that stranger to be my father.

It's been a couple of hours, and it's not anywhere as awkward as I expected meeting him again to be. I'm actually comfortable talking to him. Having the pictures, listening to the stories, was a great idea. It took the focus off me and gave me insight into my mother. Insight into the circumstances that shaped her, and why she blames me for ruining her life. I can't say that she's wrong. I ruined her life just by being born.

"Thank you for sharing this with me. It helps me understand." Not that it will change the past. I swallow the bitter memories.

"Understand?" His eyebrows squish together.

"Yeah, understand my mother. Why she is the way she is, and why she has always blamed me for ruining her life."

"You didn't ruin her life. You didn't force her to make the choices she made. You didn't make her an alcoholic or a junkie. She made those choices on her own. Yes, she had a messed-up family and being thrown out when she was pregnant with you was a terrible thing to endure, but it's no excuse. Plenty of people have been in the same situation and made better choices."

Better choices. I've had my share of bad decisions too. All my bravado, meaningless hookups, and avoidance hasn't helped me at all. I left my mother, the only home I have ever known, the place I grew up in, but I brought my scars and nightmares with me. My mother uses alcohol and drugs to numb her pain and regret. I use sex to feel in control. Are we that different?

I hug myself and drop my shoulders, hiding behind a curtain of hair. I can't look at him now. I can't face my father. Irrational as it may be I'm afraid he'll see all my sins written on my face. Heat climbs up my neck, and my cheeks burn. I'm ashamed of my choices.

"We can't change the past, Becca. What is done is done, but we can change the now."

His words are a stab into my heart. A laser knife. Cutting and cauterizing at the same time.

He reaches with a tentative hand. Taps mine gently. "I want to be a part of your life from now on. I want you to call me when you need help, or just to say hello. I want to have a real father-daughter relationship with you. I can't change the actions that made me absent from your life. But I can choose a different direction."

I nod, still not able to face him. I squeeze my eyes shut and forbid the tears to spill. But tears are traitorous little bitches and do whatever they damn well please.

"I choose you." He squeezes my hand. "I choose you, Becca."

I stop hiding behind my hair and look at him, his face blurred by my tears. I blink until he comes into focus again.

Like turning the little dial on a pair of binoculars until everything is clear. I look beyond the words and the gestures, and what I find is kindness. And hope. And love. It stirs something in my chest, and a little piece of my armor falls, and in this moment it's easier to breathe.

No one has ever chosen me before. Not even myself.

"I hope that with time, you can learn to trust me," he says.

I don't know why, but I already do.

CHAPTER ELEVEN

BECCA

I HESITATE, HAND ON THE DOORKNOB—HOLDING OFF FOR a few extra seconds before I have to step out of my room and face the world again. I close my eyes, rest my head on the frame and try to push away the thoughts that have taken residence in my brain.

One last time, I allow myself to relive the meetings with my father. His words about changing the past weigh heavily on my chest, even though they were about him and not directed at me. Much of my life was out of my control. Other people forced their wills on me.

"But the last four years, that's all on you Becca," I whisper to no one. "You made a mess out of yourself." The choices I made to take control of my life are not something I'm proud of. Or something I ever allowed myself to look into too close.

I need help. I know I do, but I have no idea where to start, and the thought of sitting with someone face-to-face and speaking the truth terrifies me. I push the thought away, open the door and take the stairs out of my dorm. Monday classes await.

"Hey there!"

"Ahhhhhh!" I jump and step back. The scream is out before I realize who tapped my shoulder.

"Sorry?" Puppy dog eyes beg me for forgiveness, but Tommy's laugh betrays him.

"Tommy?" My heart is trying to escape my chest.

"That's me."

"What are you doing here?"

"Hmm, waiting for you to walk to class together."

I press a hand to my chest, my heart still beating wildly. "You scared me to death."

"You're not dead, so technically, that's not true."

I squint my eyes at him, hoping it looks like a nasty dirty look. "You disappeared for a week. You didn't return any of my messages."

All the lightness evaporates from his face. "Yeah, I was dealing with some ... stuff."

That's it? No explanation? Just stuff?

I turn on my heels, veer off the walkway and cut through the grassy slope that will take me to the Maslow building. My feet hitting the ground with unnecessary force. I trample the poor grass and grip my backpack harder, hands curving around the straps until my nails bite into my palms.

"Hey, wait up." Tommy catches up with me. "You mad at me?" His pace quickens.

He tries to stop me, but I flinch away. I'm acting like a brat. My emotions controlling my reactions.

"Becca, stop!"

I keep going. "I have class, and I don't want to be late."

He jogs around me and forces me to stop and look at him. "I'm sorry, okay? I had to deal with something, and I didn't want to drag you into it."

His eyes search mine, so open and eager. He's out of breath, dark shadows under his eyes, he blinks, and wetness gathers at the corner on one eye.

All the fire inside me extinguishes. "No. I'm the one who should apologize. I have no right to be mad at you. You have a life, and I'm nothing to you."

"You are not nothing!" Tommy steps closer. "Do you hear me? You're somebody, and I care about you."

There's a golf ball-sized lump in my throat, and my eyes are trying to leak again. Talking to my father two days ago opened a faucet of endless tears, and I can't even blame it on PMS. It's not the right time of the month. *Damn it.* I dig in my bag and find some sunglasses to put on so I can blink the tears away without looking deranged. The golf ball is stuck—I don't even attempt to speak and nod at him before resuming my walk in a normal pace now. Tommy trails next to me, and we walk in silence. Him with his stuff and me with my monsters.

When I was a kid, I used to name them.

Hungry Harry.

Cold Cindy.

Afraid Abigail.

Hurt Henry.

Lost Lila.

Lonely Lou.

Stupid Sandy.

Dumb Debbie.

Whore Wanda.

Slut Sonia.

Until there were too many to name. I was naming all the things I felt and identifying them as something outside of me. Naming them had been my way of distancing myself from everything. But the distance was an illusion, and I was still

77

hungry, cold, and afraid. It still hurt, and I was still lost and lonely. And *they* still called me stupid, dumb, whore, slut.

And now, when I glance at Tommy and the pained expression on his face, it hits me. Maybe, just maybe, he's not as happy and carefree as he seems. And perhaps he has monsters of his own. Monsters with different names, but no less real.

I have a new monster to name. Add one more to the list.

Selfish Sam.

CHAPTER TWELVE

BECCA

Tommy touches my arm. "I'm sorry I went MIA. I really had some stuff to deal with."

"That's okay, Tommy. I'm sorry too. I'm cranky and took it out on you."

He shrugs. "No biggie. Want to grab some coffee after your class?"

"Can't, sorry. I have my practicum this afternoon. I'm working until five."

His brows furrow. "What's a practicum?"

We walk at a slower pace. "It's like an internship. It's the practical, hands-on part of the coursework. You need a certain number of hours to graduate and get a license."

"Huh … How many hours?"

I smile, the anger easing with each step we take together. "It varies by state, but in Vermont, we are required to complete four hundred and fifty hours."

"That's a lot of hours."

"That's nothing. The master's requires three thousand hours of supervised experience over a period of two years. I love every second." My candor surprises me. I didn't plan to be so open with him.

His eyes widen. "Whoa ... how many more hours do you need to finish it?"

I adjust the straps of my backpack. "I'm over four hundred hours now."

"Oh, so close."

"Yes. I can almost taste it. I'll complete the requirement by graduation, and then I can get my license and do some kind of entry-level human service job while going for my master's."

"And then what?"

"And then more training, more hours, more tests until I get my clinical license."

He bumps me with his shoulder. "So, what do you wanna be when you grow up?"

I grin at him. "I want to be a Licensed Independent Clinical Social Worker. Basically, I can work independently."

"That's cool. Being your own boss, huh?"

"Something like that."

"How did you even get into that?"

His question makes my steps falter. "I don't know. Something I've always wanted to do." A partial truth.

"And the university helps you find the internship?"

"Yes and no. We get referred to different places. But I work under the Queen."

"The Queen?"

I laugh. "That's not her real name. That's what everyone calls her because you better be good at your job or else heads will roll. Her name is Magda Kenny."

"Holy crap! Can't you find a different internship?"

"I wouldn't want to. She's a powerhouse of a woman. I love

working for her. She's been in the field for over thirty years. Nothing can replace that kind of knowledge or experience."

I'm so close to graduating. And Magda Kenny played a big part in getting me to this point. I worked my ass off. All the sleepless nights studying, the odd jobs I took in addition to my bartending gig, brought me a step closer to what I want. I'm lucky to have her in my corner.

We're at the Maslow building now. Tommy walks in with me. "Was it hard to get the job?"

"After she accepted me into her program, I found out she rejected nine other applicants before me. She's picky. I got lucky, I guess."

That day is imprinted on my mind. After the interview, at the very end, I was sure I'd be rejected.

"Miss Jones, you answered every question perfectly. You have a 4.0 GPA. And recommendation letters that praise you as an exemplary student. I should be thrilled with you. But I'm not."

"No?" I couldn't help myself. I was mortified as the word jumped out of my mouth.

"No. I'm not happy at all with this interview. You want to know why?"

"Yes."

Then she looked at me with eyes that could see into my soul.

"For an hour we talked, and I still don't know why you want to be a social worker."

"To help people ..." She cut me off before I could say anything else.

"Bullshit!" I was so startled by the cuss, all I could do was sit there, and open and close my mouth like a fish.

"Excuse me?"

"You didn't go through all of this, spent thousands of hours

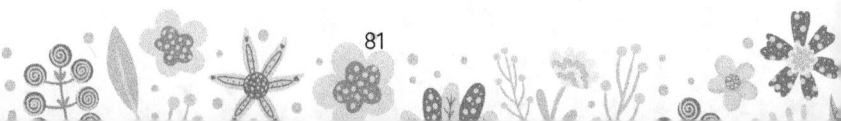

studying and busting your ass for these grades, so you can help people."

Her response incensed me. The hell I didn't. That's exactly why I was doing this. Anger got the best of me. Now that I was sure I didn't get the position, I had nothing to lose. My mouth was filled to the brim with words that needed spilling. But again, she stopped me with a raised eyebrow.

"I'll ask you again. Why do you want to be a social worker, and don't give me that 'you want to help people' bullshit answer again. Think, then speak."

I said nothing. I had nothing. As I was about to gather myself and leave, she spoke again.

"The truth, Miss Jones. All I want is the truth. The real reason you want to work for me."

Her eyes. They cut right through me. Through all the layers, carefully built, one over the other until I had a shell so thick nothing could touch it—nothing until the Queen. Until Magda Kenny.

And then I understood what she was asking. And it was harder than anything else I had ever had to say.

"Because I know."

"Because you know what?" She was not letting me off easy. Not at all.

"Because I know what they are going through. Because I know what it's like. Because it was me. They are me."

She smiles then. The Queen graces me with a smile so bright and full of warmth, it could obfuscate the sun.

"Now we're getting somewhere. I don't need super-smart kids. I don't want people who want to help because they're on a mission to make the world better. I need people who know. People who can relate. People who'll understand. And you, Miss Jones, fulfill those

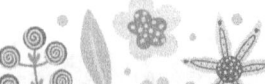

needs. But before I offer you the internship, I need you to understand one thing."

"Okay ... "

"You can't save them all. Can you live with that?"

I knew the answer she was looking for was yes. But my head was shaking even before she finished the question. "No, I can't."

"I've been doing this for over thirty years. We lose some. You can't stop it."

"I can damn well try."

"Miss Jones, it was a pleasure to meet you. You got yourself a job."

I blink away the memory. "You don't have any classes here, do you?" I ask.

Tommy is looking at the stairs with a determined look in his eyes. "Nope. Going to say hello to my brother. Catch you later." He answers without looking at me and walks to the stairs.

I've worked for over a year under Magda. Didn't take long to understand her nickname. She's not Queen because of any sense of superiority or vanity. She's Queen because she makes things happen. Where others fail, Magda creates small miracles. And some days a miracle was the only thing that kept us going.

Her keen eyes landed on me as soon as I walked into the cramped office.

"Miss Jones?" She never calls me Becca. Not unless something very serious was about to happen.

"Yes?"

"Could you please take some of these fliers and post them

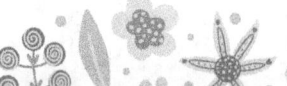

on bulletin boards around campus?" She hands me a folder and inside are about a dozen bright pink fliers. I look at them and freeze. I take a moment to find my voice again. "What is this?"

"It's a new program to help victims of abuse. Completely anonymous. Riggins is one of thirty-two universities taking part in this program, and they asked for our help."

The words on the paper float before me like a jumble of letters. I blink again and again, trying to make sense of what they say. The rapid tempo of my heart out of sync with my frozen state. I push myself to move, leaden feet drag on the carpeted floor.

IF YOU SPEAK, WE WILL HEAR YOU.

**Every 98 seconds, someone is
sexually assaulted.**

You Don't Have to be a Victim.

**Talk to us. We will listen.
We will counsel. We will help you.**

**All sessions are hosted by trained
medical professionals.**

**100% anonymous.
100% free.**

More information on the website below.

I close the folder and put it in my backpack. Turmoil takes residence in my head. I can't wait to get back to my dorm and go to the website. I need to find out more about this program. The multitude of thoughts in my mind is reaching Defcon one status. It takes a ridiculous amount of concentration to accomplish the most menial of tasks. Thank goodness all I'm doing today is entering some paperwork into the computer and nothing requiring any kind of real thinking.

Vibration alerts me to a text. I glance at the screen and find a message from River.

River: Food?

Becca: I can't. I have a lot to do.

My stomach is flipping inside out. There's no way I can eat anything.

River: But you still have to eat.

Becca: Sorry. Can't. Breakfast tomorrow?

River: Okay... :(

I turn the phone facedown on the desk.

My gaze keeps finding my bag. The folder and pink sheets peeking from behind the half-open zipper taunt me. I check the time again. The minutes tick away with the eagerness of a sloth. A hibernating sloth. A hibernating sloth in slow motion and going backward.

I need this day to end.

CHAPTER THIRTEEN

BECCA

My fingers tremble when I type in the URL for the anonymous sexual assault survivor web page. I double-check the address on the flier again and hit enter. A second later the page loads.

The page lists statistics and some generic information I've read online before.

It's simple. White with pink and purple accents. And a box to create an anonymous login.

Not even an email is needed. The website hosts a mailbox that's accessible when you log in.

They say it's one hundred percent anonymous. But I'm still nervous about it. I close the window. Then clean the cached information for good measure and close the browser.

My heart is speeding. Could they really help me? Could they get me off the track of self-destruction I'm in?

I open the browser again and go incognito. Type the URL one more time. Read the entire page, make sure I'm not missing anything.

My lungs expand with a deep breath. My hands shake. I can do this. I can talk to someone. They'll never know it's me. I push the heel of my hand into my chest, massage it, try to dislodge the building anxiety. I've never talked to anyone about any of this before.

It's time.

I release a purposeful breath.

Username. Okay. What can I use for a username? Something that won't identify me and I can easily remember. A nervous laugh escapes when I think of it.

USERNAME: Cougar22
PASSWORD: **********

There. The perfect username for me. I am a 22-year-old cougar, after all.

I hit ENTER. The page loads.

Welcome to our safe space. Everything discussed in this area is private and confidential.

Calls are not recorded and chat conversions are deleted once the chat window is closed. Our program is more flexible than traditional one-on-one therapy.

Think of us as an open-minded friend, who is here to listen and guide when needed. You can talk to one therapist or several.

You may also join a group therapy room and take part or observe.

Our therapists are highly trained, and here to help you. We have male and female therapists available 24/7.

And so there's complete transparency, male therapists have odd numbers and female therapists have even numbers. Please check below for a list of available therapists now.

"I'm so not ready for a public confession." I ignore the link to the group chat room and look at a list of available therapists.

Therapist4

Therapist8

Therapist11

Therapist14

Therapist18

Therapist22

Male or female? My first impulse is to pick one of the even numbers and ignore the lone guy on the list. But which one? Can any of them really help me? I have never done any kind of therapy or mental help before. God knows I need it, but it costs money. Self-medicating with alcohol and random sex is free.

I close my eyes and will my heart to slow down, flex my hands and command the trembling to stop.

"It's just a chat. If I don't like it, I can close the window and delete my account."

I stretch my back and turn my neck right and left, up and down.

"Shake it off, Becca!" When I open my eyes, the first thing I see is the alarm clock on the table next to my bed—big red numbers stare back at me.

11:11 PM

I look at the list of therapists and back at the clock. Then look at the time on the computer too, to make sure.

11:11 PM

"I hope to God this is some kind of sign."

I've never been one for signs and superstitions, but I'm calling for reinforcements now.

I grab a quarter from my nightstand.

"Heads, and I'll go ahead with this guy, tails, I'll forget the whole thing and log off."

I flip the coin, smack my hand over it before I can see how it landed on my bed.

Heads.

"One more time to be sure." I flip it again.

Heads.

"Really? Last chance to change your mind, universe!"

I flip the coin, and it falls to the floor with a soft thud. The sound muted by the rug. I peer over the edge of my bed.

Heads.

"Okay, Therapist11 it is. I guess I'm talking to a dude."

I click on the link for Therapist11, and a chat window pops up.

Welcome to your private chat room. You are being connected to Therapist11.

My first instinct is to close the laptop and shove it under my bed, but I stop myself. My heart is running a marathon inside my chest. I wipe sweat from my forehead with the back of a sleeve. I shiver even though it's warm in my room thanks to the illegal space heater I have on the floor.

I'm safe.

I'm safe.

I'm safe.

I breathe in and out, dragging big gulps of air into my lungs until I'm dizzy. The blinking cursor in the window mocks me. Each blink a dare.

"I can do this. It's anonymous. No one will ever know."

My hands shake so much it takes three attempts to type two letters.

Cougar22: Hi.

The reply comes seconds later.

Therapist11: Hello, Cougar22. I'm glad you joined Safe Space. How can I help you?

Cougar22: I don't know.

The reply is off my fingertips, and I hit Enter before I change my mind and shut the entire thing down.

Therapist11: That's okay. Taking the first step in talking to someone is never easy. It takes courage. You can tell me as much or as little as you want.

Cougar22: I don't even know where to start.

My throat constricts. I grab a water bottle and drink, swallowing hard.

Therapist11: You can start anywhere you want. Do you mind if I ask you a few questions? Stop me at any time or direct the conversation to where you need it to go. Maybe that will help?

Cougar22: Okay.

Therapist11: Have you ever seen a counselor before?

Cougar22: No, never.

Therapist11: That's all right. I'll tell you about how this works and we can take it from there. Is that okay?

Cougar22: Yes.

Jesus. I'm hyperventilating. Why is this so difficult? My face burns, the heat spreads down my neck and into my chest. I press the cold water bottle into my cheeks, get up, turn off the heater and open the window a few inches. The cool breeze coming in makes my skin shiver. I sit back, and he has replied.

Therapist11: We work differently from traditional therapy. There's more of a conversation. Everything you tell me is confidential and anonymous, of course. We do not save this conversation in any servers. But I would like to ask your permission to take some notes. Those notes are for my eyes only, and they'll never be shared with anyone. I'll only use them to guide me. Is that okay if I take some notes? If you are uncomfortable, I won't.

Notes? No. No. I don't want anyone to read any of it. But—but I need to get this weight, this burden out of my chest. Maybe. Maybe it's what I need to do. I came this far. I need to keep pushing.

Cougar22: Okay. If no one else will see it, then that's okay.

Therapist11: Thank you. Thank you for trusting me.

Cougar22: So, what do we do now?

Therapist11: You're the boss. I'm here to listen, to guide, to help. But we'll only talk about what you're comfortable with. You don't have to share everything right now. We can talk about something else and go back to the root of the problem when you feel safe.

I'm no longer as scared as before. The fear, the sheer panic, I felt earlier has now settled into my stomach like minor discomfort. I'm not ready to talk about the past. But I can talk about now.

Cougar22: I need to change.
Therapist11: Need or want to?
Cougar22: Need. Want. Isn't it the same?
Therapist11: No. Not exactly. Need implies something you're forcing yourself to do because of an external force or idea. Want implies that you are doing it for yourself. Because you want to. Not because of external pressures.

Do I need to change, or do I want to change? I close my eyes. My life choices flashing through my mind. I want to change.

Cougar22: I want to change.

A weight lifts off of my shoulders with each word I type into the screen.

Therapist11: What do you want to change?
Cougar22: Everything.
Therapist11: Why do you want to change everything?
Cougar22: I don't much like the person I am.
Therapist11: And why is that?

God. Tears sting my eyes, and the heat returns to my face and chest. Not even the open window helps me now. My skin is cold, and yet it burns. I wipe the wetness away with my sleeve. Bite the inside of my cheek until the sting of physical pain distracts me from the hurt in my heart.

Cougar22: I'm not a good person. I lie. I lie all the time.

He doesn't respond right away. I get a sense he's waiting for me to go on. I watch the screen, count seconds in my mind. Make it to seventeen and give up. Start typing again.

Cougar22: No one knows the real me. I let no one in. The person they think they know doesn't exist.
Therapist11: Who's this person you've created?
Cougar22: She's carefree, aloof, happy. She's a party girl who doesn't have a worry in the world.
Therapist11: And the real you?
Cougar22: She's the opposite. I'm tired of pretending. I want to change.
Therapist11: And how do you plan on making that change?
Cougar22: I have no idea.
Therapist11: We can go back to that later. Let's say you change. What is it you hope to find once those changes take place?
Cougar22: I want to find the person I could have been before.
Therapist11: Before?
Cougar22: Before. Why is this so hard?
Therapist11: Take your time. Tell me what you're comfortable with. We can talk about something else.
Cougar22: Okay.

"Oh my God. I'm doing this. I'm really doing this. I'm talking to someone about me." I whisper the words out loud to make sure this is real.

Cougar22: It's easier to talk about me now.
Therapist11: We can do that. This is your safe place to talk about anything you want.

Anything. I squeeze my eyes shut, suck in one breath and then another. It's up to me now. No more lying. "Be honest, Becca."

Cougar22: I use people. I use men.
Therapist11: How do you use these men?
Cougar22: Sex. I use men for sex. I pick men who I know won't hurt me, hook up with them for a few days or weeks, and then let them go. Move on to the next guy.
Therapist11: Does it make you feel in control when you pick those men?

Yes. That's exactly how I feel.

Cougar22: Yes.
Therapist11: Why do you phrase it like that? Using men for sex instead of saying you're dating different men?
Cougar22: Because it's not dating. I don't like them. I have no interest in a relationship. We don't go out. There's no dinner. No movies. I pick guys I know are safe, and I have sex with them.
Therapist11: What do you get from it? What do you get from these men?

A sense of power. It makes me feel in control.

Cougar22: It makes me feel like I'm taking something back.
Therapist11: What is it you're taking back?

Oh God, can I really tell him? This stranger? Tell a man? How could he ever know? Understand? I stare at the END button, hover the mouse over it. You came this far. Don't back away now.

Cougar22: A piece of myself.
Therapist11: So to reiterate. You pick men you think are safe, and you do this to feel in control and to get a piece of yourself back?
Cougar22: Yes.
Therapist11: I have two questions: What makes you decide these men are safe?
Cougar22: I watch them. Watch how they behave. And I never pick a guy who's much bigger than me. I pick guys I can fight back.

There's a lengthy pause on his side. And I know I've said too much. More than I wanted. But he has to know why I'm doing this. This is a sexual assault survivor support group.

Therapist11: That sense of control and taking back a piece of yourself. How long does it last?

How does he know? It never lasts long. I feel normal for a few days, and then the flashbacks return.

Cougar22: Not long enough.

Never long enough.
I hit the END button then, close my laptop and collapse on

my bed. My room is freezing now. Sobs and shivers rack my body. If from the cold or the never-ending pain, I cannot tell.

Later, much later, when I can make myself move again, I close the window, turn the space heater back on, nest under the blankets and allow exhaustion to take me.

CHAPTER FOURTEEN

BECCA

I'm not hungry, but I force myself to eat. The jumbled sounds of the cafeteria reflect the confusion of thoughts in my mind, as if I too, have hundreds of voices speaking at the same time inside my head.

I barely paid any attention in my classes today. It's a miracle I took any notes at all. Thank goodness I had no tests, or else who knows what would have ended up on the paper.

"Earth to Becca." Fingers snap inches away from my face.

"What?" I blink at River who is looking at me with a smirk on her face.

"There she is. Welcome back. I was beginning to think you had been kidnapped by aliens and replaced by a clone."

"Nope. No such luck." I sigh. "I'm tired, I didn't sleep well."

She snorts. "Did your boy Tommy keep you up?"

I ignore the innuendo. "No, I was alone. What about you? Seeing anyone?"

"Negative, ghost rider."

"You and your movie quotes."

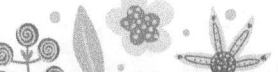

"What?" Her hands go up. "Top Gun is life."

I pick a french fry from my plate and point at River with it. "What's up with the dry spell?"

She steals the fry, dunks into the little cup of ketchup between us and takes a bite. "Dry spell?"

"Yes." I grab another fry and eat it before she can take it. She pouts and goes for my plate. "You haven't gone on a date since last semester. What's up?"

River holds my gaze for a few extra seconds, then shrugs. "Nothing. Taking a break from men and concentrating on classes with it being senior year and all."

Evasion is not in River's nature. I know she lied just now. Or at the very least omitted the real reason she's been flying solo for months. I'm too good a liar not to recognize an untruth when I see one. The way she looks at me—unblinking—that's her tell.

"That's it? A boy time-out?"

"Oh, look!" She points over my shoulder. "Your favorite professor. We should ask him if he wants to join us for lunch." Her smile is so devious, I'm afraid to look behind me.

Her arm shoots up, and she waves. "Hi, Professor Beckett. Want to join us?"

Kill.

Me.

Now.

I stare straight at River. She gives me the sweetest of smiles. I don't look back, but I can feel someone standing to my right.

"Miss Devereux. Thank you, but I have a huge pile of papers to read and grade sitting on my desk." He says this in his cold and distant voice. He pulls back the chair next to me and sits anyway.

He's inches away, and his clean scent reaches to me with

invisible fingers. His proximity overpowers my senses. The sounds of the cafeteria, the competing smells of food, the constant motion of people moving all around us fades away. Sitting this close to him, I can see a ring of green around the whiskey color of his eyes, and a tiny scar above his right eye, a thin line slightly lighter than his tanned skin.

"Miss Jones, have you seen my brother today?"

With his question, the sounds, motions, and smells of the cafeteria come rushing back in.

Was that disapproval in his voice?

I turn to face him. "I saw him this morning. But not since."

"I was under the impression you two have lunch together." An eyebrow rises.

"Not on Tuesdays. Our schedules don't line up that way." Tommy meets me for lunch often, but it's November now. He's made new friends, and I'm happy he's venturing on his own. But I don't say any of it to Professor Dick.

He looks at me for a long moment. And I can't read him. I can't tell what he's thinking. What he's hiding behind those beautiful eyes. I know he's trying to read me. Still judging me and trying to figure me out. Good luck with that. I don't even know what's going on with me. How could he?

He gets up, pushes the chair back in place, picks up his to-go salad, looks at my plate and back at his salad.

He steals two fries from my plate and pops them in his mouth. "I should have gotten the burger and fries."

He nods at River and disappears.

"What the hell just happened?" I look at River with both hands up as if I could grab the answer from the air.

She's laughing at me. "He likes you," she says in a singsong voice, dancing in her chair.

"What? No. Just no. He hates my guts. He thinks I'm corrupting his brother."

River stops the chair-dance. "Who's his brother?"

"Tommy."

"Wait, the kid you're hooking up with is his brother?"

"Yes. No. Yes. No. Ugh." I push my plate to the side and bang my head on the table.

She steals another fry. "What is it? Yes or no?"

I pull my plate back and shove a bunch of fries in my mouth before I lose them all. Chew harder than needed. Swallow. Take a drink from my water bottle.

"Yes, Tommy is his brother. And no, we're not hooking up. We never did."

"Whoa … hold the press. You're not hooking up with this kid. Why?"

"No. We're friends. I don't fuck every guy I know." I glare at her.

"I know that. I didn't mean to imply you fuck everything with a dick. I meant, I could swear you said you were with him."

"You assumed, River. I never said it."

"Huh … well, that makes things easier, then. It would be too weird to be hooking up with two brothers."

I lean into the table, lower my voice. "I'm not hooking up with either of them. Never happened. Never will."

She goes for another fry. I smack her hand away.

She rubs her hand. "Famous last words, Becca. Famous last words."

"What do you mean?"

"Ohhhh, you challenged the universe with that never. Now we have to figure out which brother you'll be with."

"None. No one. Neither one of them. I'm taking a page of your book and going on a boy sabbatical too. No more dick for me."

"Not even Professor Dick?"

"Specially not him."

CHAPTER FIFTEEN

DYLAN

Best damn french fries I've ever had.

CHAPTER SIXTEEN

BECCA

THE WEB PAGE BLURS. I BLINK. THE WORDS LINE UP AGAIN, making sense once more. My bed creaks when I shift. I've been sitting in the same position without moving for so long my whole body aches. I stretch my arms above my head, uncurl my back, circle my neck. Work off the stiffness that has settled into my muscles. Ease off the tension.

For twenty minutes I have been here. Sitting stiff as a log and telling myself to be brave and reach out again. Talk to him and be honest.

Therapist11

He's available again tonight. The familiar pressure on my chest is there, but less than before. I'm not as anxious or nervous this time around.

I click on his name.

Call or chat?

"Be brave, Becca."

The mouse hovers in the middle, between the two options. My hands shake, making the cursor oscillate between Call and Chat.

It's easier to hide behind the Chat window. It gives me time to think. Easier to walk away.

"Be brave, Becca." I whisper the mantra to myself again and place the cursor over the Call option. Squeeze my eyes shut. Click. The connection beeps, a dial tone follows, the sound loud in my ears. I scramble to grab my earbuds, plug them into the laptop and put them on just in time to hear the second ring coming through.

"Jesus! I'm a mess. Really didn't think this through."

I imagine his voice low, and maybe grouchy, like an old man. An old man with a big belly, long gray beard, and a mustache. I picture him as a cross of Freud and Santa Claus and smoking a pipe. A nervous laugh escapes my lips. He answers my call then, and that awkward laugh is the first thing he hears.

"Hello. I'm so glad you're back."

My laugh dies. His voice is neither low nor grouchy. He doesn't sound like an old man at all. Even through my old and staticky earbuds, his voice is warm, soft, and welcoming. It makes me think of melted chocolate, and the notion is so bizarre that it triggers a nervous laugh.

"It's good to hear you laugh."

"Hi." I sound timid and not like myself. I don't speak with the assertiveness and edge of anger that usually coats my words. This is good. It wasn't intentional, but I'll keep this soft and timid voice. It's another layer of protection. Not that I think whoever is on the other side of the line would ever know who I am. If I thought for a second that someone could find out, I would never have joined this program.

"Will you let me in on the joke?" I can hear the smile in his soothing voice, and I'm at a loss for what to say. I guess the truth will have to do.

"I was picturing you as a cross between Santa Claus and Freud, and it made me laugh."

It's his turn to laugh. The sound is melodious, masculine and welcoming. I like it. I like the sound of his voice, the timbre of his laugh. It's friendly, happy. It makes me feel safe.

"Sorry to disappoint, but I don't think I could pass as Freud or Santa."

There's an awkward silence then.

"How are you today?" He takes the lead.

"I'm okay." For a change, the automatic response is not a lie.

"Yeah? Do you want to pick up where we left off or talk about something else?" He doesn't mention the rather abrupt way I ended our last conversation, and I'm grateful for that.

"I don't know. I don't know how any of this works." I curl into myself, let my shoulders drop, release some of the stiffness in my back.

"Think of me as your sounding board. I'm here to help and guide you, so you can understand your emotions, create better behaviors, and relate to your thoughts differently."

The faint squeak of leather comes through the connection, and I imagine him getting more comfortable in his chair.

"Okay. And if I do all that, then what?" I can't picture myself in any other way than what I am.

"Then you can live your life the way it was meant to. Live your life to your full potential. Not as a result of circumstances or whatever happened in the past."

I snort at his words. The sound is rude even to my ears. "Yeah, I can't see this happening anytime soon."

"And yet you called. And yet you're here talking to me. And

yet, the first thing you said was 'yeah.'" He calls me on my bullshit response, but his tone is kind, not accusatory.

"What?" My feeble response is a weak attempt at scrambling for some extra time to think about what he said.

"You said you can't see *this*—this different version of you— happening anytime soon. But the first thing you said was *'yeah.'* And that tells me that yes, you see that life for yourself, and more than seeing it, you want it."

"I don't think that's how a sounding board works." I shift in my bed.

"I'm also here to call you on your BS, when I see it."

Crap on a cracker! It's like he can read my thoughts. "Get out of my brain!" The words spill out before I can stop them. He rewards my impromptu honesty with a low chuckle.

"That's what I'm here for."

I suck in a deep breath and release with a loud sigh. "I guess it makes sense. In theory, at least."

"Just in theory?"

I hear steps outside my door and lower my voice. "I can understand it on a rational level. But I haven't internalized it yet."

"Ah … yes. Assimilating a new point of view can take time."

"But it's more than just a new point of view, isn't it?"

"It is. It's a whole alternative way of thinking. And changing the way we view ourselves is far more difficult than changing the way we view others."

That gives me pause. I have to run what he said through my mind. It resonates with me. "True. Yes. I can see that. But, why? Why is it easier to change the way we see others than the way we see ourselves?"

"Because we believe the lies others tell us about ourselves.

And even worse, we believe the lies we tell ourselves too. We believe these made-up stories and proceed to make them real."

This is also true. How many times was I called a slut growing up? Even before I ever kissed a boy. They shoved the word at me on a daily basis. And look at me now? Isn't that what I am when I pick random guys to have sex with? I shake my head as if I could dispel the intruding thoughts. Get back to the call, Becca! "But how do we know they are lies?"

"You're not asking the right question."

"I don't understand." I get what he means about believing lies we tell ourselves. How often have I said I was okay and played the part of the happy and carefree girl? Too often. So often I sometimes fear I have lost my identity.

"The right question is not what are the lies."

"No?"

"No, not at all."

"Then, what is the right question?" My heart thunders in anticipation. Half of me believes he holds the key that will free me from my cell. The other half is too afraid to believe and is terrified of what will happen if I dare to step out.

"The right question is, what is the truth?"

"What's the truth?" I repeat, letting the words wash over me like rain. One drop at a time.

"Yes, truth. Forget about the lies. Ask yourself, what is true?"

"And how do I know what is true?"

"The truth, my friend, is that which never changes."

"What do you mean? Everything changes. Doesn't everyone have his or her version of the truth? People have different perspectives of the same events."

"That is not the truth, then. It's the lies people tell themselves. Truth by nature cannot be two things, especially two opposing things at the same time. Truth, in its essence, is universal."

My mind is racing with conflicting thoughts. I understand what he's saying on a very primal level, but this is making my brain hurt. And how the heck did we get to this?

"I don't know where you're going with this. How any of these ideas of lies and truth can help me." I can't hide the annoyance in my voice. "I'm gonna need an example."

"Hmm …" He hums, and I can almost see him leaning back in a leather chair and swiveling back and forth. Now that the Freud-Santa picture has been dismissed, his face is a blur in my imagination.

"Okay. Something simple. When we see a ripe strawberry, we can agree that its color is red, correct?"

"Yes."

"So for us saying that a strawberry is red is true. But the strawberry is not always red, is it? It starts green, and then turns red, and eventually, if no one eats it, it will turn brown and black. All those colors are also true at any given moment in time."

My mind is whirling, trying to keep up with him. "Which, then, by what you said before, it's not true at all because the color is always changing."

"Correct. The colors change. The outside changes, and the flavor changes too, but it is still a strawberry, despite all the changes. The changes are not the truth, the strawberry is. Now apply this to yourself, and that which remains the same is the truth."

What? What the fuck does he mean by that? I'm no fucking strawberry. I rein in the irritation and press the heel of my hand into my forehead. Massage it for a second.

"But people are not strawberries. Something as simple as

red or green can't define us. And do people really change? Or do they make you think they can change?"

"Yes and no, it depends on the person, and how committed they are to change."

I cut him off. "That's a non-answer."

And he continues as if I hadn't interrupted him. "We grow, we mature, we evolve and sometimes we change. But our true nature, our true essence, it stays true throughout those changes. So what's actually changing is not the essence of the person, but their perception and behavior. Much like the strawberry. It is still a strawberry, the colors may change—that's our perception of it—but that doesn't change the fact that, independent of its many color changes, it is still a strawberry."

"I need a minute to mull this over." I close my eyes and let what he said sink in. It's all too much. I remember a PSY class in which we had to take two different stances and defend our findings. People can change versus people can't change. I was in the "can't" group. Have I been living my life under the assumption that I have no choice all this time?

"I don't know that I agree with this idea. My mind is twirling."

"And you don't have to agree. But I want you to think about it. How does this relate to you and the choices you made up to this point?"

"Me? How does this apply to me?"

"Because the things that happened to you are not you. You are not a result of whatever brought you here. You're a reaction to it."

"What?" His words shake me. I'm tittering on a precipice.

"Last time we talked, you said you date guys you feel are safe to be with, and you can have a certain amount of control over, correct?"

I said I hook up with them, have meaningless sex with them, but I'm grateful for the more generous description he gives me.

"Yes."

"And you said you do this to get a piece of yourself back."

I nod. Hearing my own words repeated back to me have a weight of their own, and they feel heavier somehow.

"Are you still with me?" His voice is even gentler now.

"I'm still here."

"Why do you think you pick these guys? The real reason this time. The truth of it, not the perception."

I drag in a long breath, forcing my lungs to expand until it hurts. The urge to hang up and end the call makes my fingers twitch. But instead I curl them into my palms and squeeze my hands into fists. My lips tremble as I try to form words. "I-I do it to punish myself. I do it because I don't think I deserve more or better."

"And why is that?" he asks almost in a whisper.

I blink away the tears that come uninvited, suck in another breath and push it out. My whole body trembles. "That's all I know. That's all I've ever had."

"But that's not the truth, is it? That's the story you were told. That's the story you're telling yourself still."

Oh my God. The sound that escapes me is half cry and half gasp. The sound of a wounded animal. Perhaps that's all I am. Perhaps when we strip all that makes us civilized, all that's left is animal sounds.

"I want you to do something for me. Will you? Please?"

"Okay." I don't know how I manage to speak.

"I want you to think about the story you've been telling yourself. Break it apart. Find when it first started. And then find the real you in the middle of it all. Find the you that never changes. Your essence. Take a day or two to think about it, and call me back, please."

He waits for a response, and I don't know if I can answer him. I'm folding into myself, becoming smaller and smaller.

"Can you do that? Please?" There's so much kindness in his voice, it draws me out again.

"Yes."

CHAPTER SEVENTEEN

BECCA

Thursday night football games bring a lot more customers to the bar. Even my boss, Gus, is out front tonight, talking shit with our locals and ribbing the lone Steelers fan sitting at the end of the counter. The New England Pats are ahead by ten points, and the beer is flowing. Everyone is happy. Except the Steelers fan. It doesn't look good for his team.

With their attention on the game and Gus helping, I have less to do and my mind is working on overtime. I haven't been able to think of anything else since the call with the therapist. When did my story start? When did I start believing in the lies I was told? And why is it that, even though I know the stories are lies, I still believe them?

My mind flashes through a Rolodex of time and memories. Little flashbacks spark here and there as I search for the real me in the dark corners of my mind.

The one who stays constant, he said. I think I found her—the real me.

The little girl buried under all the bullshit I was fed my whole life.

The teenager who was broken beyond all hope.

The young woman who never believed she was worthy of love and kept on punishing herself again and again. Who gave her body as if it was all she was—a thing to be consumed and easily forgotten.

"Becca?" my boss calls to me.

"Yeah?"

He takes a few steps closer, a benign smile on his face. "I think that spot is clean enough."

"What?" I follow his line of gaze to the rag in my hand and the spot I have been scrubbing for the last couple of minutes.

He ducks, trying to catch my eyes. "Everything okay?"

"Yeah, fine. Just thinking. School and stuff. You know."

Gus looks at me for a moment longer, nods, and goes back to the other side of the bar. Laughs greet him. Save for Pittsburgh guy. He's not laughing at all.

I push the thoughts away and concentrate on work and all the distractions it provides. I check the game on the TV. Pats are up by seventeen now. I don't really care for football. Or any sport. The sheer size and strength of those athletes alone can send me into a panic. I avoid them at all cost.

It's halftime now, and the bar clears a bit, some people heading to the bathroom to make room for more beer, others leaving to catch the second half at home. The bell over the door chimes with each exit, a barely audible ding over the sounds of the bar, now a lot quieter without the game going.

The sharp screech of a barstool being dragged hurts my ear. I have a new customer.

"Be right with you." I close the cash register and give Pittsburgh guy his change. He's had enough teasing for tonight. He pushes a five back into my direction.

I smile. "Thanks! You never know, they could come back."

He touches his cap. "Maybe."

I pocket the money and turn to my new customer, still smiling. My feet stop so suddenly, I almost pitch forward.

Professor Dick. What the heck is he doing here? I look over his shoulder and back toward the door, and then again in the restrooms' direction.

"No, Tommy is not here. It's just me, Miss Jones." He taps the scratched wood top, answering my unasked question.

I want to ask what the hell is he doing here, but rein in my inner bitch. "What can I get you?"

"A Dos Equis." It's a repeat of what he had the last time he was here. I don't ask if he wants the lime this time, just add it to the bottle, and slide it in his direction, making sure to avoid the few inches of space between my hands and him. He catches it, pushes the lime all the way in, and brings the bottle to his lips. He has beautiful hands, long fingers, like a pianist. Hands that create instead of hurting.

"Do you play the piano?" The question is out of my mouth before I realize what I'm saying. What the hell? What do I care if he plays or not?

He hesitates, the tip of the bottle paused on his bottom lip, a tiny lime pulp touching it. His gaze on my face. He lowers the bottle without drinking, the tiny pulp stays behind, and his tongue comes out and captures it. My entire body freezes. I hold my breath, and then inhale as if by doing so I could rewind time like the old VCR player we had when I was a kid. As if I could take that question back or my eyes away from his lips.

My toes curl inside my sneakers. I cross my arms over my chest, chin up in defiance. Muscle memory takes over. I brace myself for mockery or insult. Neither comes.

"I play. Did Tommy tell you?"

My head denies his question first with a slight shake. "No."

He tilts his head; curiosity tinges his beautiful face. "How did you know?"

I shrug.

His long and tanned fingers with short, clean nails tap the aged wood top of the bar again. He waits for an answer.

I force my shoulders to relax. Uncrossing my arms, I gesture toward his hand. "Your hands. You have the hands of a pianist."

His eyes widen, his brows arching in response to my words. He's surprised by my answer. I like that I put a chink in his shallow view of me.

He grabs his beer, takes a long pull. The lime inside bobbing with each gulp.

He points at me with the bottle's neck. "Do you play?"

"No, always wanted to. Never learned." Jesus! Why am I talking to him?

"Never too late."

"Yeah, well, piano lessons are expensive. And time consuming. I'm running on a time deficit as it is."

He chuckles at that. "Aren't we all? Time is like a dog chasing its tail. Just when you think you got it, you have to let go, and start all over again."

"Much like a dog chasing its tail, I don't think we're meant to catch time."

He takes another drink, the bottle almost empty. "No?"

"No. To use your dog analogy, if time is the tail, then it should be as nature intended. It stays behind while you look forward. Time will pass anyway. Trying to look back and catch up with it only wastes the time you have now." The words come to me with such a clarity. I've been thinking so much about my past over the last few days, weighing what the therapist said against my own perceptions. And now—just now—because of what Professor Dick said, everything clicks into place. Like a dog chasing its tail, I've been chasing and holding on to my past. And like a dog, when it finally catches up and bites its tail, it only hurts itself.

He looks at me, eyes narrowing with intensity, the amber color hidden behind thick, dark lashes. The bottle dangles an inch above the bar top by three fingertips. He takes the last sip. Tilts the bottle on its edge, rolling it back and forth in a semicircle, the neck dangling from his fingers.

"That's an interesting concept, Miss Jones." He lets go of the empty bottle, and it wobbles for a second before standing still. He reaches for his jeans pocket and pulls out a twenty. "Good night, Miss Jones."

Why does he always say my name like that? In that cold tone? He's gone before I can react.

What the heck is happening?

I need somebody to tell me I'm not having a hallucination right now. I grab my phone and text River.

> Becca: You're not gonna believe what just happened.

> River: What happened?

The reply comes in seconds, she must have been holding her phone.

> Becca: Professor Dick left here a minute ago.

> River: What?

> Becca: Professor Dick was here.

The phone vibrates in my hands, and the screen shows River's face. I tap the green button to answer the call.

"What? What do you mean Professor Dick was there? Where are you? What did he do? What did he say?"

Wow, take a breath, girl. "I mean exactly that. I'm at work, at the bar, and he showed up. Asked for a beer, drank it and left." But that wasn't all, was it?

"That's it? He said nothing else?"

"Well … we talked a little."

"I knew it!" River shrieks so loud I have to pull the phone from my ear.

"Knew what?" There's nothing to know. Or is there?

"I knew he has the hots for you."

"You're insane."

"Nope. I know these things. He's hot. You're hot. You two are gonna burn the sheets! It will be like KABOOM and WHOOOSHHHH." She makes special effects sounds and giggles.

"No! He's a professor. Of ethics, no less. He would never, ever get it on with a student. Ever!" I'm already regretting calling her. River will never let me live this down.

"I call dibs on the maid of honor spot—"

"You really are insane."

"And you have to name all your babies River." She goes on as if I hadn't said a word. I have to laugh. River never knows when to stop. I need to put the breaks on the delusion train and stop the madness.

"I have to go, River, it's getting a little busy here."

"Coward." Yeah, she got me there, I don't want to talk about this any longer.

"Forget I said anything. I have to get back to work. Bye now." I hang up before River has a chance to say anything else, but my mind lingers on what she said. Especially the burning-the-sheets part. Sound effects and all. And I'm not averse to it. Not at all.

CHAPTER EIGHTEEN

BECCA

Tension melts away with each step I take closer to the babies. The NICU is my happy place. Most people wouldn't think of a place where at-risk newborn babies are kept as happy, but for me, these babies are a clean slate, a haven, a home for second chances. And God knows I need all the second chances I can get.

I'm about to get into the scrub room when the text message comes. I'm not surprised to see his name on the screen. My father has been texting me every couple days.

> Robert: Good morning, Becca.
>
> Robert: Hope you are okay. It's been a few days since we met.
>
> Robert: I would like to see you again. Maybe grab breakfast?

He wants to meet again—for breakfast this time. Seems like all the meetings revolve around food. Like the universe is trying to compensate for all the days and nights I went hungry. The universe can be a bastard sometimes.

I think of everything that the therapist said … and about the odd conversation I had with Professor Dick last night. I don't even know where that came from, but the thought hit me with such a clarity, with so much depth and certainty, I knew it to be true the moment the words left my lips. I've spent my entire life chasing my past like a dog chasing its own tail.

The therapist's words come back to me again: *That which never changes.*

The truth is I've been waiting for my father my entire life. Even when anger replaced hope, and resentment replaced longing, that want was still there—dormant, silent, biding its time until it showed up again.

Can I fit my father into my life now? Is there room for him in it? Is there room for me in his life? He seems to believe there is. He seems to believe that we can heal and make up for the lost time.

I search for the pain that shadows all thoughts of my father —the barbwire that wraps itself around my heart whenever I think of him—and it's not there.

What happened to it? Where did the resentment go? I want to deny this vacancy in my chest where anger once existed. It's too soon, too fast for forgiveness. I'm not ready to let go. I want to chase the hurt, bite its tail, hold on to the familiar pain.

I stand there staring at a screen long gone dark. Is my misery a habit? My bitterness a choice? A companion I choose to keep at my side?

It hits me like an avalanche.

A sob rises up my throat, and I clamp my mouth shut, press my lips together, keep it all in.

This is not the place.

This is not the time.

I won't sully the NICU with my dark and dirty past.

I put my phone and bag in the locker behind me. Scrub my hands and arms until the skin is pink and tingles. If only it was this easy to wash everything else off of me.

I dry my hands, put on a gown, shoe covers, a cap. Walk into the room. Look at the dozen or so babies. I envy their innocence, their raw potential, their unmarred lives.

Nancy smiles at me. Baby Jay in her arms is a reminder that not every life starts unmarred. It humbles me. I force myself out of my pity-party for one and allow my love for this child no one wanted to swallow me. I take Baby Jay in my arms, immerse myself in the warmth of his small body and breathe in his sweet scent. I listen to his little cries, close my eyes and sing.

Two hours is not nearly enough. My time is up.

I leave the hospital and get to my car, shivering while I wait for the crappy heater to come to life. I grab my phone, my father's text messages still on the screen. I unlock the phone to respond.

> Becca: Breakfast would be nice.

Dots dance on the screen. The inside of the car is still not warm enough. My hands shake while I wait.

> Robert: Wonderful. How about tomorrow?
> Around 9:30? I can pick you up.

I'm not ready to be this close to him, to be confined to the

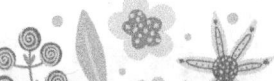

small space of a car without a way out. The sting may be gone for now, but who's to say it won't come back?

> Becca: Thanks. But I can drive. Where do you want to meet?

> Robert: How do you like the Waffle Bear? I got reservations.

Waffle Bear? That place is impossible to get in. You have to wait hours for a table. And they don't take reservations.

> Becca: I'd have breakfast with the devil if he got me into the Waffle Bear. How did you manage that? I thought they didn't do reservations.

And a part of me wonders if I'm having breakfast with the devil tomorrow.

> Robert: The owner is a long-time friend. We served in the army together.

> Becca: Wow, okay. I'll meet you there tomorrow at 9:30.

> Robert: Great! Talk soon.

I don't reply. I plug the phone into the car charger and turn up the radio. The temperature inside is finally a few degrees warmer than the outside. I drive to Riggins with a flood of thoughts.

My father also has a story. We all do. We're telling ourselves stories and listening to other people's stories, and sometimes those stories don't go together. Sometimes two stories have chapters that don't overlap until much later.

This is the kind of story I have with my father. There's a prologue, and then we skip straight to chapter twenty-two. Looking at my life as chapters, only written as I go along, makes it easier to look forward. But looking back becomes that much harder because I get to see how well I didn't do.

I spent so many years blaming my mother for everything that happened to me. And yes, she was responsible for a lot of things. Her neglect, her hateful words, what she allowed to happen right under her roof. But if I'm being honest with myself, when I was older, I could have chosen differently. I could have asked for help. I didn't have to believe the stories my mother or Theodore told me. There comes a time when one has to take responsibility for their actions.

The only way to move forward is to leave the past behind.

I can choose to be who I want to be. I can create a new story.

A story in which I'm worthy of love.

So, I say yes to meeting my father again.

I say yes to the love he wants to give me.

I say yes to starting a new story.

It terrifies me.

CHAPTER NINETEEN

BECCA

Waffle Bear is madness, especially on a Saturday morning. The parking lot behind the two-story log cabin-style restaurant is full, and I maneuver my car to the back where I find a spot under a tree bare of leaves. The naked branches reach for the sky like fingers looking for the warmth of sunlight in the chilly morning.

"I know how you feel, tree." I shake my head. "Great. Now I'm talking to trees too. If I didn't need therapy before, I do now."

I step out of my car and lock the door. Tilting my face up, much like the tree, I soak up the weak warmth. The cornflower sky is clear of clouds.

My phone vibrates, breaking the moment.

Robert: I'm here. By the big bear.

I pocket my phone without answering and walk around to the front of the building. Despite the chilly morning, there are people everywhere with pagers in hand waiting for their turn.

I visited Waffle Bear only once before during my first year at Riggins. River treated me to the best breakfast I've ever had. Now I'm here again in my last year at Riggins. If my father hadn't invited me, I don't know that I would have returned. I'm in the habit of denying myself things I love. The insight digs into my brain. Learning my worth is a battle I must wage against myself.

I find my father next to the big bear—a nine-foot grizzly carved out of a single log. My heart speeds up, and I scratch at my chest. He looks younger than forty in dark jeans, a T-shirt and a gray jacket.

A smile lights up his face as soon as he sees me, and my steps falter. I cover my hesitation with a wave.

"You're here!" He steps closer, arms out as if welcoming me with a hug. I stop short of reaching him, shove my hands in my jacket pockets. This is much too soon for touching. Even if a part of me craves the love and attention he wants to give me.

"Yep. I'm here." I look around at all the waiting people milling and huddled into each other. Couples, friends, families. No one could guess that this is only my third time meeting my father.

He gestures to the door, smiling at me still—his whole heart shines in the crinkles of his eyes, in the curve of his mouth—he's happy I'm here. A part of me wants to do something mean and wipe the joy from his face. But I stop myself. Repeat the question that's now a mantra, a prayer, a guiding light in my web of self-harm and misdirection.

What is the truth?

Who's the real me beneath all the crap and all the lies I tell myself?

I find comfort in the question. It keeps me in check, giving me something to hold on to and stop me from drowning in misery.

I search for the me who holds babies for hours, who volunteers in soup kitchens, who helps strangers. I hold on to her and smile at my father.

"Ready?" His arms drop, and he steps closer to the door, pulling it open for me.

I walk through the massive glass and wood door. "Thanks."

The loud hum of voices, laughter, and the familiar notes of a country song I can't name greet me along with the sweet scent of waffles, sugar, cinnamon, and the sharp smoky and salty smell of bacon. My mouth waters like Pavlov's dog. I wasn't hungry before, but I'm hungry now.

We're greeted by a girl about my age.

"Hi." My father steps closer to her.

"I'm Robert Anderson, and this is my daughter Becca. Our names should be on the list."

The girl taps away on her computer screen and smiles at us. "Oh, yeah. The boss said to give you the best seat in the house." She waves a waiter over and gives him two menus. The waiter wears a friendly smile and Harry Potter glasses. We follow him to the back and up a wide set of stairs. We sit across from each other at a booth set along a thick glass wall facing a lake.

"I've never been up here. I didn't even know there was a lake. You can't see it from the street." The view is spectacular with the lake nested among evergreen trees like a blue gem reflecting the sky. The restaurant sits alone on a road flanked by trees and nature everywhere.

"It's so much quieter up here."

My gaze darts all over, taking everything in. The glass and log walls lined with booths, the many carved wooden animals propped into niches and the totem pole that stands in the open center through both. It's just as busy up here as down below, but the conversations are more sedate. The atmosphere less chaotic. And despite the opening in the middle, the sounds from below don't quite reach us.

"Yes, Michael added soundproofing between the floors and a white noise machine around the opening."

"Is that your friend? The one who owns this place?"

"That's him. Michael Bear."

"Wait, Bear is his last name?"

He smiles. "You didn't know that?"

"No, never really put much thought into the name."

"We both served in the army. Together in the same unit for three years." His smile falters a little, and shadows dim the light in his eyes.

I can't imagine what kind of tortured memories he holds. I guess we both have some darkness to overcome.

The awkward silence stretches between us, but neither looks away. We're saved by our waiter when he arrives with water, lemon and orange slices dancing inside the pitcher he places between my father and me.

I glance up and freeze. The waiter mistakes my reaction for interest and smiles at me. A hint of cockiness in his face. He reminds me of Theodore—a younger version of the man who still haunts me inside my mind. The way he hovers at the edge of my seat. Looming over me. I'm trapped between him and the wall. He's too tall, too muscular, too smug. I scoot away an inch or two, drop my gaze to the general direction of his chest.

"Need a couple more minutes?" he asks.

"Yes, please," my father answers him.

I pick up the menu and use it as a shield. Put some space in between us, hide my face behind it. Close my eyes, push away the anxiety creeping up my spine like a spider. I want to recoil from both the feeling and the man standing next to me.

He walks away, but I still hide behind the menu, hoping my father didn't notice my reaction to the waiter. I drag a slow, silent breath expanding my lungs to the count of ten. Hold until my chest hurts with the need to release the stale air and then exhale. Do it again and again. Slowly the sounds of the restaurant come back, the tinkling of glass, snippets of conversations, laughs. The anxiety attack at bay. For now.

I lower my menu without having read a single word. When my gaze meets my father's, he's looking at me with so many questions in his eyes.

I look back at the menu, my hunger gone now.

"You okay, Becca?"

I could ignore his question. Make believe I didn't hear it. He would let it go, I know. But I lower the menu and let him see me. "Yeah, I'm fine."

"You know that man?"

"No, never saw him before, why?" I can't help the way my shoulders square out in defiance.

"You went a little pale, that's all. But your color is returning now."

I nod. "I get a little anxious around people sometimes." That's the most honest thing I have ever said to him. His eyes linger on me, but before he can say anything another man stops at our table. This time an older man, my father's age. Shaved head and built like an armoire. My father is on his feet a second later, and then they're doing the man-hug-slapping-backs thing.

"Becca, this is my good friend Michael. Michael, this is my daughter Becca."

I try to get up, but he waves me off and gives me his hand to shake instead. It's huge and callused. This guy is not sitting around collecting the profits from his restaurant.

"Nice to meet you." I shake his hand and thank God for not slipping back into anxiety. Perhaps knowing this man is my father's friend lends him a certain amount of trust. This surprises me. It's an unexpected thought.

Michael puts a hand on my father's shoulder and points at him. "This guy over here saved my life."

My father immediately shakes his head.

"Now, he's too modest to tell you. But he did. I got shot and knocked unconscious, but he dragged my sorry ass through a hellfire of bullets and got me to safety."

I look at my dad, and he averts his eyes, blinks a few times. Dad. This is the first time I think of him as such.

"Did you pick what you want to eat yet?" Michael asks us both.

I look at the menu and back at him. "Not yet. Any recommendations?"

"I'm not one to brag, but everything is good."

My father interrupts him. "Don't believe a word he says, he brags about everything."

Michael has a hearty laugh, and I can't help but to laugh with him.

"Tell you what? How about I surprise you? Do you trust me?" He points at me with both index fingers and a huge smile on his face. I look at my father, and he shrugs.

"Okay ... surprise me."

"Any allergies or foods you hate?" he asks.

"None, and I like everything."

"Awesome! Sit tight. I'll be back."

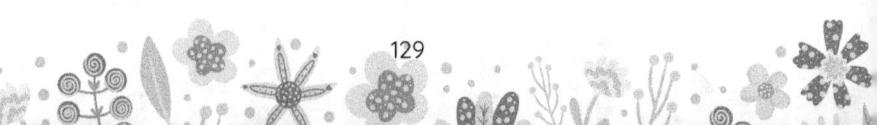

I watch him go for a few seconds before turning back to my father. "He's kind of intense."

"That he is." He fills both our glasses with water.

The same waiter shows up with a coffeepot and a carafe of orange juice, setting both on the table. "The boss-man sent this." He winks at me. "And said he's taking care of your food himself. Anything else I can get you?"

I curl my fingers into my palms, the sting of my nails biting into the tender flesh grounds me. Before I can say anything, my father dismisses him. "No, thank you. You can go now. I'm sure you have other tables to tend to." His tone is cold and dry, the opposite of the way he talks to me. The waiter walks away, but not before looking at me again.

My father picks up his phone and starts typing. It dings with a reply a few seconds later. "He won't be coming back again."

"Who? The waiter?"

"Yes."

"What did you do?"

"Asked Bear to send a waitress instead. I didn't like the way he was looking at you."

I look at him, speechless. I'm trapped in a kaleidoscope of conflicting emotions. Each taking a turn and trying to fill my field of vision. My chest warms in gratitude—that he cared enough to do this, to protect me from my perceived threat. Then it burns with indignation. How dare he interfere with my life? And finally caves in, scared he saw how uncomfortable the waiter made me feel.

"I can take care of myself, you know. I have been doing it alone my entire life." Anger, and old habits, win.

He nods, palms turned up. "I know, Becca. I know. But maybe you don't have to go it alone all the time anymore. We're family. Let me take some of the burden. I want to be here for you."

Family. I've longed for it, for the sense of security the word triggered in me my entire life. I blink away the sting of tears. I will not cry. I will not cry. I will not cry.

I reach for the orange juice and fill my glass, look at him, and he shakes his head, reaching for the coffeepot instead. I drink, filling my mouth with the sweet and tangy juice so I can buy myself some time.

"Listen, this is probably too soon and too much. I know we only met twice before. But we—I," he corrects himself. "I wasted too much time already. And I don't want to waste another second of not having you as a part of my life."

I drink another huge gulp, the liquid pushing at the knot in my throat.

"I was in the army for nearly ten years. Met someone a few months after they discharged me. We've been married for nine years now."

I set the glass down with shaky fingers.

"Her name is Linda."

I find my voice. "Does she—does she know about me?"

His face relaxes, his shoulders release the tension and drop. "Yes"—he smiles—"and she wants to meet you."

"She does?"

"Yes, she does. And there's more."

"More?" I'm reduced to parroting everything he says. I have no words of my own. I know what's coming, I'm not sure I'm ready to hear it.

"We have two kids." His voice drops to almost a whisper.

A small gasp leaves my lips. The knot returns to my throat and grows into a boulder.

"You have two siblings, Becca. A brother and a sister." He

131

leans into the table. "And they can't wait to meet you." He says this with so much love, with such a tenderness. It's too much. I don't know how to react or what to say.

"Becca? Stay with me, please." My gaze finds his, and I see fear. Fear of rejection. Fear that I will walk away.

I speak around the boulder, and my voice cracks. "They want to meet me?"

"They can't wait to meet you. They wanted to come with me today, but I want to give you the choice of how and when."

Give me a choice? Dear God. I have a brother and a sister. Something warm spreads in my chest and melts the boulder away.

"I thought maybe you could come over to our home. Have lunch, hang out and get to know your family?"

"My family?" I repeat.

"Yes, your family. They—we are your family. We want you."

"Here we go. I got you all my favorites." Michael Bear is back with an enormous tray, and I'm thankful for the reprieve. An older lady follows him and sets down a tray-holder. He places the tray on it and starts placing plates of food on the table. There's enough food to feed ten people.

"Wow. That's too much food." My mouth waters at the sight and heavenly scents of waffles covered in fresh fruit, pancakes drizzling with syrup, omelets bursting with cheese, bacon, sausages, home fries. There's French toast and whipped cream, and even breakfast burritos.

"Well, whatever you don't eat, we pack up, and you can take back with you. I know they don't have food this good at Riggins." Bear winks.

"I don't even know what to eat." I want to eat everything.

"Dig in. And this is Mariah. She'll be taking care of you. If you need anything, she's your woman." And with that, he's gone before I can even say thanks.

My father looks at me, I think he's also grateful for the reprieve.

"Eat." He points at all the food. And we eat.

We sit across the cleared table, the uneaten food packed in a brown paper bag on the seat next to me. I have enough leftovers to feast on for the next few days. The only things left on the table are two water glasses, condensation building on the sides.

I know my father waited until we were done with our meal to talk again. His eyes meet mine now.

"The whole family wants to meet you. Not only us, but your grandparents too."

"My grandparents?" Vivid images of all the pictures of his parents he showed me come to mind. My grandmother's kind face, my grandfather's mischievous smile.

"Yes, them too. Linda wants you to come for Thanksgiving. I know that might be too much for you. Too many new people, too much extended family. You're welcome to come to Thanksgiving, or we can meet the day after if you prefer, just the five of us."

"I don't know what to say." I can't believe they want to meet me.

"Say yes. We are your family. It's way overdue that I have all of my kids together."

I want to say yes. I want to say yes so badly. But he doesn't know me. He doesn't know about all the terrible choices I made. I'm toxic. I'll drag them down. I can't do that to them. I

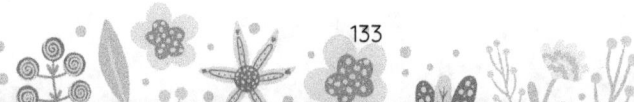

can't tarnish their family with my bitterness and all my dirty secrets.

I shake my head. His hands come up to stop me. "Wait." He grabs his phone and opens the photo app. The first thing I see is the smiling faces of two kids. A girl with brown hair and the same color eyes as me. The boy has white-blond hair and aqua-blue eyes. My sister and brother. They're beautiful and happy and innocent.

He taps the screen. "This is Mara. She's nine going on thirty. She thinks she's an adult and tries to boss everyone around. She's ecstatic to have a big sister. Since the moment we told them, she's been talking nonstop about meeting you and having girl time." He swipes to the next picture. The face of a boy fills the screen. His hair is long, reaching his shoulders and curling at the ends. He looks angelic. "Don't let the angel face fool you. He's a master manipulator. He gets you with that sweet smile and huge eyes. We call him our little heartbreaker." There's so much love and pride in his voice. He swipes again. Another picture of the two of them together. In PJs this time, sitting on a large bed, books all around them.

My heart fills with something I have never felt before. Not like this. I'm bursting with a love so fierce I know I would do anything to protect them. To keep them innocent and clean. To leave them untouched by the ugly in the world. To keep them from being tarnished by me.

A cry bursts from me, and the need to run overwhelms me. "I can't." I try to get up, but the bag of food blocks my way out.

"Becca." The quiet in his voice stops me.

I look at him. He reaches into his jacket and pulls out an envelope. My name written on it with a bright pink crayon in the sloppy handwriting of a child. "Mara wrote you a letter. I have no idea what it says. She sealed the envelope and told us we couldn't read it." He stretches his arm across the table. "Please?" All the joy is gone from his face, replaced with such a sadness, it wets his eyes. I did that. I turned his joy into sorrow. That's what I do.

I take the envelope with a shaky hand, move the bag of food. Get up.

"Take the food with you. Michael made it for you." He nods at the food with a watery smile. I take the food and leave.

CHAPTER TWENTY

BECCA

I DON'T EVEN REMEMBER THE DRIVE BACK TO MY DORM room. I left the restaurant and my father behind, but I couldn't leave all that weighs me down behind with him. Shame and regret follows me like a faithful, unwanted dog. The letter is burning a hole through my back pocket, but instead of reading it, I make space in my mini fridge by taking out water bottles and replacing them with the food. I fold laundry, dust my desk, and sweep the floor. All to buy myself another thirty minutes, but I can delay it no longer.

My hands shake when I pull the envelope out of my pocket and unfold it. I sit on my bed and smooth it against the mattress. Crayon drawings of pink flowers with yellow centers cover the envelope. My name is written in a childish calligraphy in the middle. I flip it over. On the back, a drawing of a unicorn, and her name, Mara, written inside a heart. On the corner, in a smaller writing, it says plus Hunter. My sister and brother.

I let the letter drop to my bed, grab my laptop and turn it on, going to the support website now so familiar to me, but

Therapist11 is not available. I knew he wouldn't be. He's never available during the day.

God, how did I come to rely on him so fast? I don't know if this is good or bad, but talking to him centers me. Talking to him helps me get out of my head and see things with more clarity. I close my laptop again, sit back on the bed, cross my legs, close my eyes and take a deep breath.

"It's just a letter. It's just a letter from a kid. There's nothing in this envelope that can hurt you, Becca." Why does my heart feel so small, then?

I take a breath and hold, release it. Do it again.

My hands shake when I slide a finger under the fold and carefully open the envelope so as not to rip it. I stop. Close my eyes. Take another measured breath. Then I slide out two sheets of paper. Unfold them.

My eyes track the childish handwriting without reading the words on the lined paper. There are little doodles all around the margins—flowers, butterflies, hearts, and stars all done in different-colored pencils.

I am not ready to read it, but I do it anyway. I can't delay myself any longer.

Dear big sister Becca,

I'm so happy to know I have a big sister. I've always wanted a big sister.

Daddy told us that a long time ago he had a baby, but he didn't know about it because the mommy never told him. Why did your mommy never tell my daddy he had a baby?

Was it a secret?

But then he found out all about you, and he said you're so beautiful, and so smart.

I'm so excited. I can't wait to meet you. I want you to come over so we can talk, and I can show you my room, and my drawings, and my books. Do you like to read? I love books, but mom won't let me read hers. She said I need to be thirty before I can read them.

Daddy said you're studying to be a social worker. I didn't know what that was, but he said that's a job where you help people who are a little lost. I think that's a very nice job. I would hate to be lost.

I'm in fifth grade and will be going to middle school in one more year. I'm a little nervous, but my mom says it will be okay because lots of my friends will be there too. Mom and Dad try to make me feel better, but they don't understand. I mean, they're old. They don't know what it's like to be a kid today. Hunter started first grade this year, but I think it's different for boys because he wasn't nervous at all.

Did you get nervous when you started college? Can I come and visit you? I've never been to a college before. I think it would be fun. Maybe it will make me less nervous about middle school. Then I can say, I went to college before I went to middle school. That would be funny.

I can't wait until we meet. There's so many things I want to do with you. We can go to the mall, and we can watch movies, and we can try different clothes on, and you can teach me how to use makeup because my mom says I'm too young and she won't let me even try.

My brother, Hunter, is also very excited to have a big sister. He says he wants you to pick on me, so I know what it's like to have an older sister. But you know what? I'm so happy to have a big sister that I wouldn't even mind if you picked on me.

Hunter can't write very well yet, so he made you a picture. He

said to tell you he loves you very much and he can't wait to meet you too.

Dad says he's inviting you over for dinner and that maybe you can spend Thanksgiving with us too. Please say yes.

I can't wait to meet you. Lots of love from your little sister,

Mara

I can barely see the words through the streaming of tears on my face. I press a hand to my mouth, trying to hold in the sobs, but they escape through my pressed lips.

God, why are you doing this to me? I wipe the tears with the back of my hand to no avail. I grab the edge of my T-shirt and do a better job this time, but rogue tears continue to break free.

With trembling fingers, I look at the second sheet of paper. And now I'm crying even harder. My hands shake so much I have to lay the letter and drawing on my bed. I grab a box of tissues, take several sheets and mop the mess that's become my face. I curb the tears and sobs, and look at the drawing again.

It's a regular piece of printer paper, but the drawing is everything I ever wanted and hoped for. There are five stick figures on the paper. To the left side of the page, the first stick figure is a tall man with light brown, honey-colored hair, his body done in navy blue. The word DAD next to it. Across the page, on the right side, another stick figure. A female, with a green dress and long brown hair. MOM is written to the right of the figure. Right in the middle, there's a drawing of me. My hair is the same color as my father's. My name above my head. A big smile on my face. He drew me wearing black pants and a gray shirt—the same colors I was wearing the first time I met my father. To the left of my stick figure, a little boy with yellow hair and dressed in blue, and HUNTER written next to him. And to my right, a little girl with brown hair and, in pink, the word MARA above her head.

Above the five stick figures, a rainbow, the colors in the right order. And written on top a single word. FAMILY.

I can't hold it in anymore, the pain comes out like an avalanche, ripping apart everything in its path with me in the middle, tumbling, tumbling, and so, so cold. The pressure in my chest robs me of air. My mouth hangs open, but no sounds flee. The silent wail so very telling in this moment. Even as I break, Theodore's voice whispers in my head.

"Quiet!"

"Shut up!"

"If you tell anyone, I'll kill you and kill your mother."

"No one would believe you."

"You're nothing. No one loves you. No one cares."

"I know you like it, you little whore."

I fall apart, fold into myself, make my body smaller, melt into my bed. I've kept his voice at bay for so long, but he finds me now. His ghost haunts me still. The pressure builds like magma inside a volcano until I crack wide open. Erupt. Let it all pour out like lava running over rocks. It scorches my heart. My shame is fire, and it's burning me alive.

CHAPTER TWENTY-ONE

BECCA

I DON'T KNOW HOW LONG I CRIED BEFORE EXHAUSTION and sleep claimed me. My room lay in shadows. There's no light coming through the window. The sky outside is winter gray, even though winter is still a month away.

I shiver. A hot shower will make me feel better. I force my limbs to move. Everything weighs me down. I'm heavy and lethargic. A pounding headache beats against my temples. I gather a towel, bath robe, and shower supplies. Looping my keycard lanyard around my wrist, I make my way to the common showers, glad it's on this floor and only two doors down the hall. I don't even know what time it is. But it's probably too early to get ready for a night out. I should have the space to myself.

Weeks ago, I would be at a party. On the prowl for someone to numb myself with. That's no longer an option. I'm not that girl anymore. I don't know why or how it happened. But the idea of a meaningless hookup repels me.

I glimpse myself in a mirror. Stop. Turn to it. My reflection doesn't lie. Pale skin, puffy, red eyes and dried, black mascara tracks on my cheeks. I see my mother's face in mine.

Her hollow empty eyes sunk into dark circles stare at me in my dreams sometimes. It's been nearly four years since I last saw or spoke with her. I don't even know if she's alive. She must be. If something had happened to her, I would have heard about it. Someone would have found me. She never tried to contact me. It would have been easy enough to find me. She knows where I am.

The door to the shower room opens with a creak that begs for oil. It's followed by voices, and I retreat to the back. I find a shower stall, close the thick, opaque curtains and hang my things. Stripping, I then turn on the water and step into the spray before it's warm enough to be comfortable. I welcome the initial sting of icy water as it jolts me out of my head for a few blessed seconds.

But as the water warms, the thoughts come back. All I've ever wanted was a loving family. A mother who cared and protected me. A father. Siblings. I've never known the meaning of family. But today, a nine-year-old and five-year-old taught me more about the love of a family than I could ever have imagined.

I want that. I want that so badly it scares me. What if they let me in? What if I allow myself to love them, and they find out about me? If they find out how unworthy I am. How unlovable. How I cheapened myself with sex.

I turn the water hotter, wash my hair, wash the mascara and makeup off my face, scrub at my skin with soap and a loofa until it stings. It's been years since Theodore last touched me. Years since he died, but some days I can still feel his fingers on me, the press of his much larger body on mine. I can still smell the stink of weed, alcohol, and sweat.

I've scrubbed my skin raw too many times before to know that no amount of soap and water can wash off the memories in my head.

I want to say yes to my father. I want to meet my sister and brother. I want to go to Thanksgiving with them. I want all the things my father wants to offer me, but I know they'll ask questions. I know they'll be curious.

My mind plays a hopscotch game, jumping from one thought to the next.

I don't want to lie. I'm tired of lies and deceit, but how can I ever tell them the truth?

I turn off the water, dry myself. Put on the robe that's so big on me it swallows me whole. I grab my things and walk back to my room, making no eye contact with the few people in the hall. I lock my door behind me. Night has fallen, and I close the curtains and shut out the outside world of Saturday parties, hookups, and carefree fun.

I check my phone. I have text messages from both River and Tommy. Nothing from my father. Perhaps he changed his mind, and it's already too late. Perhaps he decided for me.

I find my laptop. Log in. Grab my headphones. Navigate to the support page. I sink to my bed in relief when I see his name in bold. He's available.

Therapist11. I click on the icon and wait.

"Good night." His voice is warm, welcoming.

"Hi." Mine quivers.

"What's wrong? You sound like you've been crying." He immediately picks up on my mood.

"How-how can you tell? I said one word."

"You sound sad." Now his voice sounds sad too.

"I'm having a hard day."

"Want to tell me about it?"

"Do you ever get tired of hearing people's complaints all day?"

He chuckles. "No, not really. And I don't get a lot of calls."

"No?"

"No. Besides you, I've only had two other people pick me."

"I guess the being-a-guy thing might scare some girls off." I'm still surprised I had the guts to pick a dude too, but I'm glad I did.

"Why did you pick me? You had other options."

"You going to laugh at me?"

"Hmmm … maybe?"

"You're supposed to say you won't laugh at me."

"But then I might laugh and that would be lying, and the one promise I can make you is to always be truthful with my words."

"I appreciate that." Funny, being that I lie all the time.

"So?" he prompts me.

"It was … I don't know. Fate? Divine intervention if you believe such things." I pull a blanket over my legs. "I saw the flier, and when I checked on the website it was eleven eleven."

"Ah, and my number is eleven."

"Yes, but it's more than that. I tossed a coin too."

"You tossed a coin?"

"Yes. Got heads three times."

"I see." He doesn't sound like he sees it at all.

"You do?" I challenge him.

"Yes. You left it to fate to decide on who you would talk to."

"Yes, my past choices haven't been that great. I figured if I removed myself from the equation, I might have better luck. I think it worked."

"Well, I'm glad you picked me. I enjoy talking to you."

There's a hesitation in his voice at the end. Like he didn't mean to say that last part.

"I enjoy talking to you too. It … it's easier than I thought."

A silence falls between us and extends for a few seconds more. I know he's waiting for me to speak, to tell him why I'm upset. And I'm grateful for the extra time he gives me to get around to it.

"I met my father today."

He waits a beat before speaking again. "Is that good or bad?"

"I'm not sure. Good, I guess."

"Go on."

"I met my father for the first time several weeks ago."

"How did that make you feel?"

"At first, it enraged me. After all this time, I thought, why come to find me now?"

"Did you ask him that? Why now?"

"Yes. He said it was time."

"You said when you first met your father you felt enraged. How do you feel about him now?"

"Not enraged. Sad. I'm mourning all the lost time." I didn't know that's what I was feeling until I said the words, but they ring so true the sting of tears comes back to my eyes.

"Despite the fact that he wasn't in my life this whole time, he's a good guy."

"What are you going to do about it?"

"I have no idea. He wants me in his life. Today he told me he has a family, wife, kids. I have a brother and sister, and he wants me to meet them."

"Do you want to meet them?"

"Yes. No. I don't know."

"Okay. I can see how finding out you have siblings can be a shock. Let's break it down into small bites. Yes?"

My chest expands with a deep inhale as if I'm preparing to go under water. "Yes."

"Tell me how you feel about letting your father into your life."

I drop to my bed, lie on my back and adjust the buds in my ears. "I think he really cares about me. He told me all about growing up, showed me pictures of his parents and grandparents. He told me he regrets not being in my life. He didn't know about me at first, and when he found out, my mother pushed him away, and he let her. He sent her money, but he didn't stay around to check on me."

"So, he cares about you. He regrets not being present in your life and wants to make amends. Do you want him in your life?"

"Yes, but I'm scared."

"What are you scared of?" His voice softens, and I push my buds in to hear him better.

"Disappointing him. Disappointing myself. I don't know."

"I think you know."

Jesus. "This is hard. Why is it so hard?"

"We all fear speaking out our innermost thoughts because that makes them real. Secrets, pain, shame—all of it thrives in the dark. The more we bury and hide them, the stronger and bigger they grow. Speaking up doesn't make them real, it weakens them. The fear is a result of the lies we tell ourselves to feel safer. But we don't feel safer at all, do we?"

"No. I don't feel safer."

"Why not?" He waits for me to connect the dots.

"Because I'm always afraid."

"Afraid of what?"

"That someone will find out. That someone will figure out all of my secrets." And pain and shame.

"Exactly. So we trap ourselves in this never-ending loop. Bury the secrets and the shame as deep as we can so no one can find them, and then we live in fear of someone finding out. We hold ourselves hostage to our own humanity."

"We hold ourselves hostage to our own humanity," I repeat, letting it sink in.

"Yes. No one is perfect. Every single person on this planet has skeletons in their closets and shame over them. It's our collective flaw as a human race."

"How do we fix that?"

"We deal with shame the same way you'd deal with someone who's blackmailing you."

"Pay them off?"

He laughs. "No. The way to stop someone from blackmailing you is to remove what they hold over you."

"I'm not getting it."

"Someone can't blackmail you if you expose whatever they have on you first. You come clean and show the world whatever is the thing that has a hold on you. You beat them at their own game."

I'm shaking my head before he even finishes speaking. And as if he can sense it, he speaks again.

"Stop it. That's shame and fear talking to you right now. That's shame and fear blackmailing you into thinking you have to hide and run and give in to whatever it wants. It's not true. It's a lie."

"You don't know what I have to hide."

CHAPTER TWENTY-TWO

BECCA

He pauses after that. Each second taking a millennium. One thousand years.

Two thousand years.

Three thousand years.

Then he breaks the silence. "No, you're right, I don't know what secrets you keep. Each person's pain is uniquely theirs. Even if their experiences are similar. We all process differently. But I've worked at this for a while now. I have delved deep into people's darkness, and I can assure you that nothing you can say would shock me."

"That's sad and horrifying." My chest constricts with the idea of other little girls and boys living through what I did.

"Yes, it can be. I've seen all matters of darkness, of pain and hurt, and hopelessness. But I also have seen people learning to love themselves. People learning to forgive the past, letting go, and figuring out how to be happy."

I pull a blanked over me, cocoon under its cover. "That sounds kinda impossible right now."

"No such thing as impossible." There's no hesitation in his reply.

I laugh at that. "I don't know, Doc, I have never had much faith in the goodness of people."

"You don't need to have faith in the goodness of other people. You need to have faith in your own goodness."

God. His words hit me like a slap to the face. "I guess … I'm even more screwed, then, because I'm not good." The words hurt when they leave my lips.

"I don't believe that. Those are the lies you tell yourself."

"How could you possibly know if I'm a good person or not? You don't know me."

"I know you are a good person because you care. Because you want to do better and be better."

I don't respond. He has me there. I want to be better. I want to be someone I can be proud of. And I care.

"Tell me what happened today? What upset you?" he asks me.

I hesitate, spread my fingers on the bed. "I met my father for breakfast this morning."

"How did meeting your father for breakfast upset you?"

"It's not his fault I'm upset." Why am I defending my father?

The faint sound of a creaking chair comes through my earbuds. "I never said it was."

No, he didn't.

"Go on," he says.

"This is only the third time I met him. He wants to be a part of my life, he wants to get to know me."

"How does that make you feel?"

"Why are you always asking me that?" My voice is louder than I intended.

He chuckles. "Because, my friend, how we feel is the crux of the problem."

"How should I feel? What is the right feeling?"

"There is no right or wrong. Emotions, feelings, just are. How we relate to them, and what we do about them, is what matters."

"Ugh. That's not an answer."

"It's the only answer I can give you for that question. You are evading my original question, though. How did meeting your father make you feel?"

I pull the blanket tighter around my shoulders. "Everything. It made me feel everything."

He waits. I know he wants me to elaborate.

Why is it so hard to put words to the storm raging in my chest? "The first time I met him, I was so angry. I ... I wanted to hurt him. I wanted him to feel the same pain I felt. But I also wanted to know him. I wanted to find out why he never came for me."

"You said, 'the first time you met him you were angry.' You're not angry anymore?"

"I don't know what I am. I'm splintered into a hundred pieces, and each tiny piece feels and wants something different."

"Okay, I can see how meeting your father for the first time as an adult can be confusing and conflicting. Let's name some of those pieces now. We can tackle them together."

I already feel like someone put me through a meat grinder. I want to say hell to the no, but I don't. "Okay." I put as much enthusiasm in my reply as I can, but I'm not fooling anyone.

"It's not a root canal without anesthesia. It's just talking. Let's do this out of order. You said you met your father three times. Tell me about the second time you met him."

I almost wish for the root canal instead. "We met for lunch a few weeks ago."

"What did you talk about?"

"He showed me pictures of his parents and grandparents. Told me about his life, said he wants to get to know me better. To have a real father-daughter relationship."

"And—"

"I know. How did that make me feel? I don't know. I want that father-daughter relationship more than anything else. But a part of me is so angry still. It wants to tell him to fuck off. I think it will be angry forever."

"Hmm."

Hmm? What does that mean?

"Do you communicate with your father often in between those meetings?"

"He sent several texts in between. I didn't answer most of them."

"Why not?"

"Because I wanted him to feel like I felt my entire life."

"And what was that? How did you feel your entire life?"

"Abandoned and waiting for something that would never come."

"But now, it is here. The something you were waiting for—your father is here. And it challenges the truth you've been holding on to all these years. That he would never come. You don't have that to hold on to anymore. It's no longer true."

He's right. I have been holding on to my anger for so long it has become a lifesaver in a rough sea. But now that lifesaver has been pulled from me, and I'm adrift with nothing to hold to but the lies I tell myself. Knowing this doesn't make it any easier.

"I know you're right. I can rationalize it, but I'm still trying to hold on. Why is it so hard to let go?"

"Because it has become a habit. Because you don't trust that it's real. You're waiting for the other shoe to drop, for him to disappear again."

"I am." He's right again. I'm afraid to hope. And what does that "hmm" mean?

"But what if he stays? What if your father becomes a real father to you?"

I ignore the question. "What did you mean by 'hmm' before?"

"Ah, that. I was pondering at your choice of words."

What did I say? "What choice of words?"

"You said, 'I want that father-daughter relationship' and that a part of you was 'angry.' You referred to what you want as 'I,' but to the anger as 'it.' You didn't say you are angry. You said a 'part of me.' This part is angry, not you. Anger is a separate entity. But the want for your father is you."

What the hell am I supposed to do with that? "It's just words."

"Is it? You have to find your true self. Anger is not your true self. It's simply an aspect of your personality that takes over to protect you from what experience has taught are very real possibilities. Our emotions are always trying to protect us. If you didn't have to protect yourself, how would you feel? That's closer to your true self."

Whoa ... back up a minute. "My true self?"

The sound of steps accompanies his voice. "Yes. You said yourself that you are holding on to your old beliefs and anger. Holding on is as much a choice as letting go. But when you let go, when you truly let go, you are suddenly filled with empty spaces. You miss the burden, the comfort, of what is familiar.

As destructive and painful as anger and unforgiveness are, for most people they're still better than nothing. That anger validates them. Makes them righteous. None of that is your true self."

I'm almost afraid to ask. I'm getting a headache. "How—how do I fix that? How do I learn to let go and become my true self?"

"It's different for each person. You can let go a little at a time or all at once. But the key of truly letting go is to fill those empty spaces with something else, so whatever you let go of has no room to come back."

I rub my temples. My cold hand soothes the building headache. "What do I fill the spaces up with?"

"That's up to you. Love, hope, kindness, charity. Fill that space and time up with whatever you want as long as it is something good for you and those around you."

"That's a lot to think about."

"Yes, and I'll let you ponder about that on your own. We have two more meetings to talk about. Tell me about the last time you met your father. You said it was today."

"We met for breakfast and talked. He's nice. A good man. The kind of man I always wanted as a father. But now that he's here, I don't know what I want."

"Don't you?" he challenges me.

"What I want is impossible. What I want doesn't matter. It will never be." Why can't he understand that?

"If by impossible, you mean change the past, then you are right. You can't change it. But you can change the way you look at it. You can change the way you relate to your past. That's within your power."

I laugh. "Power? I have no power."

"But you do. And we are getting sidetracked again. Working

with what you have now—having your father back in your life
—what do you want?"

I give in, put into words what I have told no one before. "I
want to be loved, cared for. I want someone to care."

"And your father? What does he want?"

I bite my thumb until it stings. "Forgiveness and to be a
part of my life."

"And why did that upset you so much?"

"Because he already has a family. A perfect one. He has a
wife and two kids. I have siblings. I have a brother and a sister.
And my father wants me to join them, he wants me to be a part
of his family."

"Isn't it what you want too? A family?"

"Yes. But how can I? How can I let him—them get closer?
My brother, my sister. They're kids and innocent. How can I let
them be tainted by me? By all the horrible things I did?"

"What horrible things?"

"Can we talk about the first time I met him now?" I wait
for a response, not sure if he will let it go or ask again.

"Sure. We can. Tell me about the first time you met your
father."

"The first time I met him, it was not what I expected at all."
I turn onto my back and stare at the ceiling in the darkening
room. "I expected him to be some kind of sleazy asshole. But he
wasn't. He's young, clean cut, attractive even. And I have his
hair and eye color. It was a shock to see so much of myself in
this man I had never met."

"Why did you expect him to be some kind of sleaze
asshole?"

"The way my mother always talked about him. She lied. She
lied about so many things."

"What did your mother lie about?"

"Everything. She lied about everything. About his reasons to stay away. About him. Even about me. He didn't even know he had a daughter. Not until I was seven. And when he found out, she lied to keep him away from me so she could continue to get high and drunk on the money he sent her for child support." I push the heels of my hands into my forehead and closed my eyes to keep the tears away. "I was so angry. At her for all the lies and at him for believing her and never trying to find me until it was too late." God. I said too much.

"Why was it too late?"

And there it is. He caught that. I knew he would as soon as I let it slip out. I drag a breath in and pull the blanket over my head, closing my eyes inside my already dark cocoon. The air grows warm and stale in the confined space.

"Because if he had come for me, if he had seen where and how I lived, he would have taken me away, and then Theodore would never have hurt me." It's out. I said his name out loud for the first time in years. And it didn't break me. Not like before when he made me say his name again and again while he hurt me, while he wrapped his hands around my throat and robbed me of air, while he raped me.

The silence that follows is heavy with meaning. "Who's Theodore?" His voice is so soft, so filled with kindness—I can't refuse him.

"He was my mother's boyfriend."

"What else?"

I could hold my response. I could hang up right now and never call again. No one would know. Except me. I would know, and I'm tired of hiding, lying, and being a coward. "He was my tormentor, my molester … my rapist."

"Where is Theodore now?"

"Rotting in hell."

CHAPTER TWENTY-THREE

BECCA

T HE M ASLOW BUILDING GREETS ME WITH ITS MIRRORED windows and beautiful lines. I overslept, and I'm late. I hate being late. This disruption of my routine spikes my anxiety and need for control. I'm running now, my heart racing with the exertion, my breath rapid and shallow. With only two minutes before classes start, the halls are mostly empty. I take the stairs two at a time and make my way to the second floor—and come to a halt—my sneakers squeaking on the tiled floor.

I nearly crash into Professor Dick. Inches between us, close enough to inhale his clean scent. It hits me in layers.

Soap.

Aftershave.

Fresh laundry.

He's wearing a baby-blue shirt under the navy jacket. The first couple buttons are open. My gaze gets snagged in that small space of tanned skin just under his throat. He exhales. A minty taste touches my lips. I look up and find his eyes fixed on me. The color more honey than whiskey in the sunlight filtering through the tall windows.

His size doesn't instill fear in me like so many other bigger men do. There's no aggression in his stance, no dominance, no cockiness. He has a solid and stable presence, an inner-calm that reaches out to me and tries to dull my sharp edges. He makes me feel safe. Safe enough to get mad and be rude. That familiar twinge of irritation that shows itself every time we cross paths is slowly awakening and dragging me out of my stupor. Is this a defense mechanism? Because he embarrassed me all those years ago. Because of Tommy? Crap on a cracker! The therapist has me analyzing everything now.

We're standing still, trapped in a virtual tug-of-war. Neither looking away nor making the first move.

He blinks first, opens his mouth, his body sways a little, his head tilts, he leans in, and—all hell breaks loose. Doors slam above and below. The last few people in the halls are running. The insistent vibration of my cell phone in my pocket has me reaching for it. Professor Dick reaches for his phone at the same time. We look at our screens.

LOCKDOWN
ACTIVE SHOOTER ON CAMPUS.

I freeze.

He doesn't.

Professor Dick grabs my wrist and pulls me down the hall, I resist, my feet dragging with a squeaking sound. My body wants to fight him—flashbacks of another hand grabbing me and dragging me fleet before my eyes.

"Becca, please!"

The plea in his voice snaps me out of it. We run up two flights of stairs to the fourth floor. My heart is beating so fast it is pounding in my ears. He comes to a stop so abruptly that I slam into his back. He doesn't even register it. He lets go of my wrist and pulls a set of keys from his jacket pocket. His office. The door opens. He urges me inside first and locks the door behind him. I stand still, paralyzed by indecision. I don't know what to do. He wedges a chair under the door handle. Then he steps back and pulls me with him to the floor. We sit with our backs against a bookcase. His chest expanding and contracting with each rapid breath. I'm breathing just as fast, my chest burns with each inhale. The phone buzzes in my hand again. I look at the screen, but the same message as before appears.

Jesus! I never expected to see that message in the campus-wide notification system. We get weather-related messages. Classes canceled because of a snowstorm. But nothing like this. My hands tremble, and I lay the phone on the floor next to my backpack.

"W-what will h-happen?" I'm shaking so much my voice stutters. Tears sting my eyes, and I can't catch my breath. I suck in air in big gulps, but it's not enough.

We're sitting shoulder to shoulder.

He moves and puts an arm around me. "You're safe."

Of all the things he could have said, this is what I needed to hear most.

He tugs me closer. "Shhhhh, it's okay. It will be okay."

His presence, his scent, his voice, the heat of his body pressed against mine—all of it seeps into me layer by layer, slowly breaking into my panic attack and dragging me out of it.

His touch, the gentle pressure, calms me down. I should be terrified right now. I should be terrified because I'm locked in a room with a man who could easily overpower me. And no one knows I'm here. And yet, I feel safe. Perhaps because he's Tommy's brother, and I trust Tommy. Perhaps because he never made me feel like an object to be used.

Whatever the reason, I'm glad he's here to talk me off the ledge, to guide me back into reason. Relief washes over me like a tidal wave, slow to rise and then all at once. I shudder. He pulls me closer, tucks me into his chest. His chin rests on my head, and he makes soothing sounds while rubbing my back with one hand and my head with the other. The hum so quiet, it's more of a flutter against my skin than a melody. Gentle fingers comb through my hair. I don't resist. I don't pull away. I wrap myself around him, nestle closer still. Allow myself to be in this moment, drinking in the heat of his body and the comfort of his embrace. Savor the safety of hands that mean no harm. I close my eyes.

Our breaths slow, his beating heart under my ear is strong and steady. Minutes pass. His hands slow until they just hold me.

I should move. I should stop this right now. But I stay. I don't dare even speak. I don't want to break away. I don't want to burst this bubble. I'm in an alternate universe. I like it here. Time stands still inside his embrace.

Our phones vibrate. We don't move. We stay. There are sounds now. Coming through the door. Steps, people talking. Movement outside. More messages on our phones. The sounds out in the hall get louder, dozens of voices. The outside coming in, breaking this—whatever this is.

His lips press against the top of my head. Not quite a kiss. He inhales deeply. I do the same and fill my lungs with his scent. I want to hold on to this moment, freeze time, and stay here. I crave his touch, the safety of his arms around me. I mourn the impending loss of his embrace. How can I yearn for something I never even knew I wanted?

He disengages from me. Pushes me back with tender hands. We touch no more but the physical sensations linger. My skin prickles under the intensity of his gaze. But coward that I am, I don't meet his eyes. I look around instead.

I've never been in his office. It's small. The walls painted sage green. There's a dark wooden desk, a chocolate-brown leather chair and a bookcase behind us. The window lets the sunlight in. The rug under us is also dark brown. The space is masculine, austere even. But spotless. No dust, no empty bottles or old coffee cups. He gets up, standing in front of me. I stare at his shoes.

"Becca?"

I look up, his hand waits for mine. I take it, and he pulls me to my feet.

"You okay?" He bends his head, trying to catch my eyes.

I look up. "Yeah, thanks. I'm okay." There's no judgment. No inquisition. No coldness in his gaze or voice. And it's like I'm seeing a different person. Or like I'm seeing him for the first time. Who's this man standing in front of me? So cold one moment and so kind the next? What is he hiding behind the harsh façade?

I want to take a step closer to him, push into his chest and lock his arms around me again. Find that safe place I've craved my entire life.

I don't recognize him or myself in this moment. We are two different people, pushed together by circumstance and playing a role neither is sure of.

It's too much. I grab my backpack and cell phone from the floor. There are several messages. Some from the school with updates. They got the guy. The shooter. They have canceled classes. Students are advised to stay in their dorms or leave campus. There are messages from River and my father. And one from Tommy.

I look at him. "Tommy is okay."

He looks at his own phone, and his eyes widen. "Jesus. Tommy! I forgot about him."

He mouths the words, but I read his lips. The words are as clear to me as if he had said them out loud.

"What?" I try to catch his gaze, hold on to the magic a little longer.

His face goes distant. His shoulders straighten back, becoming rigid. Does he blame me for not thinking of Tommy?

He steps aside, moves the chair away from the door. Opens it.

"Miss Jones." He gestures toward the hall.

Message received loud and clear. He wants me out. Whatever happened in this room is now gone. And I don't think I'll ever find it again.

CHAPTER TWENTY-FOUR

DYLAN

"How could I forget Tommy?" My brother. My only family.

And what for? A girl I barely know, but can't stop thinking about.

I pace the small space in my office, talking to myself.

"But she was so scared." All I could think of was keeping her safe. Taking her from harm's way. Protecting her. I want to reach out and erase the pain I see in her eyes. And hurt whoever put it there.

"If something had happened to Tommy, I would never forgive myself."

I can't have someone else die because of me.

CHAPTER TWENTY-FIVE

BECCA

The campus is total chaos. There are people everywhere, some crying, some huddled in small groups, some hugging and some standing as if in shock. Students, police, and EMTs litter the way. I cut through the throngs of people and walk to the dorms, catching snippets of conversations here and there.

There was a shooter on campus.

The police got him.

He was at the Jane Austen building.

No one got hurt.

My phone keeps buzzing in my hand. There are messages from my father, from River and Tommy. I ignore all of them, instead rushing for the safety of my room. For the only space that's mine, even if it's temporary. I need to put distance between myself and the moments I shared with Dylan. I miss his touch. I miss the comfort of his presence and the care with which he held me. The time we spent together brought to light a hole in my heart. An empty space I wasn't aware was there. And a sweet ache of longing I never imagined possible.

What is this? How could he have done so much damage to my defenses in so little time?

I make it to my room and lock the door behind me. I fall against it, my body heavy like lead. The space from the door to my bed may as well be miles away. I let my backpack drop to the floor, kick off my sneakers, stagger the few steps and fall backward into my bed. I stare at the ceiling as if it could give me answers to questions I don't even know how to ask.

My phone buzzes again.

> River: Are you okay? Where are you?

I drop the phone to my chest, squeeze my eyes shut, drag in a breath, release. Shake my hands as if the physical motion could also shake off my thoughts. Pick up the phone again.

> Becca: Yes, I'm fine. I'm in my room.

My hands still tremble. I can barely type.

> River: Jesus! Why didn't you respond before?

I call her. She answers before the first ring ends.

"Where were you? I've been texting you for over an hour." The worry in River's voice is unmistakable.

"I'm sorry. I was in Maslow. Almost to my classroom when the alert went out." I sit up, and I'm momentarily dizzy.

"I saw people from your classroom, they said you weren't there."

"No, I never made it inside. I was in the hall when all the doors began to close and lock."

"Oh my God, where did you go?"

"I was … I was with Professor Dick." I can't still believe it myself. Did I imagine it?

"What? How?" Her voice drops to a whisper.

I lie down again. "He was in the hall too. I nearly slammed into him running up the steps to the second floor. When the lockdown message came through, he grabbed me and we ran to his office."

"He saved you!"

Did he save me? "Technically, I was never in danger because the guy was not in Maslow."

"Pfft," she makes a dismissive sound. "He didn't know that, and neither did you."

I shift the conversation to her. "What about you? And Skye? Doesn't she have most of her classes in the Jane Austen building?"

"I was in my class. Everyone is fine. But Skye—God. She was there. And the guy, the shooter? He's one of her professors' husband. And Skye was in that professor's classroom."

I almost drop my phone. "Jesus! Is she okay? That must have been terrifying."

"She's okay. Her boyfriend got her out."

"He's a cop, right? Was he one of the officers who went into the building?"

"Yes. That much I know. But I've heard nothing yet. I made Skye take a Xanax, and she's sleeping now."

"I can't even imagine what Skye went through."

"What I can't imagine is you holed up with Professor Dick —Beckett in his office. Now you have me calling him Dick too."

"It was n-nothing." It was not nothing. My voice cracks.

"What are you not telling me, Becca?"

She'll pester me until I say something. "It was weird." It was ... amazing.

"Weird how?"

"We got to his office, locked the door and sat on the floor. And then ..." Jesus. Did that really happen? Or did I imagine it?

"And then what?"

"He hugged me. He put his arm around my shoulders and pulled me into him and held me the entire time until we got the message that the lockdown was over."

"Aww. That's so sweet! I told you he likes you."

I snort at that. "He doesn't like me. He was just—I don't know, trying to be nice, comfort me. I was freaking out a little."

"No, not buying it. He didn't have to hold you."

"And he sang too. Not with lyrics. He hummed a song while he held me and rubbed his hand on my back. It was ... it was calming. I felt safe. Protected."

"Whoa ... he sang? For you?"

"He hummed a song. It was familiar too. But I can't remember the name."

"Dude. He likes you. That's more than just being nice. I told you. I have a sixth sense for these things."

"Well, you were wrong about Tommy. I never dated him." I drop an arm over my eyes to block the light.

"You let me believe you were."

"You assumed, River. I never said I was hooking up with him." There's a moment of silence that extends for several seconds.

"Now what?" River asks.

"Now what nothing. There's nothing. I was freaking out, and he comforted me. End of story."

"Nooooo. No end. This is the beginning, my friend. I need more."

I sigh. "There's nothing, River. As soon as the lockdown was up, he kicked me out of his office. It was so awkward."

"Of course it was. He's a professor, and you are a student. He has to tread carefully."

"Jesus! Sometimes you're like a dog with a bone, you know?"

"No. It's more like Professor Dick is the one with a boner." She cracks herself up with the joke.

"Lame, River. So lame."

She goes quiet again. "It would be a nice change, you know? Date a real man instead of those boys you pick up. You deserve a guy like him."

My head is shaking with each word she says. "You know a guy like him would never be with me. He's far too classy for the likes of me. He probably has a super smart girlfriend too."

"What do you mean the likes of you? You're smart. You're pretty. You can be classy too."

I laugh at that. Me? Classy? I'm white trash. My mother is white trash. She's a slut, and I guess I'm not much better than her. She uses men to get money and get high. I use them for a different kind of high. I'm exhausted from the roller coaster of emotions I've been through in the last hour alone. I'm blindsided by my own feelings. It's like an upper cut to the soul. "You have no idea what you're talking about. And he's a professor. I'm a student. That would never happen."

"You're not *his* student. And you're both adults. You can be discreet. No one has to know."

"I'll know. And he will know. Do you really think a guy like him would break the rules for me?"

"Yes, I really do."

My phone vibrates with a new text message. Tommy. "Hey, River? I'm getting a ton of texts. I have to go. Glad you and your sister are okay. Call me later?"

"Yes, coward. Go. But I'm not dropping this. There's more to this story, and I know it."

River hangs up before I say anything else.

I tap the screen and open the text message app.

> Tommy: Hey. My brother said he saw you and you're okay. But talk to me. I want to make sure.

> Becca: Yes, I'm fine. I was nowhere near the Austen building. Crazy stuff. What about you?

> Tommy: I'm okay. I was in my dorm. Crazy for sure.

> Tommy: Want to hang out tomorrow morning? We haven't done that in a while.

> Becca: Can't. I'm at the hospital in the morning and have work after.

> Tommy: Hospital?

Damn it. I'm too distracted. I didn't think. I don't like telling people about my volunteering at the hospital. There are always questions.

> Becca: Yes. I volunteer there sometimes. I gotta go. Talk later?

> Tommy: Sure. Don't ghost me. :)

I shove the phone under my pillow and drift off to sleep.

Loud banging on my door has me nearly jumping out of my skin. How long did I sleep for? There's light coming in from the window still, so not long. My heart is racing, and my groggy brain is trying to catch up. The banging comes again.

"Becca? Are you there? Open the door."

I shake off the last hint of sleep and stumble to open the door. "Who is it?"

"It's me." The voice comes as I unlock the door.

My father charges into the room in a blur of limbs and tackle-hugs me. For the second time today, I'm in someone's arms.

"Oh my God, oh my God, oh my God. You're okay. Thank god you're okay." He holds me at arm's length as if to check I'm in one piece, then pulls me back into a hug again.

I freeze. I don't understand what's happening. I extricate myself. "What are you doing here?"

"I drove. I got in the car as soon as I saw it on the news."

He lives over an hour away. He must have raced all the way here.

I'm so confused. "How did you find my room?"

"I went to the admissions office, showed them my driver's license. My name is on your birth certificate. Threatened the poor kid working there if he didn't tell me your dorm room number."

He hugs me again with the ferocity of a mother bear. "I thought I had lost you. I just found you, and I thought I had lost you." His voice breaks with a sob.

"I don't understand." Why does he care?

He pulls away, his hands on my shoulders. "You're my

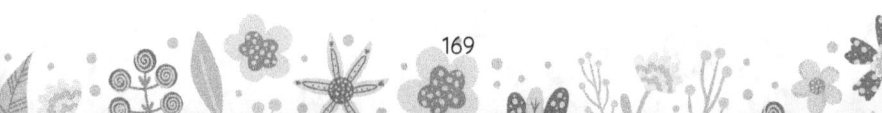

daughter. I love you. Of course I had to come and see you with my own eyes."

It's too much. "But … you don't know me."

"It doesn't matter, Becca. It doesn't matter I didn't know you existed for the first seven years of your life. It doesn't matter we only met a couple of months ago. I loved you from the moment I knew you existed, even if I was never a part of your life. I loved you from far away." His eyelashes are wet, tears track down his face.

I don't know what to say. I never heard those words before. I craved them. I wished for them, even begged for them, but no one ever said they loved me before. My chest fills with flutters I can't quite identify and something cracks inside of me. A layer sheds away, and turns to ashes, burned by the warmth spreading through me. My father loves me.

CHAPTER TWENTY-SIX

BECCA

My bed creaks as I settle in and drag my laptop next to me. No more avoiding talking to the therapist. Our last conversation still fresh in my mind. Now he knows about my past. Part of it, at least.

For the first time since I started talking to him his name on the screen is grayed out. He's not there. I need to talk to him. I need to hear his voice. And he's not there. Heat flares in my chest and spreads to the rest of my body. My hands clench. I want to grab the laptop and toss it against the wall.

Why isn't he there?

Why am I so angry?

When did I become so dependent on him?

I hate feeling this way. Like he left me. I know he didn't. I know he has a life outside these calls. He's not a friend or family. He's not even an acquaintance, and yet I feel betrayed.

I need him, and he's not there.

Like my mother.

Like my father.

I stare at the screen so long my vision blurs. I close my eyes and concentrate on breathing. Breathing and counting until emptiness replaces the surge of anger.

I open my eyes and blink against the bright glare of the laptop. Blink again.

His name is in bold now. He's back! My shoulders drop with relief. My hand moves to the mouse, but I hesitate. I can't allow myself to rely on him. To have this kind of reaction when he's absent. That's not normal. But then again, nothing in my life is.

I put my earbuds in and click the icon to call him. I won't talk about my mini tantrum.

The connection rings once. "Hello. I'm glad you called."

His soothing voice relaxes me.

I sink into the bed, fold the blanket over my legs, and adjust my earbuds. "You are?"

"Yes. I watched the news about the shooter last week. I have no idea where anyone is calling from, but I worried that some of my callers might have been affected by it."

"I was nowhere near the shooter." A small lie. I was, and I wasn't.

"Do you want to talk about it?"

"Nothing to talk about. I was safe." I can't hide the trace of anger from my voice.

He picks up on it. "Why does my question upset you?"

I fudge, total honesty be damned. "I was upset before I called you."

He waits me out. I breathe in deep and release. "This will sound crazy."

"I assure you that whatever you say will be fine."

"When I first logged on, you weren't there." Oh my God. I'm so stupid.

"I wasn't there—oh, you mean I was not available?"

"Yes. And for some irrational reason it made me mad." *What the hell am I doing?*

"Not entirely irrational. You created an expectation that I would be always available. And when that expectation failed, you got angry. Is that correct?"

"Yes."

"That's normal. People do this all the time. They create expectations about other people and things, and when those expectations don't meet their idea of what should happen, they get disappointed. And disappointment leads to anger."

"So you're saying I shouldn't have expectations?"

"No, not at all. I'm saying that you should have realistic expectations. And don't get upset when something happens that's outside your control."

"How do I know if my expectations are realistic or not?"

"It's unrealistic to expect I will be available twenty-four seven. I have a full-time job and other life commitments. But it is realistic to expect I'll continue to be available as much as I can for the duration of this program."

"Okay." I sigh. *I'm behaving like a brat.*

"Last time we talked, we left things off in a hard place."

"Yeah ..." It still amazes me I told him some of what happened to me. And that he believed me and didn't judge me for it.

"How have you been since?"

"Okay, I guess." *Surprisingly okay.* I thought I'd have some kind of breakdown, but I didn't.

"You guess?"

"No. I know. I'm okay."

"This is great. We are making progress. But I want to talk about how you feel about the shooting incident too."

"We already did."

"Not really. How did that affect you?"

"I don't think it affected me at all."

"But you said you were safe."

"I was—" I almost say Maslow building. "Nowhere near it. And I wasn't alone. I felt safe where I was."

"Were there many people with you?"

"No, just one person."

"I'm glad you weren't alone. Is this person a friend you can trust?"

He got me there. I hesitate, then let it out anyway. What's the point of these talks if I can't be honest? "Not exactly. Just a person I know."

"What makes this person safe?" Honesty comes back to bite me on the ass.

"I don't know. We're not even friends. He's someone I know, but I feel safe with him. I know he wouldn't physically hurt me."

"Not physically? But could he hurt you otherwise? Has he hurt you before?"

That's a hard question to answer. "Yes. No. I don't know. He seems to judge me sometimes."

"Is he judging you, or are you judging yourself and projecting it on him?"

"Ouch, Doc. That was harsh."

"Was it? I'm playing devil's advocate. I'm here to ask the questions you are not asking yourself."

"Tough love, huh?" I joke with him.

"If that's what it takes." I can hear the smile in his voice.

"I guess tough love is better than no love." I laugh.

He chuckles. "It's good to hear you laugh."

"It feels good to laugh. I haven't found reason to very often."

"You should. If you go around looking for reasons to laugh and be grateful instead of finding reasons for being upset, you're bound to be a lot happier."

"You really think so?"

"I know so. Life is a mathematical equation. It is part what happens to us, part what we make happen and part how we react to either of those things. But it is not as simple as two plus two equals four."

"Nope. It's more like two plus apple equals blue. Unless it's a Tuesday, in which case it equals taco."

His laughter is guttural and free. Like something that had been building up for a while and now has a chance to escape. It's contagious, and I laugh along with him.

"Ah, she can make a joke. This is good. Better than good. This is great. If you try to look at everything through the lenses of humor instead of prejudice, life is a lot more fun."

"Not always easy, though. There's a lot of angry people out there." Myself included.

"Also true. But those people have nothing to do with you. What they do and how they act have no bearing on the way you behave or how you live your life."

"But it does. It affects me." I push the heel of my hand into my forehead. A headache is coming.

"Does it?"

"It does. For every action, there is an equal and opposite reaction, right?"

"Yes, if we're talking about Newton's third law of motion. But life, it's not always like that. In life, a non-action can happen. Or the reaction can be much greater than the action that triggered it. Either way, the choice lies with the person in that situation."

"Hmm. Is this how therapy works? I thought it was like the

patient talking and the therapist asking, 'how does that make you feel' and taking notes the whole time."

He has a good laugh about that.

"Yes. Traditional therapy differs from what we are doing here. This is more of a conversation between friends. And while I have the credentials, we are working outside the norm."

"Is it like that with everyone?"

"I can't discuss other callers with you."

"No, I'm not asking about their problems, or what you're talking about. I was wondering if the other people calling you —never mind. I don't know what I'm asking." But I want to know if he's the same with other people, or if the way he talks to me is different. Special somehow. Because it feels special to me. And I want to be special for him too.

He lets it slide. "We need to move to the next step." He always includes himself—always says "we" instead of "you."

"The next step?"

"I have a little homework for you. An exercise if you will."

I want to grunt but hold it in.

"You don't seem happy with the idea," he says.

What? "I didn't say anything."

"I think I heard an unhappy sound coming from you."

I guess I didn't hold my grunt in. "No one in the history of the universe has ever been happy about homework."

"Maybe." He concedes.

"All right, what's this homework?"

"I want you to think of people you can trust. Can you think of anyone you trust?"

"Yes." I have a limited array of friends. There's River, Tommy, and Lucas.

"I want you to find a friend. Someone you trust implicitly and talk to them about some of the things you shared with me."

Sheer panic assaults me like a jab to the gut. No, no, no. I don't want anyone to know this. I don't want their pity or judgment. What if they don't believe me? What if they blame me? The idea of telling someone face-to-face immobilizes me. He carries on as the battle raging inside me runs rampant and tries to take over.

"I know it won't be easy. But I believe this is an integral part of your recovery."

I swallow to push down the knot in my throat. "Okay."

"Let's do a little exercise right now. Think of a friend. Hold their image in your head."

The most obvious person is River. I know she won't judge. She might try to go to my mother's house and beat the crap out of her, though. Tommy is far too sweet and gentle. I don't want to tarnish him with all my dirty secrets. Lucas already knows a little about me. He knows I don't go home or get along with my mother, but that's it.

I flash back to the image of Professor Dick and how he held me while singing to me a few days ago. I cringe at the idea of telling him all of my deepest, darkest secrets. Oh, he'd love that. Lots of material to judge me on.

"Do you have a person in your mind?"

"Yes. I have someone in mind. But why? Why do I need to talk to someone?" My teeth grind together.

"You need someone in your life who's more than a voice on the other side of a screen."

It stings. "But I talk to you so I don't have to dump my trashy life on anyone else."

"Your life is not trash. Your life is as worthy as mine or anyone else out there."

I'm not so sure about that.

He continues. "I want you to find someone you can trust and rely on. Find one person. And talk to them."

"What if they hate me? What if they judge me or pity me or stop being my friend because of what I say?" Nausea swells in my stomach.

"I think you're smarter than that and you know who you can trust."

The only person I can talk to is River. I know she won't turn against me.

I give in. "I have someone I can trust." My voice trembles.

"It's scary, I know, and I don't want to push you. But I think you are ready. And you don't have to reveal every little detail. You can be brief and generic. And you can choose what and how much to reveal. But it's import to find someone in your life you can talk to."

"Are you telling me this because I said I was mad when I couldn't talk to you right away?"

"No. I'm telling you this because healing requires light and trust. Hurt has a way of festering and getting bigger and darker than it already is when it stays hidden for too long."

If that's the case, mine must be the size of Godzilla by now.

CHAPTER TWENTY-SEVEN

BECCA

My phone rings somewhere on my bed. I dig under the blanket. River's face flashes on the screen.

"Hey, River, I only have a minute. I'm running out. Have a test in fifteen minutes."

"I can't believe you have a test. It's three days before Thanksgiving!"

I hold my phone against my ear with a shoulder while I lace a sneaker. "I know. They had to reschedule it for today because of the canceled classes last week."

"A lot of people left early. They should have canceled the rest of classes until after Thanksgiving. Have the tests then. And you should have come home with me." Her voice sounds muffled. I finish lacing the second sneaker while she rants on.

I stand up. "It's okay. The campus feels so weird, though. The halls are so quiet." Even more so than normal before a big break or holiday. The shooting five days ago still hangs over everyone's head. "I got to go. Call you later?"

"Yep. Good luck on your test."

"Thanks." I hang up, shove the phone in my back pocket

and grab my backpack. I open the door to leave my room and nearly crash into Tommy.

"Jesus Christ, Tommy! You scared me. I almost peed myself."

His laughter echoes in the empty hall.

I push at his chest and close the door behind me.

He pulls me into a hug. "You avoided me the entire weekend. Not cool, Becca, not cool."

I hug him back, his gentle chastising stings and makes me even more awkward. Why is it easier to hook up with a stranger than to accept the affectionate hug of a friend?

He pulls back and drapes my arm over his like we're an eighteenth-century couple. We walk to the elevator.

He pushes the down button. "So, I came here on a mission, and you can't say no."

I already don't like it. "What are you trying to get me into?"

"Nothing bad. I want to invite you for Thanksgiving."

My head is shaking like it's on automatic pilot. I'm so used to declining invitations like this. I don't do family holidays. And now I have three invitations. My father, River, and Tommy.

I still remember Thanksgiving freshman year. River dragged me along to her family's farm. It was beautiful and heartbreaking. I got to see firsthand what I'd been missing my entire life. I never imagined there could be such a love. I have missed and envied it since. No. I don't need another reminder.

His smile falters at my silent rebuttal.

He tugs at my hand, and we walk outside. "Come on, Becca, say yes. Please." Tommy makes puppy eyes at me and holds his hands up in a begging motion. The weak sunlight makes a halo around his head and gives him an even more angelic and innocent face. My walls crack.

"I'm not much of a family-getting-together-Thanksgiving

kind of person." I hike up the straps of my backpack and quicken my pace.

"Nothing to worry, then, it's me and my brother. And now you."

"Just the two of you? No family or friends?"

"Just the three of us," he corrects me.

Thanksgiving with Tommy and Professor Dick? How weird and awkward would that be after the moment we shared in his office?

"I don't think your brother likes me very much. Not sure it would be a good idea for me to show up at your house."

"Of course, he likes you. He always asks about you. I don't know where you got that. It was his idea to invite you. Not that I wouldn't suggest it, but he beat me to it."

The concept of Professor Dick asking about me and liking me is so alien I trip on my feet. Tommy holds my arm and steadies me. "Please, don't go breaking a leg just to avoid dinner."

Should I? Should I accept this invitation? A part of me is screaming that I'm crazy for even considering. But another part —a bigger part is all too eager and curious. I haven't seen Professor Dick since the shooting. I want to go. I need to see if what we shared that day is still there, or if it was my imagination.

"Just the three of us?"

Tommy is bouncing on the balls of his feet, giddy like a little kid on Christmas morning. "Yes, just the three of us, I promise."

I should say no. Why am I even considering going? This is crazy. But I need to see him again, and Tommy is so happy, I don't want to refuse him. "Okay. I'll come."

He throws himself at me, and we crash into a hug. I can't

help but laugh. I guess I'm getting used to his simple affections that ask for nothing in return.

This means I'll have to say no to my father's invitation. I already said no to River's invitation. But at least now I have a real excuse.

"What can I bring? I can't really cook or bake anything, dorm life and all."

"Nothing. Dylan's a great cook. Bring your sweet self around three o'clock."

Three days. I have three days until Thanksgiving. Three days to change my mind and come up with an excuse that lets me get away without hurting Tommy. Or three days to push through.

CHAPTER TWENTY-EIGHT

DYLAN

SHE'S LEANING ON THE GLASS WALL TAKING IN THE morning sun, face tilted up, eyes closed and lips barely parted. She's partially hidden by a column and so still passersby don't notice her presence. I may have missed Becca as well had I not been looking for her.

There's more to Becca than meets the eye. What secrets is she keeping under her sharp tongue and abrasive demeanor? She's so unguarded now, she looks like a different person.

Softer.

Gentler.

I want to hold her again, inhale her scent, touch her without the barrier of clothes. My fingers tingle with the need to feel her skin. I want to kiss her and find out what she tastes like. My body aches with the familiar want. My heart thunders faster as I give in to the fantasy.

"Who are you, Becca? What secrets do you guard so ferociously? And why do you act like you hate me?" I speak the words silently, hoping somehow the answers will come to me.

The ruckus of loud voices and laughter breaks the spell.

Both mine and hers. She's watching the men now. Riggins football players. If theirs faces weren't already well known, their sizes would give them away. The four of them move together like a wall made of muscle and bones. In sync, in and out of the field.

Becca's no longer enjoying the sun.

The closer the men get to her, the smaller she gets. Shoulders curving in, face angled down, hiding behind a curtain of hair, eyes downcast watching their feet. Her entire body rigid with tension so thick I can feel it from where I stand. The voices get louder, Becca gets smaller, her hands ball into her chest, she turns away from them, just enough to become even more invisible, but still watching their every move.

They walk by, and she freezes. As their voices fade, and each step adds distance between them, Becca unfolds. Hands open, fingers flex and arms drop, her shoulders uncurl, her face tilts up, and as she reverts to her original spot, her eyes dart around. But I'm the only one watching her, and before Becca can see me, I step back into my classroom.

CHAPTER TWENTY-NINE

BECCA

I squeeze my hands around the steering wheel to stave off the trembling of my fingers. I've been sitting in my car staring at the house for minutes. The well-cared-for lawn is still green, but it won't be long before snow and bitter cold dulls its color to a muted yellow. It's a beautiful house in a middle-class neighborhood with lots of space between homes, and nothing like the cramped, crappy house I grew up in.

As welcoming as this neighborhood is, all I can hear in my head are the words, *you don't belong* on repeat.

I suck in a breath and release it. I turn off the car and grab the wine bottle I bought so I wouldn't come empty-handed. Stepping out, I look at the house again. Like most of the houses on the street, it has two floors and sits in a nest of well-trimmed trees and shrubbery. The home is so inviting with its cream-colored siding and stone face—my nervousness is temporarily abated. Movement through a large bay window catches my gaze. Someone knows I'm here. No going back now.

Tommy opens the front door before I'm halfway up the

walkway. He rushes out on socked feet and pulls me into a bear hug, squeezing all the air out of me.

"She's here," he yells over his shoulder as he drags me into the room.

Rich mahogany hardwood covers the floors of the open-concept home. From where I stand a few feet inside the door, the living room is to my left. Bookcases line the wall opposite of the bay window. The far wall houses a huge wood fireplace with an even bigger flat-screen TV on top. Soft chocolate-brown leather couches face the fireplace. The center table is made of a single slab cut from a tree and at least three inches thick, polished to perfection and beautiful with its uneven shape and knots. A deep red carpet underneath it all makes the space cozy. Paintings and other artwork cover the walls. In the back corner, there's a baby grand piano.

My fingers itch to touch it, even if I can't play.

The home is such a discrepancy from my own, I'm momentarily off-kilter. Like an alien looking in through a window. I shut down the insistent voice telling me I don't belong and take a deep breath.

The smells of baking and roasting invite me farther in, and when I turn around, I see him. Professor Dick—Dylan. He wipes his hands on a dish towel and drops it on the counter before crossing the space between us with an extended hand. Dark-wash jeans and a black Henley make him look younger. Like Tommy, he wears socks only.

"Miss Jones. Welcome to our home. Glad you could make it."

So formal. "Call me Becca, please." His hand is soft and warm against mine.

"Is that for me?" He points at the wine bottle I'm hugging against my chest like a shield.

"Yes. I'm not sure if you like wine. I can't really cook or bake living in the dorm. Tommy said you didn't need any food and had everything covered. I figured a bottle of wine would be okay." I'm babbling. My voice sounds hoarse to my ears and a little wispy too.

I give him the wine and realize he's still holding my hand. There's an awkward moment when we let go and look away from each other. When I look up, he smiles, his face lit up. My body sways a little. I want to touch that smile with my fingertips, memorize it on my skin, save it for later.

Tommy clears his throat. "Okay. This is cozy. Dylan, shouldn't you go back into the kitchen before something burns? And you, Miss Becca, come with me and help me set the table." Tommy smirks like the Cheshire cat.

I forgot he was there. What the hell is wrong with me?

Dylan blinks and steps back with the wine.

Glad I'm not the only one zoning out.

Tommy takes my hand. "Take your boots off, you'll be more comfortable." He lifts a foot and wiggles his toes, showing me his sock with a turkey leg design and separated toes like a glove.

I laugh and take my boots off by the door, glad I have my favorite and warmest socks on.

I help Tommy set the table. "This is a beautiful set." I admire the antique rose and gold pattern on a plate.

"Yeah, Dylan saves them for the special occasions, Thanksgiving and Christmas, and that's it."

"Is it a family heirloom?"

"Yes, belonged to our grandparents. They're gone. They're all gone now." His voice deflates.

Tommy looks at the table as if lost in memory. Perhaps

happier memories. Then he glances up and offers me a small smile.

"I'll be right back." He walks down a hall.

Not sure of what to do, I walk back to the living room and look out the window. Wind knocks down the last few stubborn leaves from the trees, they dance in the air for a moment before falling to the ground. Everything gets knocked down eventually. I blink away the negative thought and turn away from the window. The bookcase draws me in. I run my fingers over the spines of several books, the kind you'd expect to see in the Harry Potter library. Old leather-bound books, antiques by the look of them. There are photos too. Several of a couple, probably in their forties, smiling at each other. More frames with the same couple and two boys, Dylan and Tommy. Tommy is very young in most of the pictures. Maybe six or seven years old. Dylan is a teenager, tall and skinny. He smiles freely. These are happy pictures. There's so much love in them. In the way they touch, in the way they look at the camera, so open and carefree.

I search the walls of the room for newer pictures and find none. My gaze drifts back to the image of a smiling Dylan. A smile not unlike the one he gave me earlier. The kind of smile that melts cold hearts.

"That's our parents." Dylan's voice startles me. He is inches away.

I breathe in. A hint of his cologne teases my nose—fresh, clean, wintry.

He hands me a glass of wine.

I take it, my hands surprisingly steady. "Sorry. I didn't mean to pry."

"Nothing to be sorry about. The pictures are out in the open for anyone to see."

"But something tells me you don't get a lot of visitors." What the hell? Why did I say that?

Dylan tilts his head. "How can you tell?" He sips his wine.

I look around. "I don't know. Just a feeling. This house looks like it was well-loved, but now it feels a little empty." *Fuck a duck! What's wrong with me? Shut up, Becca!*

He nods, takes another sip. "True. The house is mostly empty now. With Tommy in the dorms, it's only me here."

"If this was my home, I'd never leave." *Oh. My. God.* I look at the wine I have yet to touch. I can't even blame it for the deluge of words coming out of my mouth.

Dylan smiles openly, like in the picture. My heart flutters into an uneven tempo.

"This house used to be filled with voices and laughter and noises. There were always people over. So much so I had to go outside to be alone."

I like this open version of him. I like this Dylan. There's no Professor Dick here right now. I hesitate, not sure where we stand—if this is proper or not—but I've already put my foot in my mouth, may as well shove the entire leg in.

"What happened?" I think I already know, but I don't want to speak the words in case I'm wrong. And I hope I'm wrong.

"We lost them—our parents, years ago in a car accident on Halloween." He gestures at one of the pictures with the almost empty glass. His father and his mother, her hugging him from behind, wrapped around his shoulders.

On Halloween? That's why Tommy ghosted me. I'm so stupid. "I'm so sorry. I know it's just words, but I really am. Looking at Tommy and you and this house, it's easy to see this was a happy home."

He shrugs.

"You said it was years ago, but Tommy is eighteen. Who raised him? And you?"

Silence stretches out as the seconds tick. Dylan takes a long gulp, finishes the wine.

"I raised him."

"You? You must have been a kid yourself."

He presses his lips together and, his shoulders go rigid for a second. "I was. I had to grow up fast."

"I can't imagine how hard it must have been." I don't know what's worse. To have never had loving parents or to have them and lose them at such a young age.

"Some days I still can't believe I managed it." Dylan looks at his empty glass and then at mine, full still.

"I had to fight for custody. I couldn't let him go to a foster home."

"You had no other family?"

"No. It was the two of us. No uncles or aunts, and our grandparents died years before. But luckily my parents had life insurance, and that was more than enough to pay for everything we needed."

I press a hand against my chest, rub at the ache blooming for him. For Tommy. For all that loss. I want to reach out and touch him, soothe the pain I see in his eyes. But I can't. I hold myself back. Curl my toes into the floor to keep from moving. "But how did you do it?"

He nudges the corner of a frame, taps on the shelf. "I switched colleges and moved back here to be with Tommy and care for him. I changed my major, organized all my classes around his schedule so I could be home when Tommy was home. The first couple years were the hardest. But after a while we got used to our new routine." He takes my glass and drains the wine.

The gesture is simultaneously intimate and abrupt. A myriad of emotions fleets through his face. He's not over the loss regardless of what he may have said or how long ago it was. The need to pull him into my arms and hug him as tight as I can until all the pain I see in his eyes disappears, grows. The impulse is so strong I have to cross my arms and dig my nails into my palms to keep from doing exactly that.

He looks at both empty glasses, a questioning expression on his face as if he didn't know how he ended up here and what happened to the wine.

"I think we both need a refill." His voice is husky.

He walks away, and I watch him retreat into the kitchen. He refills both glasses and looks at me across the room.

Neither one of us moves.

The ding of an alarm makes us both jump. He sets the glasses down and turns back to the kitchen. He moves around, opens the oven and fusses over whatever is inside. The delicious scent of something roasting draws me in and makes my stomach grumble in appreciation.

I don't know what's going on between us. We have this odd connection I can't explain. I've known him for a little over a year, and most of that time I spent hating him for judging me. But now I have to ask myself, who's judging whom? I walk into the kitchen and wash my hands. "What can I do? Put me to work."

He hesitates for a second, then opens the fridge and takes out several vegetables. "Do you know how to make stuffing?"

"I've never made it before, but tell me what to do, and I can work on that."

"We need to chop the vegetables first, all in even sizes." He grabs a bag of baby carrots, opens it, eats the first one and offers me the bag. I take a carrot and crunch on it while he cuts up a few carrots to show me how he wants it done.

"You work on the carrots, and I'll wash the mushrooms and celery. I know you're not supposed to wash mushrooms, but I could never bring myself not to. Wait? Do you like mushrooms?"

"I like everything." Starving kids are not picky.

"I'll cut up the onions, they get cooked first." He chops the onion in seconds and puts them in a pot with a drizzle of avocado oil.

"Avocado oil?"

"It's better for you. Even better than olive oil, but with a much milder flavor."

"Tommy said you're a talented cook." The more I see Dylan outside Riggins, the more I realize he's nothing like I imagined him to be.

We settle next to each other with cutting boards and a growing pile of cut-up veggies in a bowl between us. It's mindless, simple work, but I'm aware of how close we are and how our elbows brush every so often. We fall into silence—the sound of chopping and knives scraping on the wooden boards oddly comforting.

He turns to the stove and stirs the onions. The fragrant smell adds to the already heavenly aromas in the kitchen. "We should put some music on. That's usually Tommy's job, but he's gone into hiding, looks like."

"I hope it wasn't something I said," I whisper to myself, but he hears me.

"What do you mean?" He looks at me, wooden spoon in hand, such a common and yet unfamiliar image I have trouble reconciling the Professor Dick I know with him. Dylan.

"When we were setting the table, I said I loved the dishes,

that they were beautiful. He got quiet and said they were your grandparents' china, and that they were all gone. After that, he went upstairs."

Dylan nods and goes back to stirring the pot. "He gets a little down this time of the year. But he's also in the habit of disappearing when there's kitchen work. Don't worry. It wasn't anything you said."

I nod, not sure how to reply, and add the last of the veggies into the bowl. I take the cutting boards and knives to the spotless sink. Dylan is a clean-as-you-go guy.

He sets the spoon on the side of the pot. "What kind of music do you like?"

"Hmm …" I don't think anyone ever asked me that before. "Something mellow?"

He smiles and the corners of his eyes crinkle. It tugs at something inside me, like the loosening of corset strings. I can breathe better.

"Something mellow it is." He pulls a cell phone from his pocket, taps the screen a few times and sets it on a small dock on the granite counter. The first strings of a song filter through hidden speakers in the walls.

"I put Pandora on. Is this song okay?"

I nod. But as I listen to the lyrics, I feel less and less okay. It's as if the singer can see inside my soul. This song could be my anthem, I too have voices in my head that say I'm not enough. "What's this song?" I'm sure my voice betrays me.

He walks back to his phone and squints at the screen.

"You Say by Lauren Daigle. You don't like it?"

"No, the song is beautiful. I never heard it before, that's all."

"I can change it if you don't like it." He nods his head at his phone. "Why don't you pick the next song?"

"That's fine." I turn away from him and turn on the faucet.

I wash the cutting boards and set them to dry on the dish rack. I don't look at him, but I can feel his gaze on my face as I wash the knives, taking way longer than necessary so I don't have to meet his eyes. Not yet.

He grabs the bowl and dumps all the veggies into the pan and stirs. Then covers it and reduces the flame. I watch his back and how the ends of his hair graze the collar of his shirt, how his muscles flex and stretch with his every move.

"Ouch." Damn it. I cut myself.

He's by my side in a second. "What happened?"

"Nothing, it's a small cut, I'm fine."

He turns off the water and grabs some paper towels. He takes my hand in his and presses the folded towel into the heel of my palm where the small cut wells with blood.

"That's okay. It's nothing." I try to pull away, but he holds me in place.

"It's not nothing. You're hurt." His hands are so warm around my mine, and he holds the paper against the cut with such gentleness. Everywhere we touch, my skin tingles.

"Let's have a look-see." He lifts the paper, and blood wells again. He puts pressure back on the cut. He's so close, his face inches away from mine. My hand cradled in his. I'm faint. Not because of the cut or the blood. I'm faint because of him, because of how close he is. I'm drunk by his proximity.

"Come on, let's take a little walk." He tugs at my arm, holding my hand still, and I follow him down the hall. He pushes a door open and turns the light on. It's a bathroom, with sage-green walls and gleaming white tile floors. He guides me backward. "Sit."

I obey and sit on the side of the bathtub. He reaches under the sink cabinet and grabs a red first aid case, never letting go of my hand, the paper towel still pressed between his fingers and my palm.

He kneels in front of me. Pulls the paper towel away and tosses it into a garbage pail. The cut is no longer bleeding, but it's stained red and stings a little. He opens the first aid kit and takes out disinfecting wipes, ointment, and Band-Aids. He cleans the cut and bandages it with the accuracy of a surgeon.

I'm in awe of him. My whole life, I've never had anyone care for me like this. I've never had anyone mend my scrapes and bruises. "Thanks, Doctor Dylan." I try for levity.

He looks up at me. He smiles and my cheeks burn, heat spreading into my neck.

"I had to mend a lot of scraped knees. Tommy was accident prone growing up."

"I heard that!" Tommy pops around the doorframe, half of his body leaning into the small space. He makes me jump. I lose my balance and start to fall backward into the tub. Dylan grabs my arms and pulls me back. My body shifts forward. We both fumble to the floor, me half straddling him, the first aid kid tumbling with us.

Tommy cackles and steps back. "And I'm the one who's accident prone," he calls from the hall. "Carry on, kids, take your time. I'll check on the food." His laugh echoes behind him.

Dylan and I look at each other, the blush on my face burning hotter. We're a tangle of limbs and scattered Band-Aids. I try to get off him, but I can't quite push myself up. Not without touching him, not without pushing against his chest for leverage and not with only one good hand.

He holds my waist and tries to lift me up. I press a socked foot into the floor, slip, land on him again. He bangs his head on the cabinet behind him.

"Ouch. You okay?" I reach for his head, my fingertips brush his hair before I catch myself and pull my hand back.

Awkward doesn't even begin to cover this moment. We're like two octopuses in a wrestling match. I allow myself to look at him.

"I'm fine." His lips spread in a smile, then a laugh. His entire body shakes with it.

I can't help but laugh with him. "This feels like a game of Twister gone very wrong."

"Or very right," he says.

My face is on fire. And other parts of me are on fire too. His muscles flex under me—hard and strong. I need to get off him, but I don't want to.

He leans back, his shoulders pressing against the cabinets. Gives me a hand. I take it with my good one and push a knee onto the floor. He guides me up. My legs are shaky. The moment we no longer touch, I miss it. I miss the heat of his skin. I miss the strength of his body, and the press of his legs tangled in mine. I want to go back. I want a re-do. I want to be near him again and this time ignore the awkwardness and just feel.

He sits up and picks up the scattered contents of the first aid kit, putting the kit in the cabinet again once he's done. Not a trace of the last few minutes remains. The moment undone. And yet, his touch lingers on my skin, even as I miss it.

Want it.

Crave it.

CHAPTER THIRTY

BECCA

The kitchen is getting smaller by the minute. Every time he moves or reaches for something, my body vibrates in anticipation of his proximity.

Jesus! What is this prickly, sweet ache in my chest? My hands itch to touch him again, to have him touch me. The space around us seems to disappear.

We dance around each other, stirring pots, chopping veggies, washing dishes, inches between us and sometimes not even that. A casual brush here, an awkward bump there. We weave around the chemistry of food preparation and overactive hormones.

Dylan grabs a spoon, dips it into the cranberry-orange sauce he's making from scratch, and brings it to my lips.

"Careful, it's hot." His voice wraps itself around me like melted caramel.

I blow into the spoon and take a tentative bite. He tips his hand up. The sweet and tart liquid is an explosion of flavor on my tongue. I close my eyes. Savor it. Savor his nearness. "Oh my God, that's amazing."

He's even closer now, his gaze darkened and locked on my mouth. I swallow. Heat pools low in my belly. I'm aware of his every breath. Lust like I have never felt before swirls inside me. It's a demanding and hungry beast, and it wants to be fed now. Right now.

The spoon drops with a loud clatter against the tiled floor. We both jump back and freeze.

I break eye contact first and kneel to pick up the spoon at my feet. My gaze traveling down his body. Tracing the wide chest and flat stomach.

Don't look at his crotch. Don't look at his crotch. *Do not* look at his crotch.

I look at his crotch.

Fuck.

Me.

He's hard.

My face burns, and the heat spreads into my chest.

I force myself to look down and stare at the spoon.

The thumping of feet on the stairs reaches us.

"Duuuude, we need better music. Hey, where's Becca?" Tommy's on the other side of the kitchen island.

"Right here!" I wave the spoon like a flag over the island top. "Dropped the spoon." I pop up, face still burning.

Tommy frowns. "You okay? You look a little weird …"

That would probably be the deranged smile on my face. "Yep. Fine. Got a bit of a blood rush from bending down. It happens." What the hell? Shut up. I turn to the sink and wash the spoon way longer than is necessary. Take a peek when I see Dylan moving again. He's messing with his phone. The music changes.

Dylan raises an eyebrow. I smile and nod my approval of his song choice. And so does Tommy. He launches into a full-on act as he sings along with Bohemian Rhapsody and gives a great imitation of Freddie Mercury.

Their attention is no longer on me. Thank God for Queen.

Dylan sits at the head of the table, I sit to Dylan's right and Tommy to his left, across from me. The table is beautifully laden with the foods I helped prepare. There's turkey, stuffing, mashed potatoes, green beans, and roasted butternut squash tossed with fresh baby spinach, dried cranberries and pecans. And the cranberry-orange sauce—I can't look at without a tightening in my belly.

"Finally! I'm starving. Growing boy over here, you know?" Tommy points at himself with a thumb.

The different smells make my stomach grumble. Loudly.

Dylan fights a laugh. "Hungry?"

"I'm no growing boy, but I could eat."

Dylan picks up his glass and raises it to his brother, but looks at me. "We have this little tradition." His gaze on me still. "Tommy, you're first. What are you thankful for?"

Tommy picks up his glass. "I'm thankful for all this food, and for my new friend Becca."

Dylan laughs. "He's always thankful for food. Your turn. What are you thankful for, Becca?"

The way he says my name makes my heart jittery. I haven't had many things to be thankful for. But I'm thankful for this. For now.

"Here. Right now. I'm thankful for this moment." I raise my glass.

We wait for Dylan's response. "I'm thankful for …" He looks at me like a bear looks at honey. "For possibilities and

what the future holds." He clinks his glass to mine first, and then Tommy's. "Dig in!"

Possibilities? And the way he looked at me … what does it mean? Tommy doesn't seem to think any of it was odd, but then again, he's more concerned about eating than paying attention to gratitude declarations. Dishes get passed back and forth, and then I'm holding the cranberry sauce, Dylan's fingers brushing mine.

"I think you liked this one. Have more." His voice is husky.

Is he flirting with me? Or am I imagining this pull between us? His gaze dips to my lips and back to my eyes again. No. Definitely not imagining it. This is crazy, right?

"You guys done playing tug-of-war with the sauce?" Tommy's eyebrows wiggle unevenly, one at a time like drunken caterpillars.

"Manners, Tommy. Guests first."

My face heats, I quickly scoop sauce on top of my stuffing and give the dish to Tommy. His plate piled so full I don't know how he will fit anything else in.

He makes a well in the middle of the mashed potatoes, and I have my answer.

Dylan shakes his head. "It's like he hasn't eaten in weeks."

I swallow a delicious bite of stuffing. "Oh, he's eating all right. He raided my snacks yesterday. Left me with crumbs."

Dylan's eyes narrow for a fraction of a second before smoothing over again.

Is he mad about Tommy coming to my dorm? He can't possibly still think I'm sleeping with his brother. Not after all this raw … lust? Attraction? Connection? Whatever this is, I think it goes both ways.

"This food is fantastic. Where did you learn to cook like this?"

Dylan takes a sip of water before answering. "Cooking shows and the internet mainly. There's only so much mac and cheese from a box and peanut butter and jelly sandwiches one can eat. Can you cook?"

Between my mother's neglect, not having enough food around for most of my life, and living in a dorm the last four years, I've never had much of a chance to learn. "No, not really. I can't cook in the dorms."

"How about when you go home?" Dylan's question is so innocent, and yet alarm bells go off in my head.

I don't want to lie. But I can't tell him the truth either. "I don't go home much." Not a lie. Not the full truth. I never go home.

"No? Why not?" Tommy jumps into the conversation. Half of his plate is already cleared. Where did he put all that food?

I shove a big bite of potatoes into my mouth to buy time. Chew, swallow, get a drink of water.

"You know, the same old story. I don't get along with my mother. It's best to stay away." The truth this time.

Tommy is silent, hurt tinges his gaze, and in this moment I understand his pain. He lost his parents. He'd give anything to be with them again, and he can't understand me giving that chance up when he has no choice.

He swallows. "How about your dad? You don't go to see him either?"

"My parents were never married. But I get to see my dad this weekend." Jesus! Why am I babbling my business all over the place? I glance at Dylan. He's stopped eating and is watching me with keen interest and intelligent eyes. I'm an insect being dissected. Take off a wing, see what she does. I hate being seen like this. But I brought it on to myself.

A different kind of heat bubbles up in my chest. The

therapist's words come to me. Find someone you can trust and talk to them. I'm not about to tell them my whole sordid story. But I can do a test drive on this trust thing. Talk about crap that doesn't give away all my secrets. Lots of people don't get along with their families. That's normal. Expected even. Aren't Thanksgiving dinners famous for getting families into fights? *Breathe, Becca.*

I grasp my fork harder, acknowledge the turmoil inside, and let it go. I don't need the anger right now. There's no threat here. I take another sip of water.

"My dad is okay." The truth. It surprises me. My father is okay. Better than okay. He's a good person. One good parent out of two is good odds. *Too bad he was never a father when you needed him.* The voice of doubt rears its ugly little head.

"How about—"

"This is dinner, not the inquisition, Tommy." Dylan interrupts him.

Tommy weaves his fork. "Well, we can talk about me, then."

I'm grateful I'm no longer in the spotlight. Relief is a warm embrace, and I welcome it. Did Dylan notice my discomfort and stop Tommy's questions? I think he did. I don't like that he can so easily read me. I don't know what to do with the small kindness.

Tommy cuts into the turkey on his plate. "I met someone."

"You did?" Both Dylan and I speak at the same time.

Tommy laughs. "Down, boys and girls. I said I met someone, not that I was getting married."

Dylan watches me even more closely. Is he looking for a negative reaction? Perhaps a part of him is still looking for hints of a hookup with his brother?

"I need to know more." I can't stop grinning.

I may be skeptical of relationships, but I'm a complete sucker for other people's happy endings. Which I guess makes me a hypocrite when I don't believe in love for myself.

"We met at a coffee shop outside campus." He shoves a forkful of stuffing in his mouth and points at me. "You took me there. Pat's Café?"

I nod for him to go on.

"She's a freshman, too. Bio major. And we got along really well."

"Tell me more? When are you seeing her again?"

"Next week. She went home for the holiday. She lives in Boston."

"What's her name?"

"Julia." Tommy points at me with a knife this time. "Back to you. Why aren't you dating? I haven't seen you with anyone since we met."

I sit back, put distance between us, between the question and me.

"I'm taking a break from dating." *Truth.*

I twist the napkin in my lap. "Not interested in anyone." Lie. I glance at Dylan, who has stayed quiet during the whole exchange. What is he thinking? They're both still watching me.

I shrug. "Anyway, dating is overrated." *Smooth, Becca. Seriously? Is that what you came up with? Overrated?*

Dylan leans into the table, gets closer to me. "I don't know. Dating can be complicated. And with the wrong person, overrated, yes. But sometimes you take a chance on someone you never imagined being with, and the results can be surprising and not overrated at all."

CHAPTER THIRTY-ONE

DYLAN

SHE LOOKS AT ME AND BLINKS AS IF IT COULD CLEAR AWAY the confusion I see in her hazel eyes. I have been an ass, and my flirting with her today is the last thing she expected me to do. But, God, I'm done denying myself. I'm done pushing her away. Riggins' rules and ethics be damned.

I hope she doesn't hate me.

I hope I'm not too late.

I hope we can be together …

If she will have me.

CHAPTER THIRTY-TWO

BECCA

I can't believe I'm doing this. Driving to my father's house to meet his family. *My family.*

Guilt at bailing on his Thanksgiving invitation had me promising to meet them over the weekend. We agreed on Saturday. I planned on coming up with an excuse. But I didn't. I spent all yesterday thinking about Dylan and nibbling on Thanksgiving leftovers. He's a puzzle I can't put together. It's like he's two different people. The cold professor I see at Riggins and this kind and funny guy I saw at his home. Something about him is so familiar.

"Destination in one hundred feet," the GPS announces, and I slow down, taking in the neighborhood. Single-family homes, landscaped lawns, lots of trees now bare, the leaves long gone.

"Arrived. Destination on your right."

I park at the curb, tap the screen to end route, and sit taking in the house. Not too big or too small. Two floors. A path leading from the driveway to the front door. Toys, two bikes, and a soccer ball are scattered around the lawn.

I walk up the driveway and to the path that leads to the

front door. Before I can ring the bell or knock, the door opens. My father is on the other side, a huge smile on his face.

"Come in." He steps back and opens the door wider.

I hesitate for a moment, then step in. What sounds like a stampede grows louder, and before I can react, I'm embraced by little arms. Small hands clutching at my coat. High-pitched squeals and laughter. Two pairs of bright eyes looking up at me. One pair hazel like mine and the other bright blue. My sister and brother wrap themselves around me. I never expected this … this openness, this welcome, this much affection. They don't know me, and yet they act like they do and they've missed me.

"Guys, guys, guys, give her some space." My father steps in and picks up the boy, Hunter.

My sister, Mara, releases me but grabs my hand in both of hers. "I'm so happy you're here."

I blink several times, pushing away the tears trying to well in my eyes. "I'm happy to be here too, Mara." She jumps and squeals again. The boy kicks his legs to be let down.

"Come on, guys, let her come in." I look up. A woman stands a few feet away, drying her hands on a dish towel. She's smiling. The boy runs to her and hides behind her leg.

"What? Are you shy now?" She looks at her son with so much love it makes my heart ache.

Mara tugs at my hand. "Come! Mom made cookies, and we're not allowed to eat them until you got here."

"Mara! Manners, please. I'm Linda," she introduces herself.

I step closer to shake her hand, but she pulls me into a hug.

"We're a hugging family." She gestures to the kids. "And these two little monsters you just met are Mara and Hunter."

My father touches my elbow. "Come on in. The good stuff is in the kitchen." His smile takes his entire face.

We all follow Linda and settle around the table, Mara never

leaving my side. Linda grabs small paper plates and napkins. The kids take over and set the table.

"Coffee, tea, hot chocolate?" Linda asks.

"Coffee is fine, thank you."

A plate of chocolate chip cookies appears, little hands make a grab for them.

"Guys!" Linda tries to get their attention. "Guests first."

"She's not a guest, she's my sister." Mara speaks around a mouth full of cookies.

"My sister too!" Hunter mimics her.

And it hits home. Sister. Their words make it real. My heart gallops, the sound of a thousand hooves in my ears. I blink, willing the tears to stay away. Linda sets a coffee mug in front of me. My father takes my hand and squeezes it. The kids watch me with wide eyes. And I crumble.

A sob escapes, and then another. And in an instant, I'm surrounded by all of them. My father, my sister, my brother, Linda. The four of them hug me, hold me, keep me from falling apart.

"That's okay."

"Everything is all right."

"Don't worry."

They whisper and soothe me and cry with me. They put me back together, ease the ache in my chest, decrease the thundering of my heart, shift the weight off my shoulders, bear the pain I carry.

I suck in a breath and release. One by one they step back, but stay close, within arm's reach. I find their faces, their eyes, and smiles. And as if by mutual accord, we all laugh at the same time. The hurt erased by the joyful sound, my heart a thousand pounds lighter.

CHAPTER THIRTY-THREE

BECCA

I'M PACING BACK AND FORTH, WALKING WHAT SEEMS LIKE miles in the same five or six feet of space, while I wait for River. I stuff my hands in my pockets, remove them, repeat. My feet itch to run and get away. I dig in my heels. Wait.

She walks down the path toward me. She waves.

I respond with stilted movements. My arm leaden. "Hey, thanks for coming."

She hugs me. "Of course. Like I could say no after that text message. I've been wondering all day what this important talk is about."

The afternoon breeze blows hair into my face, and I tug it behind my ear with a shaky hand. Distant voices float from somewhere down the path, but this part of the campus is quiet. A garden bench sits empty a few feet from where we stand, but I need distance between us and other people.

"Let's walk."

I step off the path and onto the grass, now more brown than green, and squishy under my feet. River walks next to me. My head down, I watch each measured step. River matches her steps to mine. I'm sure she can sense my anxiety. She has always been able to, even though I denied it each time.

This part of the campus is always quiet, but even more so this late in the season. The sky is the clear and a crisp blue that's only present in the coldest of days. But the sun makes being outside pleasant, even if what I came here to do is anything but.

I inhale, the frigid air stings as it fills my chest. "You know how I said I was going home for Thanksgiving?"

"Yeah." River's tone is cautious.

"I lied." The confession barely above a whisper.

River stops and looks at me in silence. Her expression is open and patient. I want to look away. I want to turn and run. I want to take back the words.

But I don't.

I can't.

I face her and drop my armor. I face her and open my heart, perhaps for the first time while looking someone in the eyes.

River doesn't ask questions, she gives me time.

"I'm not going home for Christmas. I didn't go home for Thanksgiving. Or Easter. Or summer break. Or spring break. Or any other holiday for the last four years."

Her eyes widen, her lips part. She still says nothing. I like this about her. She knows when to speak up, and she knows when to wait. Most of the time she's like a hurricane on crack, but right now she's quiet, and the quiet gives me the courage I need to go on.

"I left my home—no, not my home—I left the house I grew up in at eighteen for my first year at Riggins. And I never went back."

I look away from her. I knew this would be hard. Speaking up, saying the words I've taken so much care to hide, is scary. I walk again, and River falls into step next to me.

"I didn't have the life you did growing up. I didn't meet my father until a few months ago. He's actually a nice guy." I smile. The memory of meeting my siblings is one I'll always treasure. "But my mom? My mom is a different story." I look around the park again, make sure there's no one close enough to hear us. We're still alone.

The breeze picks up and ruffles my hair, most of the brown is faded, and it is nearly to my natural color. So much has changed. I stopped dyeing my hair almost a year ago. It might be symbolic. A rebirth of sorts.

I'm claiming myself back.

"My mother is an addict. Alcohol, drugs, whatever you can think of, she has tried."

River reaches out and takes my hand in between hers, and we stop again.

"My mother was never a mother to me. She was negligent on her best days. But most of the time she was abusive and angry. She blamed me for ruining her life."

River squeezes my hand. Steps closer.

"We were poor, and whatever money Mom got she spent on drugs and alcohol. I cannot tell you how many nights I went to bed hungry, or how many days I went without eating."

She squeezes my hand a little harder, and there are tears in her eyes. And she hasn't heard the worst part yet.

"I had free lunch at school. Most days it was the only meal I had. Weekends were the worst. I had no escape. She had men come sometimes. Leave money for her. I learned very early on to steal the money so I could walk to the corner store and buy food. Most of the time she was so high on something or another she didn't realize money was missing. I never took more than a couple dollars here and there. I had to hide somewhere and eat. If she saw me with food, she'd get mad."

River's eyes fill with unshed tears. "No one realized what was happening? How did you survive it?"

"People noticed. Everyone knew my mother was no good. But they were just as poor and minded their own business. I don't think anyone knew the extent of what happened, and if they did, they didn't care."

River wipes her tears with her fingertips. "How did she support herself? She didn't work?"

"No. She was on some kind of disability. And she had a string of men who came through, and they gave her money. Some were even nice. Even high or drunk, she was beautiful. And men flocked to her. I don't even know where she met them. Bars would be my guess. She brought them home, and sometimes they would stick around and try to help, bring food. Even try to get her to sober up. Those didn't last too long. She didn't like anyone who was actually nice to her." Or me.

There are tears running down River's face now, the corner of her eyes smudged in black. She wipes her face with a sleeve and pulls me into a hug.

"I'm sorry, I'm so sorry, Becca. I had no idea."

I let her hug me for a little longer before pushing away and putting some space between us. My throat tightens. I dig in my backpack and find a water bottle. Drink, push down the knot. Swallow my pain.

We walk again, River's arm through mine. "As bad as it was when I was little, it was nothing compared to when I was a teenager."

Tears prick my eyes now. I've pushed them away for so long. Stuffed these feelings deep inside, as if ignoring the hurt could make it go away. But I've learned that talking about what troubles me, bringing it to the surface, makes it easier to let go.

"My mom got a new boyfriend."

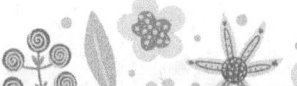

River's hand goes to her mouth, and she holds back a sob. Can she already guess what's coming?

"At first I was happy. We always had something to eat when he was around. He didn't yell at me like my mother. Or get high like her other boyfriends before him. He was kind to me when my mother was not around. But he ignored me if she was in the same space as us. She would get jealous if he gave me any attention."

I stop again and disengage. I can't be touching anyone right now.

"After a few weeks, he moved in. He had a job, he'd buy groceries, give her money, and he didn't care she got drunk or high. I didn't understand why he was with us or why he fueled her addiction, but for the first time, I wasn't hungry or cold all the time. In my limited view, that was a good thing."

I walk again. River follows at my side, keeps the few inches of space between us. I'm grateful for that.

"It started innocently enough. A ruffle of my hair, a hand on my shoulder or a hug when he said hello or goodbye. But over time, as my child's body started giving way to the body of a teen girl, that touch became a little more lingering. The hugs felt a little tighter. The hand to the shoulder would go up and down my back and sides."

Sensory overload crowds my head. *Rough hands with dirty fingernails. The smell of sweat and weed. The sound of heavy breathing.*

I bend at the waist, brace my hands on my knees, drag in deep breaths and push the wave of sickness away. It's not enough. I stand up and take a few steps away and lace my fingers behind my head, press my arms, close my eyes and squeeze them shut. Turn my back to River. Purge the images.

The only sound I can hear is my own breathing. Everything

else fades away, the breeze rustling in the trees, the birds singing, noises in the distance, it's all gone. Right now, in this moment, it's me, my thoughts, and my breath. I drop my arms, lift my face to the sky and open my eyes. Not a cloud in sight, there's so much blue—how can anything bad ever happen under such a beautiful sky?

I turn back to River. "The abuse lasted four years. He was smart and conniving. I didn't even know it was happening at first. In the beginning, it was small touches. He'd rub his hand over my nonexistent breasts. I was so skinny and small, I hadn't even gotten my period yet."

River covers her mouth with both hands. Her head moving side to side as if her shaking it could erase what happened to me.

"I was so starved for attention, for love. I never recognized what he was doing to me."

Her hands go to her chest. "He was grooming you."

"Yes. My mother never touched me, never hugged me or kissed me. She never said she loved me. I liked his attention. I craved love and connection, and I thought he cared about me, like a dad would. I was so stupid. So naïve."

"You were a child. It's not your fault."

River is right, I know, but a part of me still believes it was my fault. I should have known because I didn't deserve to be loved. My mother taught me that.

"I know I was a child, and I now know he deceived me all along." I shake my head, disgusted with myself. "But I should have guessed. I should have known something was very wrong. No one was ever kind to me. Why would this man who came to my house to be with my mother have any interest in me?"

"He was grooming you. I've read about cases like these

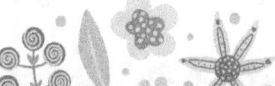

213

dozens of times. Men like him are smart, they've done it before, and they prey on kids and people who can't defend themselves."

"And I was the perfect victim." I know she's right, but it doesn't make me feel any different. "And do you want to know what's the worst part? Once I figured out what was happening, when the touches started feeling intrusive and making me uncomfortable, I told my mother. I told her he was touching me. I told her I didn't like the way he looked at me. And you know what she did?"

River shakes her head.

"She slapped me. She called me a liar. She said I was trying to steal her man. She kicked me out of the house. I was thirteen then. It was the middle of winter. She wouldn't let me back in the house. I stayed huddled in a corner against the wall, shivering for hours. Until he came home and let me in."

I hit myself in the chest with a fist. "And I was fucking grateful because he let me into the house. I hated how he made me feel when he touched me, but I was grateful because he also saved me. He saved me in so many ways. He fed me, he bought me clothes, he showed me kindness and kept my mother away from me when she went into one of her rages."

I take a step back, needing to put some distance between me and River. Between me and the memories. "And as much as I hated him, I also loved him because he was the only good thing I had, until I didn't. Until he changed, and I blamed myself for it too. How fucking messed up is that?"

I swallow the boulder that parked itself in my throat. My body is so stiff it feels as if my bones will crack. I squeeze my eyes shut. I had no choice. What could I have done? Run away? To where? Tell someone? I tried. She didn't believe me.

"They had a huge fight. But he convinced her I was confused, none of the things I said were true, that it was just teenage fantasies. He promised her he would keep his distance from me so I wouldn't feel that way anymore. And she believed him. But he lied. He continued to touch me. He threatened to kill her if I said anything again. He said he would kill her and make it look like I did it. That I'd go to jail and far worse things than him touching me would happen."

River takes a step toward me. I both want and don't want her to get any closer. I know she's trying to comfort me, but to have anyone touch me right now is too much. I put my hands up, and she stops. Tears run down her face, but she doesn't get any closer.

"He'd get me drunk. Force me to drink alcohol. Lace hot chocolate with vodka and touch me, but he said he was saving the best for my sixteenth birthday because that was the legal age of consent. He said if I ever told anyone it would be my word against his, and my mother would take his side. My age didn't stop him forcing me to touch him back."

I need to move. I need to get away. I turn away from River, take a step. Stop. Turn back. I'm moving, my feet taking charge, pacing in a chaotic loop. Back and forth I go, shaking my hands as if doing so could expunge the dirty feeling along with the words. When I finally stop, River is watching me with a hand pressed against her mouth and a stream of tears on her face.

I heave in a long breath. "By then I knew the only way to get away from him was to leave. But where could I go? I had no one. I didn't want to be another runaway just to fall in the hands of someone even worse than him. I needed to finish high school first. I put so much effort into getting the best grades possible. I knew that getting a scholarship was my only way out. I was terrified he wouldn't wait until I was sixteen. But I wasn't going to give him the one thing he wanted most."

River takes a step closer. "What was that?"

"My virginity. He liked to talk about how and when he would take my virginity. That he'd never had a virgin before. I would be his first, just like he would be my first. But I wasn't about to let him have it. A few days before I turned sixteen, I found a boy from school who was nice enough to me and lost my virginity to him."

Her eyes widen. "Oh, Becca."

"As bad as it was, it was a thousand times better than having him touch me because it was my choice." I thump my chest.

"Did he find out? About the boy?"

"Oh, I told him. It was my birthday. He gave my mother God knows what. She blacked out. And she didn't wake until late the next day. Telling him was a gift to myself. I told him with great glee that he would never be my first, that he could never have that piece of me."

"What happened?"

"He kept his promise of what he would do to me when I turned sixteen. No one came to help when I screamed or when he yelled. No one came to stop him from beating me or trashing the house. I was lucky he didn't break any bones. And he was lucky it was summer, and I didn't have school, so there was nobody to see the marks on my body."

"Oh my God, Becca."

"It took nearly a month for all the bruises to fade away. Oddly enough, he stopped touching me after that. I was tainted."

"What happened after? Is he still with your mom?"

"No. He died several months after that. Overdose."

"I thought you said he never got high."

I smile. "He did that day."

CHAPTER THIRTY-FOUR

BECCA

WE STAND LOOKING AT EACH OTHER. RIVER HOLDS HER fisted hands against her stomach. I know she wants to hug me, share my pain.

My skin crawls at the thought of allowing anyone to touch me when the confession still lingers on my lips. While his face floats like a ghost in the empty space between us. The aversion is a physical presence. It attaches itself to my back and neck, and its weight crushes me. I want to scream and run and rip at my own flesh to get rid of it.

No more.

Fuck you, Theodore.

You're dead.

Now stay dead.

I take a step closer to River, her hands open, and her arms come around me. She pulls me into a hug my body wants to reject. I shut it down. I shut it all down.

Breathe, I command myself.

River holds me, and little by little the stiffness in my muscles gives away. I ease into her embrace, and I hug her back.

Then the tears come.

River holds me until the sobs stop and the rigidness leaves me. She gives me a tighter squeeze and steps back, her hands still holding mine. "I love you, you know? You're my best friend, and you can count on me. I'm in your corner. Always."

I wipe my face with a sleeve. "I know. You've always had my back, even when I let you down."

River squeezes my hands. "You never let me down."

"I did. More than once. I didn't know how to be a friend. But I'm learning. You're teaching me."

River smiles and blinks away her own tears. I'm glad we're in the middle of a field, and there's no one close enough to see us. We're a mess.

She links her arm through mine, and we fall into step walking again. She bumps her shoulder into me. "I'm so sorry for everything that happened to you. I wish I could do or say something to make it better."

"You already have. More than you know."

She stops. "I haven't done a thing. I almost wish the bastard were alive. I have this big rusty knife at home ..."

That makes me laugh. I'm a fucking mess. I'm crying and laughing and then crying again. "But you did, River. You somehow found me and forced your friendship on me whether or not I wanted it, and you didn't let me get away. And I tried."

River shrugs. "You know I can't say no to a challenge."

"So I was a challenge?"

She holds up her thumb and pointer finger. "A tiny bit."

We find a bench and take a seat. "I'm sorry for dumping all of this on you."

"Don't." River puts a hand up. "You didn't dump anything on me. I'm glad you told me. It gives me a fresh perspective. I wish you had told me sooner. I wish I could have done more."

"I couldn't. I could never have said anything before. I've told no one."

"What changed?"

"I finally got the help I needed." I pull my legs up onto the bench and brace my knees.

"What do you mean?"

"I'm talking to a therapist."

River reaches over and squeezes my shoulder. "I'm so glad you are. How long have you been seeing her?"

"It's a he, and I never met him in person. We talk over the phone only."

River frowns. "Really?"

"Yeah. It's this program hosted by several universities, and you can text or call, and it's all anonymous. But it's not like traditional therapy, at least not like the therapy you see in movies. It's more like talking to a friend, a wise and smart friend who's on to your bullshit and calls you out on it."

River narrows her eyes, raises a hand and points at herself. I laugh. "Okay. It's a lot like talking to you, except it's a guy with a bunch of degrees who does this for a living, and …"

"And?" She nudges me with a knee when I say nothing else.

I inhale deep, the air crisp and pine scented. "And he's a stranger. It didn't matter if he liked me or not, if he judged me or not. I could walk away at any time, and no one would know." I shift on the bench so I can look at her face-to-face. "I was afraid. I was afraid you'd be disgusted and stop being my friend."

River is shaking her head even before I finish speaking. "Never. I would never be disgusted. It's not your fault. None of it was your fault. How could you think that?" Her tone is a little hurt.

This honesty and trust thing is not hurting only me. "River,

219

you have to understand. I'm disgusted with myself. Why wouldn't you be? Why wouldn't anyone?"

She grabs my hand. I drop my feet to the grass. "If I had told you the exact same things you told me, would you be disgusted with me? Blame me and walk away?"

"Of course not."

"Then why would you think that of me? And more importantly, why would you think that of yourself? Don't you deserve the same kindness you would extend me?"

Do I? My chest constricts, my body wants to fold into itself in rejection of her words. The old voices come back to haunt me.

Nobody loves you.

No one cares.

You're bad.

I squeeze my eyes shut as if by closing them I could also shun the words that have plagued me my whole life.

Lies. They're all lies. I know this. Why do I believe them?

Nobody loves you.

River loves me. My father loves me. My brother and sister love me.

No one cares.

River cares. My father cares. Tommy. Lucas. Even Dylan cares.

You're bad.

I'm not. I'm good. I'm a good person.

I rebuke the hurtful words I grew up with. I replace them with new words. Words that are true.

I open my eyes. "If you had asked me that a few weeks ago, the answer would have been no. But now, in this moment, I can say yes. I deserve kindness. I deserve better. I deserve more."

"You do. And I will be there to remind you."

"I'll need that." I'm not foolish enough to think that all is well, and all my brokenness is fixed. I may never be completely healed. But I have mended a few small pieces here and there. Now I just have to hold on to those mended pieces and patch a few more.

CHAPTER THIRTY-FIVE

BECCA

I turn my illegal space heater on, sink into my bed, and add an extra blanket. It's freezing today. I'm not looking forward to going to work at the bar tonight. I have three hours before I need to leave, but first, I want to give the therapist a call.

I adjust my earbuds, log in, and click the link to call him. The laptop screen glare is the only light in my room.

I close my eyes and wait. It rings once, twice. He answers.

"Good night." His voice has an instantaneous calming effect on me. I've grown used to this.

"Hi." I bite a nail. Pull my hands away and press them against my stomach, trying to squash the butterflies.

"Glad to hear from you. Did you have a nice Thanksgiving?"

Thanksgiving makes me think of Dylan and that damn cranberry sauce. The butterflies multiply.

"Yeah, it was very nice. I spent it with friends. You?" Well, one friend and one whatever the heck Dylan is. Frenemy? Hot-AF professor I can't stop thinking about? My next mistake?

"Same. Family and a friend."

Ugh. Are we making small talk now? I'm not good at this.

"The last time we talked you had some homework."

"Yes."

"Did you do the homework? Did you find a friend to talk to?"

I picture him leaning in, waiting for my response. "I did."

"That's great!"

I can hear the smile in his voice. "Want to tell me about it?"

"Okay." I fill my lungs, hold, exhale. "I talked to my best friend. I told her about my childhood, and how I lied about going away for holidays every time she invited me to visit her family. I told her about everything that happened to me. More than I thought I would."

There's a moment of silence. He waits for me to say more, but my mouth has gone dry.

"How did that make you feel?"

I grab a water bottle and take a sip. "Lighter. I feel lighter."

"I'm so happy for you. You've carried that burden alone for far too long."

"Yeah, I did. And I would probably have continued to if it wasn't for you."

"Nah, you did all the work. All I did was nudge you in the right direction."

"You did way more than that. And you know it."

"Okay, enough about me." He sounds … embarrassed? "And your friend? Was she supportive?"

"Yes, very much so. I knew she would be. But …"

"But?" He pushes when I stop.

"I was so afraid."

"Why? What exactly were you afraid of?"

"I don't know."

"I think you do. Remember, there's no judgment here. You didn't come this far just to retreat now. What were you afraid of?"

I close my eyes again, breathe in, out. "I didn't want her to pity me or look at me differently. I didn't want her to know how horrible a person I am."

"Okay, let's break that down. Did she pity you?"

"No. I mean, she felt sorry for me, but she didn't pity me. She got mad on my behalf."

"Did she look at you differently?" The sound of tapping accompanies his question.

"No, I don't think so. She was glad I told her. I think it strengthened our friendship."

"Are you a horrible person?"

What? His question takes me by surprise. I should have seen it coming, but I didn't. I can't answer.

"Tell me what you're thinking right now." His voice is softer.

"I have two competing voices in my head."

"What are they saying?"

"One voice is angry. It's screaming that I am a horrible person. That I'm worthless. That this whole thing is bullshit, and I'll never amount to anything." And so much more. But he doesn't need to know everything. I've said enough. Nausea rises up my throat.

"And the other voice? What is it telling you?"

"The other voice tells me I'm good, and I'm worthy, and everything else is just ugly lies."

"How does this voice sound?"

I have to think about it for a moment. "It is quiet, calm, steady."

"Do you know why this voice is quiet, and the other is screaming?"

"No."

"Because the truth doesn't need to scream. The truth doesn't need to be loud. The truth doesn't need to bully. The truth just is."

"Oh my God." *The truth just is.* Tears prickle at my eyes, and I don't stop them. He stays quiet. Waits for me to absorb what he told me. And it rings true. His words burn into my chest, dig into my heart and singe my soul like a tattoo written in fire.

"I think I'm going to need that on a T-shirt." I laugh through the tears.

He laughs with me.

All these years the two voices fought for space in my head and I've always listened to the louder, angrier voice when all along all I had to do was listen to the quiet truth that existed in me.

"Listen to the smaller voice. Listen to the voice of kindness and love. Promise me that." His voice is not so different from my own quiet voice.

"I promise." And I mean it.

"It won't be easy, old habits are hard to break. But every time the old habits and voices come after you, stop, breathe, look for the truth. It whispers. You must stop and pay attention."

"I will. Thank you."

"Good night, Cougar22." He chuckles.

I hang up. Remove my earbuds. Set my phone to wake me up at nine thirty. Sleep the best two hours of my life.

I have so many clothes layered on I look like that kid from *A Christmas Story*. Luckily, I can put my arms down, otherwise it would be a really awkward drive into work. I take five minutes to clear the frozen dusting of snow from my car. When I finally get in and turn the ignition, I'm met with a horrible dying-engine sound no one wants to hear. Ever.

"Come on. Start." I try again. Nothing.

"Be a good girl, and I'll get you premium gas next time." It's a lie, but it works. The car starts. I can see my breath. It fogs the windows.

"I should have started you first, then cleared the ice."

I hook my phone to the charger. It rings. River. I put it on speaker. "Hey."

"Hey, what are you up to? Working tonight?"

"Yeah, I have a four-hour shift tonight. From ten to two AM. Leaving for work now." I back out of the parking space and drive.

"Ugh. That sucks."

"At least I don't have to be up early in the morning." Look at me being all optimistic and shit.

"Are you up for some company? I'm bored. I could stop by."

I hesitate. "You don't have to check on me, you know. I'm okay."

"No, dude. Logan is here with my sister, and I can't make the TV loud enough to block all the monkey sex they're having."

I laugh. "Monkey sex?"

"Yeah, by the sound of it, they must be hanging from the ceiling or something."

"Skye would be so mad if she heard you."

"Ha! Skye is too blissed out by multiple orgasms to care. I'll let you go. Drive safe. See you soon."

She hangs up, and I'm still laughing. Then, for no reason at all, I think of Dylan. And monkey sex.

CHAPTER THIRTY-SIX

BECCA

THE BAR IS NOT AS CROWDED TODAY THANKS TO THE COLD and ice. Just my regulars and a few college students. It means less work for me, but also fewer tips. Thursday night football on all the TVs keeps the handful of customers entertained.

I'm restocking the beer fridge when River comes in. As expected, all heads turn to her. She sits at the opposite end from my regulars and away from the other Riggins students taking center stage in front of the biggest TV.

I wipe my cold hands on my apron and walk to her. River sets a plastic container in front of me. "I come bearing gifts. Skye made cookies. I stole them. She owes me after putting me through all that noise."

I'm not saying no to homemade cookies, especially ones made by Skye. "Thank you!" I grab the container and hide it under a shelf. "How are the monkeys?"

She laughs. "Dude, you don't understand. I love my sister, and Logan is the perfect guy for her. But if you told me at the beginning of school that this would be Skye today, I would think you're crazy."

"Good for her." I like Skye. She's the sweetest. It couldn't have been easy growing up in River's shadow. "What can I get you?"

"Nothing alcoholic. I need my wits to drive in this weather." She rubs her hands together and blows on them.

"I can make you a mean hot chocolate." Her eyes widen at my suggestion.

"And fries? Can I have fries too? I ate too many cookies, I need something salty."

"Sure. Anything for my best friend."

I call in the order and check on my regulars. They're still nursing their first beers. The college guys call me over. "We want to buy her a drink." The one in the middle nods his head at River.

Every time. It never fails. "No, dude. You don't want to do that. Not if you want to keep all your limbs attached to your body and be able to walk."

He blinks at me.

"What do you mean?" the guy on his left asks.

"I mean her boyfriend is an ex-con covered in tattoos and the size of a barn. He doesn't take kindly to other guys hitting on his girl," I lie.

"Well, he's not here right now, is he, doll?" This is from the slimy guy on the right. If they were the Three Stooges, he would be Moe. I let the doll comment slide.

"Her boyfriend? No, he's not here. But his associates are. She never goes anywhere without someone watching her." I look over their heads pointedly. All three look back, glancing over their shoulders. I hold back a laugh. Their gazes dart over the few people sitting at the tables. Two guys stare back. All three turn back to me.

"You're bullshitting me." Moe sneers.

"Hey, I don't care. It's your broken legs, not mine. What should I get the lady?"

There's silence. "Maybe we should just watch the game." This from the guy on the left.

"Shut up, Larry," Moe shushes him. I guess this makes the guy in the middle Curly. I crack up. I can't help laughing. His name really is Larry.

"What's so funny?" Moe shoves his empty bottle at me. "Get me another beer."

I know his type. I hate his type. Rich, entitled, thinks he's better than everyone else. I grab him another beer. Make sure it's not a cold one from the back. "Is that all?" I look at the other two. They nod.

I walk away to make River's hot chocolate. Heck, I'm making two.

I heat whole milk in the cappuccino machine and go back into the kitchen for chunks of baking chocolate.

"You're using real chocolate?" River leans over the top to watch me.

"That's the best way." I chop the chunks into small slivers and put them in a ceramic bowl. Pour some hot milk over it and stir until I get a creamy consistency. Add the rest of the milk and stir more. "I like to sweeten mine with agave, but we don't have that here, so I have to use sugar." I add the sugar, mix until dissolved, and then pour the hot chocolate into two large mugs. The scent is heavenly.

"Fries!" the cook calls from the pass-through window. Perfect timing. I grab the fries and a mug and put them on the bar top in front of River. She goes for the mug first. I wrap my hands around my mug, enjoying the way the heat warms my hands.

"Hmm, this smells so good." She blows steam away before taking a tentative sip.

I reach for a french fry. I love the mix of salty and sweet foods together.

"What was that about?" River holds the mug with both hands and moves a finger toward the Three Stooges.

"Oh them? That's nothing. But now you have an ex-con boyfriend known for putting guys who hit on you in hospitals."

She choke-laughs on her drink. "Thanks, friend. Super Becca comes in for the save."

A few people leave and I close their tab. The three college guys keep their eyes on the TV. I make my way back to River. Most of the fries are gone. I help myself to a couple.

River pushes the plate closer to me. "I have questions."

I knew this was coming. "Ask away." Look at me being all open instead of running for the hills.

"All those times you said you were going home for holidays, where did you go?"

I shrug. "Nowhere. I stayed on campus."

"But you can't stay on campus all year round. Don't they close the dorms?"

"You can stay on campus if you take at least one class during the breaks. I make sure to always take a class."

"I thought they had mandatory leave during certain times, like winter break."

"Yeah, during those times I had to leave. I have a friend who lives off campus, and he lets me stay in his apartment during the breaks. I love his place, it's like being on vacation."

"A friend? Who?"

"You don't know him—oh, wait. You do. You met him on Halloween. Remember that cute boy I introduced you to? Lucas?"

"The guy who was hugging you?"

"Yes, that's him. His family is in real estate, and they own the building he lives in. So he has his own apartment. It's small, but so cool."

River looks down at her mug, and when she looks back up, there's hurt in her eyes. "You know you could have stayed in my place. Heck, you could have come home with me. I invited you every time."

"I couldn't, River. Not without questions. Eventually you'd be wondering why I never went home. Why I stayed on campus the entire year. And your mom? I'm not entirely convinced she can't read minds." I make a cross sign with my fingers.

River snorts. "That's because she can. Mom's spidey sense is off the charts. But you could have come a few times. Like you did freshman year."

How can I make her understand how I felt at her home? I don't want to hurt her. "Being with your family was the best, but also so hard. I had nothing like that. I've never had family meals and all that laughter and joy. It was too much. It made me envious, and I didn't want to feel that way. You and your family were so kind to me. But I was an outsider. I didn't belong, I didn't know how to be." My stomach clenches, the truth I'm so used to denying hits me like a physical blow.

I'm saved from her response when one of the regulars waves at me. "I'll be right back."

I refill their drinks and get them a fresh batch of pretzels. The Three Stooges watch me. I glance at the TV. How much longer until this game is over? Fourth quarter. Hope they leave soon.

I go back to River. She puts a hand up before I can speak. "I want you to come home with me for Christmas. I don't want you to spend Christmas alone ever again. Please say yes."

I wring my hands in my apron. "I don't know if I can come."

"Why the hell not?"

"Because my father wants me to spend Christmas with him."

She squeals and covers her mouth with both hands. Wiggles in her chair like an excited little kid. "Oh my God. That's good, right? You said he's a nice guy."

"Yes, it is good. And guess what? I have a brother and sister. He's married, and the wife is lovely too."

"I'm so happy for you. Tell me more."

I grin at her. "I will. But first ask me what I did for Thanksgiving."

CHAPTER THIRTY-SEVEN

BECCA

"Professor Beckett? You had Thanksgiving dinner with Professor Beckett?"

"Yes. And his brother, Tommy, too." I take the empty fries plate and put it in the dirty dishes tray.

River gives me her empty mug. "Now, speak. Leave nothing out."

I put both our mugs on the tray. "Tommy invited me over. Said it was Dylan's idea—"

"Oh, it's Dylan now. No longer Professor Dick, I see." She wiggles her eyebrows at me.

I look around the bar, no one is asking for anything. The game is over, and the highlights are playing. It's only the locals and the Three Stooges hanging out now. "Hold on."

I walk to them. "Can I get you guys anything else?"

"No, I'm good." This from the guy on the left. He gets up and slides me a twenty. "Keep the change."

"Thanks, Larry."

He smiles. "Hey, you remember my name."

I smile back and turn to the other two. Curly, the guy in the middle, gets up and puts his jacket on. He was nursing a soda all night. Guess he's the designated driver. He gives me a five and both of them step back, waiting for Moe.

"You guys go." He looks at River. "I'll stay a little longer."

A chill runs down my spine. I don't like the way he's looking at her. I don't like it at all.

Larry, the nicer one of them, steps closer. "What? How you going to get back to campus?"

"I have a feeling I'll get a ride." Moe takes a long sip of his beer. His fifth for the night.

"Come on, let's go." Curly puts his hand on Moe's shoulder, but he shoves it off. "You two pussies can leave. I have plans for tonight."

Over my dead body. Time to ruin his plans.

The two guys hang for another moment, then leave. I close their tab and go back to River. "That asshole over there has plans that involve you. You're not leaving here alone. Sit tight. I'm getting backup."

"What?" River looks up from her phone and glances at the jerk behind me. "What do you mean?"

"His friends left, and he said he was staying because he has plans, and then he looked at you. I got a bad feeling about it."

She's fidgeting with a napkin, twisting it, her fingers shake. She looks nervous, which is not something I'm used to seeing on her.

"Wait. I'll be right back." I walk to the other end of the bar and to my locals. "See that guy? Can you keep an eye on him for me? Make sure he stays away from my friend?"

"We got this." One of the locals vouches for the three of them.

"I can walk out with her. I'll say I need a smoke." He grabs a pack of cigarettes from his shirt pocket and puts it on the bar top.

For once, I'm glad for the unhealthy habit. "Sounds good to me. Thanks, guys."

I walk to the back, and I can hear them engaging the asshole in conversation. I smile. They're distracting him for me. I find Gus in his small office. He's going over paperwork.

"Hey, Gus, I'm gonna need you up front for a minute."

He looks up. He knows I only come after him when there's a problem. He gets up and towers over me. I had Gus in mind when I described River's fake boyfriend. "What's up?"

"This one guy has been making eyes at my friend all night. Now his friends left, and he stayed to wait her out. I think he's up to no good."

If there's one thing Gus hates more than dealing with customers, it is slimy guys who prey on women.

"What's the plan?"

"I'll get her to leave, and you make sure he stays inside until she drives away."

"Okay. You talk to her. I'll wait a minute and then come out, so it doesn't look like you came to get me, and he doesn't decide you're the next best thing."

"And that's why you're the boss. You're smart like that." I play-punch him in the bicep. His arms are bigger than my legs.

I go back to River. "Okay, here's the plan. You get ready to leave, and when you do, Gus will stop the jerk from following you, and one of my locals will walk out with you. Put your phone on speaker and call me when you're safely away."

"What about you?" She reaches out to me, but the bar top is too wide for her to touch me.

"I'm fine. I have Gus and my local guys. Plus, he's not interested in me."

Gus comes out then, and Moe pays attention. It might be cold enough for polar bears outside, but Gus always wears a cutoff bar T-shirt, and the tattoos on his neck, arms and hands can't be ignored. Especially on a guy his size.

River gets money to pay for her drink and food. "Don't worry about it. I ate half of the fries, and we don't even have hot chocolate on the menu."

She gets up and grabs her jacket from the back of her chair. Jerk Face pays attention. He throws some money on the bar. Gus takes the money, looks up his tab and starts making change real slow. My local guy announces he needs a cigarette.

Everything is playing out like a finely orchestrated choreography.

The jerk gets up. "Hurry up, man."

"No, no. I want to make sure I got your change right." Gus gives him a vicious smile that could put sharks to shame.

I grab a rag and clean the counter. Rivers walk out with my local. Jerk Face goes after them. I look at Gus and catch him leaping over the counter and chairs with an agility I'd never imagine possible for a guy his size. I swear the ground shakes when he lands.

He maneuvers himself around Moe and blocks the door and puts his hands up. "You forgot your change."

"Forget it, man." Jerk Face tries to go around Gus.

Gus cuts him off. "No, I got your money right here." He counts again. Slowly. It's all in one-dollar bills.

I grab my phone from my pocket. What's taking her so long? Come on, River, call me already. If Jerk Face is stupid enough to push Gus, it will get ugly, and I so don't want to mop blood off the floors.

My phone buzzes. A text instead of a call.

River: Incoming.

Incoming? What the heck does that mean?

River: And before you ask, I'm using voice to text. I'm good. Driving home. Thanks, best friend.

I don't want to text back and distract her.

River: I want all the details. All of them.

I glance up at Gus and nod. He stops counting the money and steps aside. "Okay, man."

Jerk Face runs out. I stare at my phone again. Incoming. I don't understand what she's talking about.

The bells over the door ding. I look up.

Dylan walks in.

Incoming, indeed.

CHAPTER THIRTY-EIGHT

BECCA

W‌HAT IS HE DOING HERE?

Dylan approaches, his gaze on me the entire time. He looks amazing in gray sweatpants, a hoodie, and a ski jacket—last year's lift tickets still dangling from a hook. He has a couple days' scruff on his face. He takes the same seat River vacated.

I finish unloading a rack of clean glasses onto a shelf before walking to him. "Hey. I'm surprised to see you here."

"Me too."

"What do you mean?" I try to stuff my hands into my back pockets before remembering I'm wearing leggings with no pockets. I cross my arms behind my back instead.

"I couldn't sleep. Normally I'd go for a run, but not with this weather." His fingers tap a light tattoo on the counter.

"So … you went for a ride instead?" I grip my elbows.

"Yeah and somehow ended up here." His gaze is fixed on me.

We're silent for several moments. I scramble for something to say. Nothing comes to me. We stare at each other. Then the bell over the door dings again. My local is back from his smoke, and so is Jerk Face. He finds Gus talking to the other two locals at the opposite end of the bar. Takes his seat back. "Where's my change?"

His tone is accusatory, like he didn't leave in a hurry. His cheeks are red. Anger turns what otherwise would be a nice face into a caricature of itself.

I turn my back to him. Gus can deal with it. "Can I get you a Dos Equis?"

"No, thanks. Maybe something warm?" His fingers trace the wood grain on the bar top, back and forth. What would they feel like on my skin?

"A coffee, then?"

"Probably not the best idea when I already have trouble falling asleep." His eyes crinkle at the corners when he smiles.

"Hot chocolate?"

"Yes, that would be great, thanks."

I get to making the second round of hot chocolate of the night. The ingredients still next to the cappuccino machine. Dylan watches me go through the same ritual as before.

I make myself a mug to share with him. Check the time. Nearly midnight. "Do you want anything to eat? I can check if the cook is still in."

He shakes his head. "No, thanks. Not hungry."

I give him his drink, and we both take a sip, looking at each other over the rim of our mugs. This one is even better than the first.

His eyes widen at the first taste. "This is good."

"Thanks. That's a Becca special. It's not on the menu." I remember the cookies.

"Oh, I have something to go with the hot chocolate. River brought me some homemade cookies earlier." I reach into the shelf where I hid them and open the container. There's like two dozen cookies, three different kinds. Sugar cookies, chocolate chip, and, my favorite, peanut butter chocolate chunk. I offer him the container. He grabs a chocolate chip. I grab a peanut butter one. We take a bite. The moan we share sounds obscene. His eyes darken, and he looks at me like he wants to eat me instead of the cookie.

My cheeks burn, the heat spreads into my chest and belly. He licks a crumb off his thumb. The heat in my belly pools lower. This is like foreplay.

We stare at each other, blink, look away, drink, stare again. Not a word is spoken and yet so much is said. The sounds of the bar fade away. I curse and bless the counter between us. God knows what would happen if we could touch right now.

"What about my cookie?" Jerk Face interrupts us.

And with his voice comes the low murmur of conversation. The muffled song playing on the speakers. The talking heads on TV. I get yanked back into reality. Look at the asshole. He smiles like a used-car salesman. So sleazy it leaves an oily residue behind. I want to bathe in bleach.

"Sorry. You can't have any. It's against health code policies since these cookies were not made on the premises."

"He had one." Asshole points at Dylan. He sounds like a petulant child.

"He's a friend." I turn away from him, grip my mug and bring it to my lips.

"I can be your friend. What time are you leaving, doll? Maybe we can share those cookies in the back seat of your car."

I ignore him, taking another sip. Dylan is no longer looking at me. He's staring at Jerk Face with murder in his eyes. A small flame kindles inside me.

"Hey! I'm talking to you." Jerk Face's voice gets louder.

Dylan stands up.

Gus moves like a ninja and gets around the bar. Steps between Dylan and the asshole. "Time for you to go, buddy." His tone is friendly, but there's nothing friendly about his posture. Gus smacks a fist into the palm of his hand.

The three locals stand—the synchronized screech of their chairs dragging on the floor is a warning—but Jerk Face is either too drunk or too stupid because he doesn't seem to notice and doesn't back down.

"I can't go. I'm waiting for my friend Bonnie to give me a ride." He points at me.

Gus nods, never taking his eyes off Jerk Face. "Hey, *Bonnie*, why don't you go now. Don't worry about cleaning up. I'm closing early. It's *dead* tonight." Gus puts a lot of emphasis on the word dead.

I look at Dylan and whisper, "I'll be right back." I take the cookie container and walk to the back, removing my apron on the way. Grabbing my backpack, I stuff the cookies inside, grab my sweater, and put on my jacket. I fish out my keys, and I'm back in less than a minute, making my way from the other side of the bar and taking a wide berth around the asshole. Gus shifts his position, keeping himself between us.

Dylan walks to me and puts a hand at my back. I glance at Gus, and he tilts his head up in a clear indication for me to go.

Jerk Face gets up. Gus puts a hand on his shoulder. "You can't go yet." Pushes him into his seat again. "I got your change, Pretty Boy. You're going to need that to call a cab."

Dylan's hand stays on my back all the way to my car. I mourn the short distance and miss the warmth when he takes his hand away to open the car door for me. "I'll follow you and make sure you get back safely."

"You don't have to."

"I want to."

I hesitate, then get into the car. He stands by the open door. I put the key in the ignition and turn. Nothing. Not even a flicker of a sound. I try again. And again. "It's dead."

His hand appears in the space between us. "Come. I'll give you a ride. Leave the car here. We can come back tomorrow and try to jump-start it."

"But …"

"It's late, Becca. The car will be fine. Send your boss a message so he knows you're safe. I'll take you home."

I take his hand.

I get into his car.

He drives me.

We don't talk. I'm fascinated by his every move, the gentle way his hands grip the steering wheel, how he checks his mirrors before changing lanes and how his thigh tenses when he steps on the gas pedal. He's a careful driver. The ride is smooth. We get to campus far too fast.

"Where to?" He slows down when we reach the main road into Riggins.

"What?"

The corners of his mouth quirk up. "Which building do you live in?"

"Oh. The blue dorm."

He drives no more than twenty miles per hour, as if he too wants to slow down and extend our time together. "Do you know why all the dorms have different colors?" There's mischief in his eyes.

"So it's easier for people to find them?"

"That too, but that's not the original reason."

He parks near my building, but keeps the car running. We're away from the lights and hidden from curious eyes. I look at all the other buildings, each a different color. It's dark now, save for a few streetlights here and there, but during the day the buildings sit next to each other like a brick-and-mortar rainbow.

"What's the original reason, then?"

"Back in nineteen seventy-eight, an artist called Gilbert Baker created the rainbow flag in San Francisco. As you can imagine, a lot of people were not happy about it. But a few years later, Riggins, being the progressive university it was, painted all the dorms a different rainbow color as a silent support for gay rights. They never officially said anything about it. But that's the real reason. The official reason, as you said, is to make it easier for people to find their buildings."

I look at the buildings again, seeing them in a new light. "That's so cool, how do you know that?"

"My parents were professors here. They told me that when I was a kid."

"I had no idea." We stay silent for a while. Both looking at the buildings. "Is it hard? To work here I mean?"

He unlocks his seatbelt. Turns my way. "Sometimes. I have so many memories of coming here as a kid. Helping them carry papers and books. Taking classes for college credit while still in high school and stopping to have lunch with them when they taught in the summer. Sitting in their lectures sometimes." His gaze grows distant—he goes to a place I cannot follow but would give anything to experience. I'd trade the pain of love and loss for the relief of getting away from my mother in a heartbeat.

"It's bittersweet, I guess."

He nods. "In more ways than I imagined possible."

"What did they teach?"

"Dad was an economics professor, and Mom taught history.

Meals were always filled with world events discussions." He smiles, his voice lighter, happier.

"And you chose—"

"Psychology," he confirms what I already know.

"Is it something you always wanted to study?"

"Not really. I kind of fell into it, or more likely embraced it out of necessity." He looks away, half of his face in shadows—the car's interior light paints his skin blue.

"What do you mean?" I speak so low, I'm not sure he heard me.

"It was senior year of high school. A few months before graduation. I was all set to go to Dartmouth ..." He's silent for a while. I wait.

"My girlfriend and I drove together every day. That day she got mad at me because she saw me talking to another girl. It was innocent, but Annelise had always been insecure. We had a fight on the way back home. She made me pull over and got out of the car. I tried to follow her, but it was a one-lane road with barely a shoulder. When the other cars started beeping behind me, I had to go. I looped around and came back looking for her. It was less than half a mile from her house, and when I didn't see her I figured she had made it home."

He goes silent again. My heart constricts. I fear whatever he will say next.

"I texted her. A dozen times. And when she didn't answer, I thought she was still mad. I wish I had never listened to her and stopped the car."

I reach to him and squeeze his hand. He looks at our hands together, and I let go. When he speaks, his voice is so low I have to lean in to hear him better. "The call came three hours later. Someone—a jogger found her in a field. She'd been beaten unconscious and was half-naked."

"Jesus." Tears sting my eyes. We have this in common, his girlfriend and I.

"The police came after me. I was out of my mind with guilt and fear. They wouldn't let me see her or tell me exactly what happened. They kept asking me the same questions over and over. She woke up the next day and told them what happened. She was never the same."

"It was not your fault, Dylan. You know that."

He looks at me and then drops his gaze. Three fingertips tap his knee.

"Her family blamed me. She blamed herself. I tried to stay by her side, support her. She didn't go back to school. This is a small town. Everyone knew what happened. She couldn't stand to be pitied. And then there were the assholes and bullies—they sent her nasty emails and texts. I went after them, got into a lot of fights. She got help, went to counseling a couple of times a week. We thought she was getting better. But then …"

I try to get closer to him, but the seatbelt holds me back. I unlock it, pull my legs up onto the seat, and take his hand between mine. The need to comfort him greater than my fear of rejection.

He closes his eyes. "She killed herself."

"Oh my God." I hurt for this girl I've never met. My lungs lock up, and I have to make a conscious effort to breathe. That too could have been me. The idea of ending it all whispered in my ears more than once.

He blinks several times, his mouth turns down, his chin quivers. "All I could think of was the moment I stopped my car and let her go."

"You couldn't have anticipated it. It was not your fault." I squeeze his hand harder, try to break the hold the memory has over him.

He doesn't meet my eyes. "I trashed my entire room. My parents didn't stop me. They stood at the door and watched. When everything was in pieces on the floor, my mom hugged me, and my dad brought in trash bags, and we cleaned the mess."

He brings our laced fingers to his chest. His heart beats wildly against the back of my hand.

"When I started at Dartmouth seven months later, I switched my majors. I couldn't change what happened to Annelise. Or bring her back. But I needed to understand why she did it. And I wanted to make sure it never happened to anyone I loved again. I never saw the signs. Even now, knowing everything I know, there were never any signs she wanted to take her life. I'm still not sure that's what she intended to do."

I muster all the bravery I can, and I take a risk. Pulling our laced hands back, I press his fingers to my cheek and kiss his knuckles as if the small gesture could take his pain away.

Dylan shifts, disengages, tucks my hair behind my ear. His fingertips linger on my neck. I shiver. He grips the back of my head and pulls me closer, his lips inches away from mine. I close my eyes, inhale his clean scent. He leans in, breathes me in, and kisses my forehead. His lips stay there for a moment, and then he pulls away, slowly reversing his every move until we no longer touch.

Dylan blinks away the memories. "Thank you."

"I didn't do anything."

"You listened."

I could listen to him reading a math book. His voice has the same calming effect on me the therapist's voice does. Hmm ... they sound similar too. Never thought of that before. Maybe all psychologists learn to talk with the same soft tone.

He looks over my shoulder. "I'd walk you to your door, but …"

I look to the building entrance. A few people are hanging out by the door, smoking.

"Yeah, probably best for me to go alone." I'm glad it's too dark for anyone to see inside his car. Last thing we need is gossip about a professor and me.

"Can you text me when you get to your room?" He gives me his phone. "Put your number in, and I'll text you."

I hear what he doesn't say … so he knows I'm safe. I put my number in his contacts, give his phone back. We stare at each other, his gaze drops to my mouth. I lick my lips, wishing I could taste him.

"Good night, Becca."

I open the door watching him, frigid air digs its icy fingers into me, and I shiver. I step out, close the door, walk to my building, look back. He's still there. I go inside, get into the elevator. My phone buzzes. I look at it and smile.

Dylan: Sweet dreams.

CHAPTER THIRTY-NINE

BECCA

Once inside my room, I kick off my shoes and drop my jacket and backpack on the floor. Rest my back against the door. Close my eyes. "What an insane day."

My laptop calls to me, but I stop myself and grab my shower stuff instead. I need to think.

I make my way to the showers, crossing my fingers that no one is there. I'm rewarded with an empty room. My body relaxes by degrees, first by finding myself alone and then by the hot water. The tension in my shoulders washes down the drain with the suds. I'm divided between wanting to stay in the shower and leaving before someone shows up. Exhaustion and the need to avoid people while feeling so exposed wins.

I dry and dress in my cozy unicorn pajamas, wrap my wet hair in a towel and go back to my room, getting into bed. I should go to sleep, but instead grab my laptop. It's so late that I doubt he'll be there, but when I browse to the support page, I see his name. My heart picks up speed. I should be over this nervousness by now.

I shake my hair loose, comb with my fingers, get my crappy

earbuds. Wrap a blanket around me and lean against the cement wall. Cold seeps through the blanket and my shirt, making me shiver. I click his name to make the call.

He picks up on the third ring. "I didn't expect to hear from you again today."

I hoped he was up waiting for me to call again. Idiot. I'm so stupid. Why would he be waiting for me? We talked a few hours ago. He's not my private therapist, or my best friend.

"I wasn't planning on calling, but then I saw you were there." I pick at a loose string on my blanket.

"How was your night?" The sound of light tapping comes through as he speaks. An image of long fingers tapping on a desk fills my mind. It soothes me.

"It was … interesting."

"Interesting?"

"Yeah, just some work stuff," I deflect. Me and my big mouth.

"And this work stuff was interesting because …" he pushes.

"I met someone." What the actual fuck. I didn't mean to tell him this.

The tapping stops. Silence builds like a fortress. Why is he not saying anything?

"You did?"

"Yes. Well … technically I've known this person for over a year, but we never really talked before."

"And now?" The tapping resumes, but it's not as soothing as before.

"And now we did. Talk that is." Could I be more evasive?

"What changed?"

"I don't know."

"Don't you?"

What changed? He tried to protect me from the shooter. He

invited me for Thanksgiving, and he flirted with me. He said he's attracted to me. He came to the bar when he couldn't sleep. He was ready to fight that asshole to protect me, and then he drove me home. So much happened. I simplify it. "I guess we started talking, and I think I like him. It was …" Nice? Fun?

"It was what?" The tapping speeds up.

"Easy. It was easy talking to him. A little like talking to you. Except he doesn't ask me all these questions."

"Can you see yourself having a relationship with this person?" The tapping stops again.

Yes. Yes. Yes. God help me. I can. "I don't know."

"Why not?" Tap. Tap. Tap. Silence.

"I'm not sure if I'm fit for a real relationship."

"What makes you think that?"

I gaze down. My hand has shredded the corner of the blanket into a tangle of strings. "You know why. I'm a mess. I've never had a real relationship in my life. I have no idea what it even looks like."

"Okay, let's break this down. One: You're not a mess. You're a human being, and being human is complicated—"

I huff. "Yeah, but I'm more complicated than most."

"You don't know that. There are over seven billion people on the planet. Don't compare. You can only speak for yourself."

Now I'm the size of a speckle of dust. He didn't mean it like that, I know, but his words make me aware of my insignificance. "See? That's why I'm not good enough."

"I didn't say that. I never said you're not good enough. Where is this coming from?"

My insecurities. "Never mind. I'm babbling. Go on."

"No. Let's not go on. It serves no purpose for you to hold on to these ideas. Tell me what you're thinking. The truth this time."

I wrap the jumble of strings around two fingers and pull. They dig into my skin before breaking away. If only breaking away from myself was that easy. "I have nothing to offer him."

"That's not true." The soothing tapping resumes. "You're kind, and funny, and you have a huge heart."

I run a thumb through the grooves the strings left on my skin. "How can you know any of this? We've never met. All you know is what I tell you, and none of it is good."

"I know because I have been listening. You have way more to offer than you think, and—" He pauses, the tapping increases, he releases a loud breath. "And I have another homework for you."

I close my eyes and thump my head against the wall. What now? "Ugh."

He chuckles. "This should be easier than the last one."

"Why don't I believe you?"

"Your homework is to let it be. Don't automatically shut down with this person."

"Let it be? What do you mean, let it be?"

"If you're attracted to this person and feel safe with him, let it be. Don't run. See how this plays out. Give him, and yourself, a chance."

"What if I can't? It feels like too much." I'm holding myself so stiffly, my shoulders burn. I arch my back to ease the pain, but the ache burrows deeper.

"I'm not saying marry the guy. I'm saying talk to him, get to know him better. You might surprise yourself. This might end up being nothing, just another person you crossed paths with, but it could also be the beginning of something great. And you won't know until you try."

"And if it's a big freaking mess?" It's already a mess. He's a professor, I'm a student. It can never happen. But I can't tell him that.

"And if it's not?" he counters.

And if it's not … what could it be, then? Resistance builds in my chest, it constricts me, makes it harder to breathe. "Please don't tell me you believe in happily-ever-afters." Sarcasm drips from every word I say.

"I believe in happily-ever-nows. Each moment is a choice we make. To be happy or not."

His words press into my chest like a phantom CPR trying to breathe life into my deadened heart. A part of me screams that he's talking bullshit, hippie mumbo jumbo. But another part remembers all the times I could have been happy, but held to my anger and misery instead. Warring thoughts take residence in my mind, bouncing against each other. My temples pound with the beginning of a headache. Have I been making the wrong choices all these years?

"Talking to you feels like being punched in the face again and again." I didn't mean to say the words out loud.

"What? I'm sorry—"

"No, don't apologize. It's not a bad thing. It's what I need, I think. A good brain-shaking to dislodge all the crap I stuffed in there over the years." I laugh at my attempted joke. But the words spoken without thought, spoken without guarding myself, ring true with such a force they fill my ears with the sound of my racing heart. I press a hand to my chest, will it to slow down.

Silence returns. He waits for me to speak again. But I can't. I need to sit with this revelation.

The tapping comes back, slower this time. "You there?" he asks, his voice is so low I can barely hear it. I don't reply before I hang up.

CHAPTER FORTY

BECCA

Dylan's car is parked in the same spot as last night. I look around before opening the door. No one is paying attention to me. I get inside.

"Thank you for picking me up so early." The therapist's advice flashes back in my mind, and I blush and look out the window to hide my face.

Dylan starts his car. "Eight thirty isn't so early."

"It is if you don't have to get up and can sleep in, especially when it's so cold." I look down, avoid his eyes, and adjust my jacket under the seatbelt.

"My first class is at eleven, it's no biggie." He glances at me, then back at the road.

Something is different. I can't figure out what, and I can't stop thinking about it. "What changed?"

"What do you mean?" His hands curl around the steering wheel.

I debate speaking up and breaking this … whatever this is. Here goes nothing. "You were a dick to me." The words are harsh, but my tone is neutral.

His eyebrows rise in response.

"You were a jerk when we first met. Now, you're not. What changed?" We come to a red light.

His shoulders drop, and his head follows. He closes his eyes, nods, and then looks at me.

"I deserve that. And I'm sorry. I owe you an apology, and I should have apologized earlier."

"That still doesn't answer my question."

His fingers tap on a knee. "I made a harsh judgment about you based on things I overheard and things I didn't fully understand."

If I could poke around his brain and read his mind, I would, and then I could avoid the questions. But I can't. And I can't deal with not knowing or understanding what's going on. I don't know where we stand. Where *I* stand.

I look at him. "Explain." The car behind us beeps when the light turns green. "Please."

He opens his mouth, closes, opens, closes, and nothing comes out.

Another beep. He drives.

I reach to him, touch his hand on the steering wheel. "Don't hold back. Tell me what you're thinking."

His hand flexes underneath mine. "Remember the first time we met? The very first time." His eyebrows go up.

How can I forget how he found me kissing Lucas in his classroom? "Yes, you caught me kissing a boy in your classroom."

He glances at me and back at the road. "I didn't like that. When I first saw you two, before I realized it was you, I was annoyed, but I also remembered being a teenager in a college. I understood. My only intention was to get you two out of my classroom before the next lecture started. But when I saw it was you, I got angry."

That makes no sense. "Why? You didn't even know me."

"But I did. Well, maybe not in person. But I knew you, I noticed you."

"I don't understand."

He laughs. "You are an attractive woman. I'm a guy. I noticed."

I'm at a loss. I've never seen him look at anyone with anything other than cold politeness and utmost professionalism.

"You noticed me?"

"Is that so hard to believe?"

"Yes! Look at you!" I wave my hand up and down at him. "You could have anyone you want. The students, the staff, the teachers—they all have the hots for you."

"No, they don't." His eyebrows dip into a V.

"Yes, they do. And if you'd look around and pay a little more attention, you'd see that too."

He slows down, making a right turn. "It doesn't matter. I don't care about them. I would never get involved with one of my students. And we got sidetracked. I owe you an apology, so this is me apologizing right now."

His students or any student? He said *my student.* He pulls into the empty parking spot next to my car. How did we get here so fast?

"That first time we met"—he makes air quotes—"I got angry because I wanted you, and I couldn't have you." He runs a hand through his hair. "And then I heard stories about you being …" He looks at me. "This is not me saying I believe any of those things I heard, okay? I want to be honest with you."

"What did you hear?" But I already know. I've heard the same words myself.

"I heard people saying you go after the freshmen. That you have some kind of fetish for them."

My body revolts against the words, even though I know they are true. Just not the way people think. "And if it's true?"

"I have no say in how you live your life or who you date, Becca. But I was a jerk. I was jealous and took my anger out on you, and for that, I apologize." He opens his mouth as if to say more and then presses his lips together.

"Thank you. I appreciate your honesty. I dated some freshmen. But not because of a fetish or fantasy." I don't give him anything else.

He looks straight ahead. "And then I saw you with Tommy. And he couldn't stop talking about this new friend he was hanging out with. And all I could think was that my little brother was being used. I got angry."

I'm taken aback by his candor. "Tommy and I were never together like that. We're just friends. He's like a little brother to me."

He takes off his seatbelt. "I know that now. After the first time we met at the bar, Tommy came to my office at Riggins and ripped me a new one." He laughs, his gaze lost in the memory. "I had no idea he had it in him. He made me proud."

"Tommy is a good kid. You should be proud." I adjust the heat vent away from me. Why am I so warm?

Dylan shifts toward me, and with two fingertips, tucks a lock of hair behind my ear. "For the last two years I have been watching you from a distance."

"Two years?" Never mind butterflies. There are seagulls dive-bombing in my stomach.

"Yes. I never planned on acting on it. I just like to look at you."

Whoa … he likes to look at me? "I don't know if I should be flattered or really creeped out."

He grimaces. "Even before that day in my classroom, I knew you. I watched you, paid attention whenever you were around. I didn't like the things I overheard. I hated when I saw you with someone. But to be completely honest, the main reason I was mad is because I wanted that guy to be me."

CHAPTER FORTY-ONE

BECCA

He wanted it to be him? Him instead of Lucas? Something warm and unexpected tingles inside me. The sensation is so foreign to me, it takes me a while to identify. Is this a spark of … joy?

"You did?" My voice is the squeak of a bird.

He leans in and wraps a long lock of my hair between his fingers. "I still do."

I don't know what to do with this revelation. He wants me. And I want him too.

"What does this mean?" I'm in unfamiliar territory here. I have no footing.

"It means I care for you, and I'd like to get to know you better, take it slow, see where this goes."

"Where this goes?" My heart flaps around in my chest like a bird fighting its cage.

"Yes. You lead. I follow." His gaze drops to my mouth.

I'm falling, falling, falling. The ground is gone, and I have nothing to hold on to. All the barriers I carefully constructed around me, around my heart, crumble.

You lead, I follow. Those simple words did me in. He's offering me control. Putting me in charge of this … whatever this is between us. The therapist's advice comes back to me.

Take a chance.

Let it be.

My heart sprints. Each beat is a command. Take a chance. Take a chance. Take a chance.

I take a chance.

I lean in and kiss him. Our lips touch, soft and warm. We linger, not moving—not just yet. He waits for me to lead, and I do. I take charge, my mouth on his. I lick and nibble, shift in my seat and get closer, grabbing his jacket and pulling him to me. His hands go into my hair, and he anchors me to him. Our tongues play a chasing game, retreating and advancing in a dance as old as time.

Shivers dance on my skin, igniting fires everywhere. I want to climb on his lap, press myself against him, soothe the growing ache. The confined space fights us, keeps us from getting closer. It's a curse and a blessing because going slow is the last thing I want to do. But I need to. Maybe if we go slow, we can make this last.

I pull away, just enough to part our mouths, our chests heaving in the same air. He presses his forehead to mine and kisses my cheek. His lips warm and damp on my skin. We stay like this until our breaths regulate, go back to normal, and the cold outside sneaks into the car again.

His eyes crinkle in the corners, his smile easy, happy. I want to kiss that smile and make it mine. But I sit back instead, still not sure of what's happening. Heave in another deep breath. "I thought you said you didn't get involved with students."

His smile falters, and I want to smack myself. "I said I would never get involved with one of *my* students. And I never have. Or any student." He tugs at my hair gently. "But you're not my student. And I have restrained myself for far too long."

I shake my head, still in disbelief. "I had no clue."

"This kiss is worth two years of watching you from afar."

My cheeks burn. I press my hands on my face to stop the blushing. "I can't believe you've been watching me for two years."

"And now I sound like a total stalking creep." He laughs, breaks the tension.

I want to stay here with him, but I have to go.

He's watching me. "You have to go, right? Let's get your car started."

He grabs cables from the back seat, and we step outside. He has my car running in minutes, and I can't help thinking if he's also jump-starting my heart.

"I think you need a new battery. Your car may not start once you stop, and you'll get stuck again. Do you have time to get a new battery before you have to go? I know a place, it should take no more than thirty minutes."

I check the time on my phone. It will cut it close, but I can do it. "Yes, if it's just half an hour."

I follow him in my car to a place five minutes away. Dylan handles the conversation, haggles on the price and gets the battery installed and running. It's surreal. I've never had anyone do anything like this for me. Ever. I have to hold back and stuff my hands in my pockets to keep from touching him.

"I know you have to go, but maybe we can talk? Tonight?" He tilts his head, his eyes amber-gold in the sunlight.

"Tonight's okay." Wind whips my hair into his direction, as if it craves his touch as much as the rest of me. He lifts a hand, drops it. Looks around. His gaze lowers to my mouth. I can still feel his lips on mine, still taste him.

I understand. There are rules. Rules we're breaking. We're in a public place with lots of people coming and going and not hidden from view in a deserted parking lot behind Gus' bar like before.

"Tonight," he confirms before walking away.

I watch him, questioning everything that happened. With each step he takes away from me, my doubts and worry grow. He can't find out the truth about me.

So many complications.

He's a good person. Responsible. Caring.

I'm a mess. Chaotic. Tainted. Broken.

No, you're not. You're kind and smart and generous.

He doesn't need someone like me in his life. He needs someone sweet and pure and wholesome. *You can be sweet and wholesome too.*

And there's Tommy to think of.

What good can possibly come out of this?

Take a chance.

Let it be.

You don't have to marry the guy.

I laugh at the last one. As if. I'm not marriage material. I'll die the way I was born. Alone and unwanted.

Not true. You have people who love you.

Take a chance.

Let it be.

I get into my car. Relish in the warmth inside. Drive to the hospital. My thoughts are a jumbled mess of opposite messages.

Take a chance.

Why bother? He's not for you.

Let it be.

You're going to hurt him and yourself.

Dylan: Tonight.

The message comes as I'm walking into the NICU. I smile. Something that feels like hope flutters in my chest. I turn off my phone, put my stuff in the locker, and prepare to scrub. I can do this. I can lead if he'll follow.

CHAPTER FORTY-TWO

BECCA

"Good morning, Becca." Nancy is all smiles when I walk into the NICU.

I muffle a yawn. Spending half of the night talking to Dylan was worth every sleepless minute.

"Good morning. You look happy." I check myself, make sure everything is in place—gown, cap, shoe covers.

"I am. We have great news. Baby Jay is going home." She claps her hands.

I miss a step. I'm clobbered by her words. And I know she can read it on my face. Her smile fades. Her hands go to my shoulders. My eyes burn.

"Now, now. None of that. I know you've grown attached to him. And him to you. But this is good. A wonderful family will foster him. And they're moving to adopt him."

"When?" My chin quivers and my voice cracks.

She presses her lips together and squeezes my shoulders harder. "This afternoon. All the paperwork was ready to release him yesterday, but I called in a favor and asked them to pick him up today so you can say goodbye and meet the family."

A nod is all I can manage. I knew this day was coming as it has many times before. Leaving the NICU is a wonderful thing for these babies. They fought hard to live. They have earned it. Going home with their parents is the ultimate goal. Why does this hurt so much, then?

I find my little man. His thin arms shake in excitement when I lean over his incubator. "Not yours, Becca. He was never yours," I whisper to myself.

"Hi there. Ready for your lunch?" I take Baby Jay out of the incubator and nuzzle him to my chest, inhaling his heavenly scent. My eyes sting. I find an empty rocker and sit with him. He turns his head and looks at me with gray-blue newborn eyes that are too big for his face. His mouth opens and closes to form a little pout.

"Okay, sweetheart, I got your bottle right here." He takes to it with a strength he didn't possess a few weeks ago. He's ready. I know he is.

"You put weight on, didn't you?" His skin is rosy and healthy. No longer showing the tiny blue-green veins underneath. Jay feels less frail in my arms. He's a little over two months old now, and finally the size of a newborn child. He finishes the bottle, and I burp him. His hands close into fists and open again.

"Okay, okay, I know what you want." I settle him on my chest and hum all of his favorite songs while walking around the NICU and swaying back and forth with his little head on my shoulder. His strong heart beats against mine. I push all of my love and hopes for him into his chest through our tenuous connection.

"Becca?" Nancy's voice reaches me. I don't have to look at the clock to know my time with Baby Jay is over. I turn. They're standing just inside the doors. My legs bring me closer to them against my will. Next to Nancy is the hospital social worker and a couple in their thirties. They're dressed in the same sterile coverings I am. They are here for Baby Jay. The tears I've kept at bay this whole time spill. Nancy and the couple join me in the silent crying. The social worker checks her watch. Too used to such displays, and too callous to shed a tear over one more baby. I've never liked the woman. She's strict and unfeeling.

Nancy is the first to recover. "Becca, please meet Mr. and Mrs. Reynolds. They'll be fostering Baby Jay, and—"

The social worker steps closer, an open folder in her hands. "You mean baby John Doe. Naming foundlings is discouraged and—"

Nancy steps in front of the social worker and interrupts whatever she was about to say. Something unpleasant, for sure. "The Reynolds family have also adopted another NAS baby. She's three years old now and thriving." This is directed at me. She turns to the couple, her back to the social worker. "Becca, like me, believes all babies are deserving of a name, and she named him Jay."

Mrs. Reynolds gasps and tears fill her eyes anew. Her husband puts an arm around her, pulls her closer and kisses her head. When he looks at me, his eyes are wet too. "Before we found out we couldn't get pregnant, we had all our kids' names picked. We wanted four kids." He wipes the corner of an eye. "Jay was our first pick for a boy name."

"You see," the wife speaks, "both our fathers have the middle name Jay, and we always joked that one day we would have a baby boy and name him Jay. We lost our fathers last year, within five months of each other. This is like a sign they are okay, and this baby is meant to be ours."

The clamp around my lungs eases, and I can breathe a little

better. I've never been one to put any faith in signs, but this moment seems to have been etched on fate. Baby Jay coos. I kiss his head, inhale his scent one more time and give him to his future mom. "Take good care of him, Mrs. Reynolds. I'm going to miss this little guy."

She takes him from my arms, and he goes without protest. Perhaps another sign this is meant to be, that he knows he's in the arms of his mother. "He likes when you sing to him."

"Nurse Nancy told me all about you. I don't want this to be a goodbye. We live in town. We would love for you to stop by and visit."

A sound of irritation comes from behind Nancy. The social worker steps around her. "In cases like this, it's best to cut all ties with the former caregiver."

"This is not the case of a parent giving up their rights. Those rules do not apply here," Nancy speaks up.

"Let's go, please." The social worker indicates they should leave. They follow her, but Mr. Reynolds comes back and shakes my hand. He presses something into my palm and whispers so low I can barely hear him, "Nancy warned us about the old hag. Both of our numbers are there. Call us." I almost snort at his description of the social worker. Clasping the piece of paper he gave me, I cross my arms until they leave. Then, unfold the paper in my hand.

Call us.
  802-555-0712
  802-555-3849
  Steve and Claire Reynolds

I fold the paper and put it in my pocket. I will call. I'll get to see Baby Jay again. I look up and do something I never did before. I send a thank-you into the universe. To whoever the orchestrator of this day is. A day filled with surprises, and a promise of a tomorrow I never imagined possible.

A promise I'm terrified of believing in.

CHAPTER FORTY-THREE

BECCA

I sit in my car in the hospital parking lot trying to get a hold of my thoughts.

There's so much going on. This is an emotional roller coaster of a day. I need to talk to someone, hear my thoughts out loud. I know the therapist is not there during the day, but he also said I had to trust someone, and I already have. I can talk to River.

I grab my phone and text her.

> Becca: Hey! What you up to?

> River: Nothing. Chilling at home alone. Wanna come over?

> Becca: Yes. Leaving the hospital now.

> River: See you soon.

I'm glad River is home. I'm in knots and meeting her at her apartment will make it easier to talk. No witnesses or random listeners.

River beats me to the door, my hand in the air ready to ring the bell. She steps back. "Come in. It's freezing out there."

I follow her down the hall and into the first-floor apartment. The smell of fresh-baked cookies greets me. I groan. "Hmmm. Skye baked again?"

"No, I baked." River locks the door behind us.

"Yeah, right?" I laugh. "You're not into the culinary arts, unless it involves eating it."

"I did!" She crosses her arms over her chest.

I laugh again.

"I can bake!"

"Sure you can. Where's Skye?" I look down the small hall for a sign that she's here.

"She's at Logan's."

"She baked before she left?" I drop to the blue couch and hug a pillow against my chest.

"Dude! I got the cookie dough balls out of the freezer, put them on a pan and then put the pan in the oven for twelve minutes at three-fifty." Her hands go to her hips.

"Ha! I knew it. You didn't make the cookies."

"Well, no. Skye made them, and froze the extra cookie dough, but I"—she points at herself—"baked them." She's so proud of herself too. "And if you want any, you better stop laughing and follow me." She points over her shoulder.

I take a seat at the island dividing the small kitchen and living room. "I love your apartment, the open floor space, it makes the place seem bigger."

River's on the other side of the island, opening and closing cabinets. "Yeah, I'm going to miss this place when we graduate." She grabs two mugs. "Hot chocolate, coffee, or tea?"

"Tea, please. But aren't you staying here while going for your master's?"

"I'm not sure. Our lease ends in July. But the way things are going with Skye and Logan, I wouldn't be surprised if she moves in with him."

She goes through the motions of making us tea.

"Wow? That fast? Hasn't it been only a couple of months since they began dating?"

"A little over two months. Their first date was on our birthday."

I flinch a little at that memory. My faking drunkenness to cover up a panic attack. "That's kinda fast."

"Maybe? But when you know he's the one, then why wait?" She takes a sip of her tea.

I hold my mug, warming my hands. "I don't know if I believe in insta-love."

"Why not? Everything is possible, right?" The oven timer beeps behind her.

"Do you think it's possible to fall in love with someone you never met?" Jesus! What am I asking?

River grabs an oven mitt. "What? Like falling in love with someone famous?"

"No, not that. I mean a real person you've talked to, but never face-to-face."

She opens the oven, peers inside. The heavenly scent of cookies rolls over me like a warm and sweet hug.

River takes the pan out of the oven. "Like someone you met on a dating app?"

"Not exactly. More like an online friend."

"I guess it's possible. I mean, you hear stories like that often enough. People meet online, talk, have video chats, and they even have phone and video sex." She slides a sheet of parchment off the pan. Sixteen cookies on top.

"No, not like that either. What if you only ever talked or texted, but have never seen each other?"

"Never?"

"Never."

"I don't know. At the risk of sounding shallow, I think that would be harder. Attraction is a big part of falling in love, right? Usually people are attracted to what they see first, then they take the next step and get to know each other."

"True, but then you also have friendships that develop into more."

"Yes, but I'd think there was an attraction on some level there too." Her keen gaze fixes on me. "Why are you asking?"

I look away, focus on my forgotten tea. "I don't know. I've been thinking about it a lot. What's love, really? How does one know they're in love? And can you love someone you've never met, and never even seen? Someone you know absolutely nothing personal about, and yet you feel like they know you down to your soul?"

"Wow, you went way deep."

I face River now. Her sharp eyes try to read me. I tamp down my need to close myself off. My first instinct is to lie, to deflect, to run. But I hear his voice in my head, telling me to trust her.

"I think I might be falling for a guy." Dylan's face flashes in my mind. Or two.

I hold my breath. Her reaction is not what I expected. A squeal leaves her lips. She runs around the island, lunges at me and hugs me. "Spill it. Hold nothing back."

I drag a deep breath in. "Okay. But cookies first."

We move to the couch in the living room, the plate of too-warm-to-eat cookies between us.

I pull my legs up and under my body. Grab a pillow and

rest my elbows on it. "I've been talking to someone online. For a few weeks now."

"A few weeks? And just now you're telling me?" She pokes my knee with a fingertip.

"We've already established I suck as a BFF, so no need to remind me."

She pokes me again. "Stop holding back and tell me already."

"So … I met him online, and we talk a few times a week. And he's so kind and funny."

"Go on."

"I love his laugh and his voice. His voice is so … I don't know. Calming? He speaks low, like we're sharing a secret." Because we are sharing secrets.

"What else do you know about him?"

"Nothing." I look down.

"Wait. You don't know his name?"

"No."

"His age?"

"No."

"If he's married or single?"

"No idea." I trace the edge of the pillow.

"Where he lives?"

"No clue." I feel stupider by the second.

"Does he have an accent? Does he speak well?"

"No accent. He speaks very well." I meet her eyes again.

"Well, at least you know he has good grammar. That's something."

I laugh.

River looks at me, her face scrunches. "What do you talk about?"

"Life mostly. How to deal, stuff like that."

"Do you know what he does for a living?"

"Yes. He's a therapist." River pulls back a little. Her head tilts. I can see her making the connections in her mind.

"Oh, Becca. This guy is the therapist you've been talking to. The one helping you with …" She cuts herself off.

"Yeah … I know. It's dumb."

"Not dumb. And not uncommon either. He's helping you. He gives you a sense of worth, he doesn't ask for anything back, and he's safe."

"So, you're saying that what I'm feeling is not real?"

"Not at all. It's real. But it is unrealistic. You can't be in a relationship with a voice. And as much as you feel close to him, he's just that. A voice."

All of me rejects what she's saying. My heart stomps around my chest and throws a tantrum. "But it doesn't feel like it."

"I'm sorry, sweetie. But this is good. It's a step in the right direction. You're opening yourself up to trust and love."

"Let me hold on to this fantasy a little longer." I pout.

"I'm not saying you can't. But I don't want you to get hurt."

"I won't. I know it can never be. I know nothing about his life outside the therapy sessions." And there's Dylan, too.

"What about Professor Beckett, though?"

It's as if she reads my mind. "And then there's Dylan."

She reaches for a cookie. "What happened after I left last night?"

"Where do I start?"

"Start from the time he walked into the bar after I left. Leave nothing out. I've been patiently waiting for this." She taps her wrist.

I grab a cookie, chew, swallow. "Okay. So he walked in, took the same seat you had. We talked a little, and then that jerk face turned his attention to me. Dylan looked like he was ready to throw down with the guy, but Gus stepped in."

"That's interesting …" She trails off.

"He walked me out, and my car wouldn't start. He gave me a ride to campus."

River leans in, eyes wide. "And? Tell me something good."

"We talked about different things. Riggins, and stuff like that." I'm not about to tell River all that Dylan shared with me. That's not my story to tell, and I have a feeling it's not a story he shares often either. "And he picked me up this morning and drove me to get my car back."

"Yeah? That's nice of him. To drive you twice like that." She wiggles her eyebrows.

A flashback of that kiss fills my mind.

She squints at me. "Oh, something happened. I can tell by that smile. Tell me."

I stuff two whole cookies in my mouth. Warm, melted chocolate coats my tongue. My face flushes with a fantasy of chocolate kisses. I cover my mouth and try to speak, but can only mumble an indecipherable sound.

I wash down the crumbs with tea. "I'm not smiling." But I am. I can't stop smiling.

"Becca!" My name is a warning.

I laugh. "Okay, okay. I'll tell you." I take a breath. "We were there, sitting in the car in the parking lot, and I kissed him."

"You kissed him. You? First?"

"Yes. It's crazy, I know. There was so much sexual tension. He said he wanted to get to know me better, and I couldn't take it anymore and kissed him."

"How was it?"

"It was … amazing, hot, sexy. I didn't want to stop."

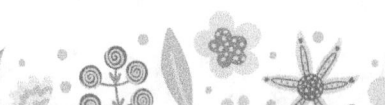

"I'm happy for you. Maybe this is real. A little risky, but real."

"Yeah, I know I'm coloring outside the lines, but—"

She snorts. "Outside the lines? Becca, I don't think you've ever been inside the lines. Ever. And ... I support this."

She's not wrong.

River folds her legs under her. "Did you guys talk about how you'll manage dating?"

"No. But I think it was understood that we'd keep it quiet. He's not the kind to brag."

She tugs at the sleeve of her hoodie. "I wonder what the rules are on staff-student fraternization."

"I checked last night. There are no official rules written forbidding it, but they frown upon relationships between staff or faculty and undergrad students. Grad students relationships with staff and faculty are more acceptable as long as the student is not under direct supervision of that staff member or enrolled in that professor's class."

"You're not his student, but you're not a grad student yet either. Not until September. But once we graduate in May, it should be fair game."

"I know. And that's why we need to keep quiet until then. And maybe even after too."

River mimics zipping her lips and throwing away the key.

I flop back onto the couch. "I don't even know what this is. The way he talked to me gave me the impression he wants more than a hookup, but maybe it's all in my head, and he's just looking for a booty call."

"Well, this is something you have to decide on, and then talk to him about. What do you want? A real relationship or another hookup?"

What do I want? "I want someone to know me, to see me

and love me. Love my flaws and all the ugly in my life. But I can't imagine myself telling Dylan any of it." The knots in my stomach ease with each revelation.

She reaches over and squeezes my knee. "We all have flaws and ugly in our lives. Is that why you think you're falling for the therapist? Because he already knows you, and you feel safe with him?"

I have to think about it. "Yes, and no. I like him. He's easy to talk to, and he calls me on my BS. He makes me see things differently."

"And Dylan?"

"I like him too. A lot. He's different from what I thought. Kind. Sweet, even. I … I don't know. Do you think it's possible to fall in love with two people at the same time?"

"Yes. I think it's possible, but I think the type of love would be different. You know what I mean? Dylan and the therapist are giving you different things, fulfilling different needs. So, you'd fall for each of them for a different reason."

"Maybe, but what am I saying? Really? This is not love. One guy will forever be a mystery. And the other I have no idea what I should do about. Just go for it? Back out? If only I could merge the two of them together and build the perfect man for me."

"Maybe Dylan already is the perfect man for you, and you need to give him a chance to prove that." She runs her hands over her arms like she's cold. "I got shivers all over. You know what my mother would say to that, right?"

"Get the salt and the holy water and run?" I joke, knowing all too well that her mom would say that's a sign. We both get a good laugh.

"Give him a chance. But even more importantly, give

yourself a chance. You never give yourself enough credit. And you're so much more than the crappy childhood you had."

Tears sting my eyes. It's been such an emotional day already after Baby Jay.

She leans in for a hug. Our arms go around each other. "Why is it so hard to believe that?" I sniff and fail to stop the tears.

"Because you never give yourself a chance. You give so much to others without even thinking. All those babies you helped for years. The volunteering at soup kitchens. The little things you do when you think no one is paying attention. Driving my ass all over the place and being my sidekick." She pulls back. Holds my hands. "You're kind, you're generous, and so smart. Now be kind and generous to you too. And put those smarts to work into changing the story you're telling yourself. Tell a better story. A happy one."

River and the therapist are saying the same thing. "I heard this before. About rewriting the stories we tell ourselves."

"We all do it. We all have stories. And it's up to us to make it a good one."

"So … rewrite my story, huh?"

"Yes. You can't change the past, but you can write your present, so better make it a good one. You know, with Dylan in it." She wiggles her eyebrows at me. "Then tell me all the juicy details."

"Sure I will," I say. But I won't. Not all of them. I'll keep the best to myself.

CHAPTER FORTY-FOUR

BECCA

WE'RE BACK AT PAT'S CAFÉ, THE PLACE WHERE IT ALL started. The place where I first met my father, even if I can't yet call the man sitting across from me Dad.

My body no longer gripped with the stiffness of anger and rejection. There's an easiness in our conversation now. We're still sharing stories and getting to know each other better. We chip away the distance one chunk at a time. Years apart being made smaller by these encounters and his willingness to meet me at my pace.

"So, that's my Baby Jay story." Telling my father about what happened makes my heart lighter somehow.

He sets his coffee down, elbows on the table and fingers laced. "Tell me more about this baby cuddling program. It sounds fascinating."

"I love every minute of it. When I first joined, I thought I'd be the one helping the babies thrive. But they're the ones helping me. I get so much joy and love from them. I can't explain." I surprise myself with how open and honest I'm being with him.

"I can. Babies are miracles you get to hold." He smiles, but there's a hint of sadness in the way his lips turn, as if the corners of his mouth have to fight to stay up.

A flash of an old memory hits me. "There was this baby about a year ago. He had been born with a hole in his heart. The parents brought his four-year-old brother in to meet him after surgery. I can still see his face vividly in my mind with his long blond hair and the bluest eyes. His name is Kyle." I blink away the tears trying to spill from my eyes. "This little boy sat in a chair swallowed by a sterile gown holding his baby brother. The parents and a nurse were talking about the hole in the baby's heart. Then the boy looked at them, and said, 'I know why there's a hole in his heart.' We all looked at him. His mom kneeled closer to him and asked why, and what he said stayed with me."

My father leans in ever closer. "What did he say?"

"A closed heart can't give love."

We both sit still for several seconds. My father sits back, mouthing the words again and again. *A closed heart can't give love.*

I put my hand on the table, palm up. "It took me a long time to realize that a closed heart also can't receive love. And I have been guilty of both."

His hand reaches to mine.

It's funny how I spent my life with a giant black hole in my chest that was empty and yet filled with a bitterness and anger I used like a shield to protect myself. But the more I let go of the past, the smaller the hole gets, and the more I drop my shields, the happier I am.

He squeezes my hand. "No more closed hearts."

"No more closed hearts." It's a promise I make to myself.

"Hello, hello."

I look over my shoulder. Tommy stands behind me. I let go of my father's hand and stand up to give him a quick hug. "Hey, good to see you."

Tommy hugs me back, but it lacks warmth. "This is Julia. My girlfriend."

A petite girl stands behind him. She has long dark hair, silky straight, and she smiles shyly at me. "Nice to meet you, Julia." Her smile grows a little bigger.

My father stands and waves at them both.

Tommy steps back and takes Julia's hand. "Have you seen Dylan? He's supposed to meet us here." There's a tinge of anger to his tone. I look around and see Dylan by the door. His eyes are cold—in a way I haven't seen in a long time. I attempt a small wave but drop my hand when he walks toward us.

There's something odd happening here. Tommy's stiffness and Dylan's cold stare. Dylan's arms are crossed over his chest and his shoulders are pulled back, making him seem even taller. Julia's gaze jumps between all of us and then away. Awkward silence ensues.

My father moves his chair back and steps around it with a hand extended toward Dylan. "Hi. I'm Becca's father, nice to meet you."

Dylan shakes his hand.

"Father?" Tommy glances at Dylan and back at my father.

Tommy shakes my father's hand next. "You don't look old enough to be Becca's father."

"Good genes run in the family," my father jokes and winks at me. There's curiosity in his eyes.

Everything clicks into place then. Tommy and Dylan thought I was with a guy on a date or something like that. They might not be the only ones. Several people watch the exchange.

Familiar faces from Riggins, mostly students, but a few employees too.

"This is my father, Robert." I gesture at my father. The word dad stuck in my throat. "And this is my friend Tommy and Dy —his brother, Professor Beckett. And Tommy's girlfriend, Julia."

My father gestures at the table. "Do you want to join us? We can get a couple more chairs."

Dylan shakes his head and speaks for the first time. "Thank you, but we don't want to disrupt your family time." He glances at me. "Miss Jones, I'll see you around."

Being called by my last name after what we shared is jarring, but necessary. Female gazes follow him across the room and to a table in the corner behind me where he sits with Tommy and Julia. The urge to look at him, see what he's doing, has me standing still.

My father sits down, and I do the same, divided between being glad and annoyed that I can't see Dylan, but he can see me.

My father's all too knowing eyes are on me. They crinkle in the corners. "A professor, huh?" There's no judgment in his tone, not even a little.

"He's not my professor." I pull my chair in.

"That's better, I guess." He is still smiling.

"What do you mean?" Honesty be damned, I'll deny this 'til the end.

"I don't know." He takes a sip of his coffee. "He looked pretty pissed until I introduced myself. And, by the way he keeps glancing at us, I'm not sure he believes it."

I hold the end of the table to keep myself from turning my body to look at Dylan. There's no way to discreetly do this.

"I'm happy for you. I like your friends. I can tell they care."

"How? How can you tell from just meeting them for a couple of minutes?" I let go of the edge of the table, grab a fork and pick at my cold pancakes.

"Easy. You didn't see them when they walked in. I did. There was pure happiness in that young boy's face when he saw you. Then his brows scrunched when he looked at me. And your"—he lowers his voice—"professor, had the same reaction, but in a much more subtle way."

I try to fight a smile and fail. "They're good people."

He looks around. Pushes his empty plate away. Leans into the table again. "I'm not trying to tell you what to do. I've never earned that right, and even if I had, you're an adult and a smart one at that." He nods once. "Be discreet and careful. And if he hurts you in any way, call me. I can still kick his ass."

I don't know if I should laugh or cry. I do both. I'm still wiping the corners of my eyes as we get up to leave. My gaze immediately goes to Dylan. His eyes soften for the space of a breath before turning aloof and away from me.

My father walks me to my car, and we hug goodbye. I unlock the driver door.

"Becca?"

He's standing on the other side of my car.

"I don't think I ever said this before, but I'm real proud of you. And I'm proud to call you my daughter." His words reach to me with invisible fingers that heal everything they touch. That gap inside shrinks and fills with something tender, fragile and unknown. My hands go to my chest. I want to cradle this moment like a newborn baby. My vision goes blurry behind my wet lashes. I blink away the wetness. My throat too tight to speak. I mouth the words instead.

"Thank you … Dad."

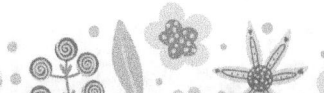

CHAPTER FORTY-FIVE

BECCA

I park in front of his house, turn off the car and watch rivulets of rain running down the window. Dylan didn't text or call after that weird encounter yesterday. It's better this way. I'd rather talk to him in person, see his face, read his reactions. "Now, if I could only get my ass out of this car and knock on his door. Yeah, that'd be great."

I don't even know if he's home. He could be on campus. If he's not here, it wasn't meant to be. I pull the hood of my sweatshirt over my head, tuck my hair in, get out and jog up the driveway, water splashing with each step I take until I'm under the safety of the veranda.

I wipe my hands on my jeans, square my shoulders, breathe in and ring the doorbell.

Wait.

Nothing. No sounds come from inside. No steps on stairs, no click of a lock. The steady drumming of the rain is the only sound around me.

I lift my hand to try one more time. I catch a movement to

the side of the house. A dark moving blur that stops inches away from me.

Dylan. He's dressed in all black. Jogging clothes plastered to his body and his hair in a disarray of wet locks.

His rapid breath sends smoke signals into the chilly air. He smells like rain and earth and something entirely him. It's a drug that pulls me closer until we're nearly touching.

"Becca ..." My name forms on his lips.

My fingertips trace his eyebrow, track a water droplet on his cheek, palm his face. I step closer still, stand on tiptoes and brush my mouth against his. He tastes like rain, mint, and hope. His skin is cold to the touch, but his lips are warm and tender. And when he kisses me back, I open up for him.

All gentleness disappears.

His mouth takes mine, hungry and possessive. His hands pull my hood back and tangle in my hair. He positions me the way he wants me and deepens the kiss.

I meet his demands willingly. Mold my body to his, the heat burning inside growing bigger despite the cold and our wet clothing. My feet leave the ground, and we're moving. He braces my body against his, one arm around my waist and the other angling my head to his.

We end up inside the house and pressed against the closed door, all without him letting go or ending the kiss.

When he pulls back, our rapid breaths mingle, the front of my clothes are nearly as wet as his. He touches his forehead to mine. "Sorry. I'm sorry. I lost myself when I saw you there, standing at my door. I thought I was hallucinating for a second. Until you touched me, I wasn't sure you were real."

"I'm real. And I'm here. I needed to see you."

He picks me up, pulls my legs around his waist, and walks

to the back of the house and up the stairs. "First let's get you a towel."

He carries me to the second floor and down a hall. He stops at his bedroom door and kicks his sneakers off before bringing me into a room painted in shades of gray. A large bookcase holds hundreds of books. Abstract paintings add bright splashes of color. The wall behind the mahogany king-size bed is darker than the rest and across from the bed there's a fireplace. He walks through another door and sets me on the bathroom counter. This room too is decorated in soft gray and white. Both rooms are spotless. He takes two dove gray towels from a shelf and gives me one of them, setting the other on the counter next to me. Dylan pulls his wet shirt up and over his head. It comes off in slow motion, peeling away from his skin an inch at a time. The wet fabric clinging like a desperate lover who doesn't want to let go.

He's all lean muscle and golden skin with a dusting of dark hair on his chest. I can't peel my gaze away from him either. He shivers when the cold air hits his bare and damp torso. I fist my hands into the towel he gave me to keep from touching him.

But why? Why should I deny myself in this? Why should I deny myself at all?

I slide off the counter. My feet taking me closer to Dylan. I rub the towel over his chest, shoulders, arms, stomach. He's frozen in place. His shallow breath is the only thing betraying his perfect replication of a statue. I circle around him, rubbing the towel on his back. *That's not enough.* I drop the towel to the floor. Trace his shoulder blades with my fingertips. He sucks in a breath. Every muscle comes to life under my touch. His reaction empowers me. I splay both hands on his back, cover every inch of naked skin, circle back to stand in front of him.

His gaze meets mine, his eyes dark and his face flushed with restraint. I start with his shoulders, run my hands over his biceps, down his forearms, the inside of his wrists, my palms brushing his until only our fingertips touch.

Then start again with his chest, graze his pecs, move down to his stomach, trace each muscle and dip in his abs and obliques. He shivers under my touch. I lean into him, inhale his scent. He smells like rain and lust. I kiss the center of his chest, taste his skin, trace a finger around the edge of his jogging pants.

"Becca …" My name is a plea.

I press my hand into his chest, his heart beating wildly under my palm. "Touch me."

His fingers wrap into my hair, his mouth is on mine, demanding, pushing in, nibbling. There's nothing gentle about this kiss. Nothing tentative. No holding back.

He kisses my neck, licks at the hollow of my throat, nips at the curve of my shoulder. His hands find their way under my hoodie and T-shirt, and his touch is cool on my heated skin.

Too many layers between us. I want his skin on mine. I pull my hoodie and T-shirt off in one go.

"This … is … not … slow." The words come out between shuddered breaths as his gaze traces the curves of my breasts.

"I don't want slow. I don't want to wait. I don't want to hold back." I have never been more turned on in my life.

"You sure?" His hands shake on my waist.

"I am." This moment is mine. This moment is for me. Just me. Not an escape. Not an eraser of the past. This is me choosing myself.

His gaze searches my face. "You can stop me. Say the word, and we'll stop."

"I don't want you to stop." I kick my shoes off. I need everything off of me.

"But if you change your mind, remember. You lead, I follow."

I unbutton my jeans, push them down my legs, socks and all. I stand in front of him in plain blue cotton panties and my bra. "This is me leading. Now take me to your bed." I don't know where this sudden confidence came from. But the certainty that this is the right choice, that he is the right person, vibrates with every fiber of my being. I have never been surer of anything else in my life. "Make love to me, Dylan." *Please*.

He takes my hands and walks backward into the bedroom. He pulls the covers back. Crisp, white sheets frame his figure. His gaze never leaves my face. He sits on the bed, pulls me between his legs, his forehead rests on my stomach. I run my fingers through his hair, soft, unruly, still damp from the rain. He brushes his lips on my stomach and hips with a thousand light-as-air kisses. His hands trace the outside of my thighs, the back of my knees, my lower back with such a tenderness it's almost unbearable. No one has ever touched me this way. With so much care and … love? Is this what a loving, unselfish touch feels like?

Dylan stands, frames my face with his hands, kisses me and kisses me and kisses me until all the breath has left my lungs, and I'm drowning in desire and lust for more. So much more.

"More, Dylan. More. Touch me."

His hands go to my back, he unclips my bra. I let it fall to the floor. Still not enough. I remove the last barrier—my panties join the bra on the floor.

His gaze slowly drifts down to my chest, stomach, and lower. He sucks in a breath. "Beautiful."

He picks me up and lays me on the bed. The sheets are cool against my hot skin. He stands still for a moment, then tugs the rest of his wet clothing down muscular legs. He's naked now.

Miles of tanned skin and lean muscles. I can't take my eyes away from him. His damp skin ripples with shivers. He reaches for a small remote control on the night table, and a moment later, orange and blue flames come to life in the gas fireplace across from the bed. His fingers touch my calf and trace up my leg as he climbs onto the bed and settles next to me. The temperature in the room is warmer now. If by the fireplace or his proximity, I can't tell. He braces himself on an elbow, a leg propped over mine.

"Can I touch you?"

No one ever asked me this before. "Yes."

He explores my body, tracing the curves, the rises, the valleys of my geography. Like a cartographer, he maps my entire body, leaving nothing untouched by hands or lips.

My body comes to life under the expert and gentle attention of his lips and tongue. My body is no longer my own, and yet I'm overcome with belonging. A riptide of sensation churns inside me until it explodes in wave after wave of the most exquisite release. I'm spent, sated, and relaxed. When I open my eyes, I find him looking at me, a satisfied smile on his lips. I trace the tiny lines around his eyes, and they spell happiness.

I ache to touch him back, to be the explorer myself. I push up with a hand on his chest. "My turn."

"You don't have to—"

"I want to." Need to.

His skin is hot under my touch, firm. He's all muscle and hard edges. He holds back for a while, letting me do as I wish, but then his control snaps and his hands and mouth are back on me. We battle not for dominance but for surrender, for who gives the most to the other. I can wait no longer. "Now, Dylan. Now." I need to feel him, all of him.

He palms my cheek, pushing the hair away from my face and making sure my gaze is on him. "You're sure?"

"Yes. I'm sure."

He reaches for protection on the night table, rolls it on himself, then hovers over me. I pull him down, his body into mine, wrapping my legs around his calves and urging him on. And when he complies, a part of me breaks away like the shedding of a skin that no longer fits. We move together in perfect synchrony, as if this was not the first time but a returning home.

At the end we lie next to each other in quiet contentment, his arm across my middle, a hand on my waist, his body molded against my side, my head tucked under his chin.

I would never have guessed that giving in and trusting someone with more than my body was the key to erasing hurts from the past and gaining a part of myself back.

With everyone before Dylan, I never felt this way—safe, and dare I say, in peace?

I don't want to move or even open my eyes. What if I do, and it's all an illusion, and I go back to being less?

Dylan's hand flexes on my side. "Shh ... whatever is going on in your head stop it. I can feel your body tensing."

"What? No—I'm not—"

He shifts to look at me, holds himself up on an elbow. "Yes, you are. I want to keep seeing you. I want us to be together. And I know it's complicated. We can't be a couple in public. Not yet. But in five months you'll graduate, and then we don't have to hide anymore." He pulls away the hand on my waist and runs it through his hair. Immediately, I miss the contact.

"I'm not very good at relationships." I shared myself with him, and yet, confessing my shortcomings makes me feel more exposed than my still naked body.

"I'm not that great, either." He traces my eyebrows with a fingertip. "But we can figure it out together." Then he traces the line of my jaw. "I want this to work. I like you, Becca. I have liked you for a long time and not being able to act on it pissed me off."

I stop his hand, hold it on my chest so I can think. "You said that before. That you watched me, but I don't understand. You don't really know me. How can you like me?"

He curves his fingers around mine. "That's just it. I noticed you the first time I saw you at the Maslow building. I paid attention every time I saw you. I have always been drawn to you." He kisses my fingertips. "I have a confession to make." He takes a deep breath. "Don't hate me, but I—fuck, this makes me sound like a creep. I know about your volunteer work. I work with Magda on a few projects." He watches me.

My first impulse is to pull away, but I force myself to stay and listen. I know all too well I can't trust my first impulse.

"I don't have any influence on hiring or how she chooses the candidates or anything like that, and I don't have access to your records either."

"How do you know, then?"

"I was at her office, maybe a couple of years ago, and you walked by the window. She said, and I quote, 'that girl has more heart than the rest of them combined.'"

"She said that?" Something flutters in my chest. Magda is not one to give compliments in vain. Or at all.

"She did. And when I asked why, she told me about some of your volunteer work and how proud she is of you."

"Magda? Magda Kenny, the Queen? Are we talking about the same person?"

He laughs. "Yes. I had the same reaction as you."

I don't know what to do with this information.

"Talk to me. What are you thinking?"

I snort. "You sound like a therapist right now."

He raises an eyebrow.

"I don't know what I'm thinking. Part of me is weirded out you knew me all this time. But then again, it's not like you had a reason to come up to me and say anything."

"I never acted on it. I never intended on pursuing you. It was always meant to be a distant veneration."

"Veneration?" That's a word I'd never associate with myself.

"Yeah, veneration. From afar is all I intended. Until you met Tommy and turned everything upside down."

"You were so mad."

"I was so stupidly jealous and angry at myself for believing the crap I never believed before. I'm a man. Men are stupid."

That cracks me up. "You're not getting any arguments from me on that one."

He brings my hand to his chest. "So, that's my confession."

I have confessions. So many of them. But he won't hear any. Not now, not ever.

His eyes light up with mischief. His hand splays on my stomach possessively.

"Have I told you about the amazing multi-spray shower I have in my bathroom? And would you be interested in a private tour?"

Yes, yes. Very much so. "Maybe?"

CHAPTER FORTY-SIX

THERAPIST11

It's been a few days since I last heard from Cougar22. When my laptop alert sounds that someone is calling in, I'm grateful and surprised to see her name.

I click to answer the call. "Good night. It's been a few days. Hope everything is well."

"Hi. Yeah, sorry about that. Everything is great."

My eyes drift closed. I missed hearing her voice. "What have you been up to?"

There's a moment of hesitation on her side. "I … listened to what you said and followed your advice."

I riffle through my notes to confirm what I already know. My last advice for her was to take a chance with a guy she was attracted to. Something that went against everything I wanted to say to her, but my professional ethics demanded I do.

"Did you take a chance with the guy you met?" My fingers tap on the desk, and I count.

"What's that tapping sound? I hear it all the time when I'm talking to you."

I stop tapping. "It's a grounding technique. It helps me focus. Sometimes I don't even realize I'm doing it." Not entirely true. I also use it when I'm anxious.

"And it helps?" The sound of faint tapping accompanies her question.

"It does. It's a habit now."

"Interesting. I might have to try that sometime."

"You didn't answer my question." I fist my hand to stop the tapping.

"I was getting to it." She blows a breath. "Yes, I met that guy, we talked, and we got together, and … and I think I like him."

Got together … I know what that means, and Jesus Christ, I might need therapy myself. Didn't I get *together* with someone myself yesterday? Why does knowing this bother me? "Will you be seeing him again?"

"Yes. I think I will. It was good … nice. Different."

"Different how?"

"Just different. I don't know. Maybe because I think for the first time I was with someone for me, because I wanted to, and not as a rebellion or to erase the crap from my past."

"This is good, this is very good. And it's great you have this awareness."

"It was good, but I'm not talking about the sex."

"Oh?" I feel embarrassed on the behalf of men everywhere.

She laughs. "No, I don't mean the sex was bad. It was amazing. I meant that it never felt like I was using him or that I was being used. It was an even exchange. Two people who mutually agreed they wanted to be together for no other reason than they were attracted to each other."

"I'm happy for you." And I am. Even as I recognize a tinge

of jealousy toward this guy. I care about her. About this young woman who calls herself Cougar22. There's a connection between us. I have come to think of her as a friend.

"Thanks. But that's not why I called."

"No?"

"No. I think things are going in the right direction now. I can see my life taking a different turn. I'm happy. I found my father and a new family with him."

She sighs. I wait. I can guess what she will say next, and I don't want to be right.

"I called to thank you for everything. You have done for me —more than you can ever imagine."

"You're welcome."

"And to say I'll probably not call again."

It hurts. I didn't think it would feel like this. This hollow space in my chest. "I can understand that."

"You can?"

"Yes. You want to move on and leave all reminders behind, and I'm a reminder."

"Yes, something like that. I'll miss our talks. I really enjoy talking to you. Even though I don't really know anything about you, not even your name, I feel like I know you."

"Jameson. You can call me Jameson." Why did I reveal that?

"Jameson? Is that your name?"

"Yes. It's a family name. After my father, grandfather, and his father and so on."

"You're tapping again." She laughs.

I look at my hand. I am tapping. I curl my fingers and force myself to stop. Again. "You could still call sometimes. Say hello to an old friend." What am I doing? I've always known that this day would come. It's time to let go.

"I might. I need good friends in my life."

"We all do."

"Goodbye, Jameson."

"Goodbye." She hangs up and I don't even know her name.

CHAPTER FORTY-SEVEN

BECCA

THE ENTIRE STREET IS DECORATED FOR CHRISTMAS. Inflatable snowmen and Santas sway in the gentle afternoon breeze. Lights twinkle and dangle from trees and roof lines. The air smells like snow and fireplaces, but none of the white stuff is falling yet. The neighborhood screams middle-class, happy families. Driveways are piled with cars, and I catch glimpses of people through the decorated windows. This is something I have only ever experienced in movies. My first real Christmas. It's … surreal.

I park at the bottom of the driveway and turn the engine off, but I don't leave my car just yet. I take in the house. A huge Christmas tree takes up most of the bay window now. The tree was not there the last time I was here.

"Get on with it, Becca," I tell myself.

I grab the pie I purchased for tonight, the gifts I got for Tommy and Dylan and a wine bottle. I cut through the dull yellow-green lawn. Grass dusted with frost crunches underneath my boots. My hands are full, and I use my elbow to ring the doorbell, the sound melodic and inviting.

The door opens, and Tommy's arms come around me, crushing me to his chest so fast, I barely have time to hold the pie away from my body and avoid it getting smashed between us. "I'm so happy you're here. Merry Christmas Eve!"

"Tommy? Let my girl in, and close the door, please." Dylan's voice comes from somewhere in the house.

My girl. It's only been a few weeks, and I'm still trying to wrap my head around being with Dylan. In hiding, but together. Except for River and Tommy, no one else knows.

"Merry Christmas Eve to you too."

Tommy takes a step back into the house and pulls me in, closing the door behind me. He relieves me of the pie and wine. "Come in, make yourself comfortable. Let me put these away." I follow Tommy into the kitchen to drop the gift bags on a chair. Dylan's back is to me as he pokes into something inside the oven. It smells delicious, whatever it is he's working on. The last few notes of *It's a Wonderful World* plays quietly over the house speakers. Another mellow song starts.

I hesitate a few feet away, unsure of what I should do. Dylan closes the oven door, flops a dish towel over his shoulder and comes to me. He wraps an arm around my waist and kisses me on the cheek. "Merry Christmas," he whispers into my hair. Shivers run down my neck. I want more than that chaste kiss. The corners of Dylan's mouth turn up, his smile makes wordless promises.

"No nasty during Christmas, kids. It's a sin." Tommy's voice reminds me we're not alone. Dylan tosses the dish towel at Tommy's head and points at him, shaking a finger. Tommy ducks and catches the towel in the air, laughing.

Dylan's hand goes back to my waist. "You hungry? Everything should be ready in thirty minutes."

"Starving." It's true. I was so nervous earlier; I couldn't eat anything.

"Want something to nibble on? Wine?"

"Water?"

Dylan goes to the fridge, and I grab the gift bags and walk to the bay window.

The Christmas tree ends a few inches from the ceiling, and the scent of pine gets stronger with each step. I tuck the bags next to the other gifts. A mismatch of ornaments decorates the tree. They look old and cherished. I can't help myself from touching a few.

A blue birdhouse, two tiny birds atop it, a little train with "Dylan." Another that says, "Tommy's First Christmas." The entire tree is covered in them. Little pieces of memories molded into plastic figurines, each telling a story.

Dylan brushes my shoulder, his hand on the small of my back.

"It's so beautiful. I've never had a Christmas tree before."

"Never?" He's holding a water bottle.

I can't step back. I'm trapped between him and the tree, and I have said too much. Racing thoughts cloud my mind. I need to say something, but what? The therapist's voice comes to me. I settle for a version of the truth.

"My family wasn't religious. We didn't really celebrate anything." Damn it! I said too much again.

Dylan kisses my head and lets it go. I'm sure he can sense my resistance on the subject. All the times we got together since that rainy day—and there have been a lot of times—I've never talked about my past.

He points at a Millennium Falcon ornament. "This one was always my favorite growing up. I'd steal it from the tree every

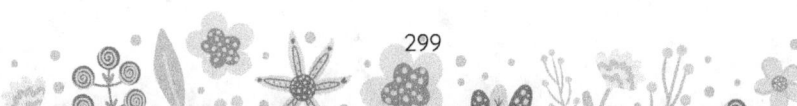

Christmas thinking I was sneaky, and then I would forget about it and leave it somewhere for my mother to find."

"Did you get in to trouble?"

"Nah, Mom was never mad. But she put it up higher and higher every year as I grew until I was taller than her." His face softens with the memory.

"What did she do then? And how old were you?"

"I was twelve. She'd get a chair and put it all the way to the top. By then it was a game we were playing for years. I'd take it and leave it somewhere she could find. And she would hide it again on the tree. Back and forth we went until the tree was down and the ornaments put away."

"I love that. It was your thing."

"It was our thing, our own little game we played only at Christmas." His hand grips my hip.

"Maybe it's a tradition you can keep going with your own kids someday."

He looks at me then, blinks away the memory and the hint of sadness in his eyes. "I'd like that."

The beeping sound of a timer breaks the moment. I open the water bottle and take a long drink, following Dylan to the kitchen. "What can I do?"

He looks around, checks everything. "Nothing. I think we're done. Tommy even set the table earlier. Let's eat."

The three of us settle in the living room, the fireplace flickers with orange and blue flames, and on the TV, *Die Hard* is playing. We're full and content. I don't remember ever being this safe, this happy, this … at peace.

"Hmm, I'm not sure *Die Hard* is a Christmas movie." I pull

my legs under me on the couch. Dylan is sitting next to me, an arm over the back of the couch, his fingers twirling into my hair.

"Blasphemy!" Tommy stands up.

I cover my mouth to try to keep my giggles in but fail. My body shakes with laughter.

Tommy points a finger at the TV. "Dylan, do something! Side with me on this one."

Dylan puts his hands up, presses his lips together and shakes his head. "I take the fifth."

"He's lying. We watch *Die Hard* every Christmas." Tommy points at Dylan now. "I know what you're doing. You're siding with your woman so you can get lai—"

A pillow flies and hits Tommy on the face before he can finish his sentence. "Watch it!" Dylan says, but there's no heat in his voice.

A pillow fight ensues, and by the time all pillows have been tossed and fallen too far for reach, I'm lying on the floor laughing so hard I might pee myself.

I've never been happier, and it terrifies me.

"It's gift time!"

"It's not midnight yet, Tommy."

"It is in Europe. Come on, I want to know what Santa got me. And the sooner I open my gifts, the sooner I go to my room and leave you two little lovebirds alone." Tommy wiggles his eyebrows and rubs his hands like a nefarious villain. The only thing missing is the evil laugh.

"Well, in that case …" Dylan jumps from the couch and grabs several boxes from under the tree.

"Guest of honor first." He gives me two boxes, beautifully wrapped in a metallic red paper. A silver ribbon finishes the gift. It's almost too beautiful to open.

"Me?" Gifts have not been a constant in my life. I'm not always a gracious gift receiver. Don't quite know how to react.

"Go ahead." He nudges me with a toe, his socked foot touching mine. "Open it. The big one first."

I put the larger box on the coffee table, kneel on the floor and remove the bow, slipping my finger under the tape and carefully unwrapping the paper. A black box with a gold logo I don't recognize reveals itself when the paper falls away. I pull the top off and wade through black tissue paper. Nested in the box is a winter coat so soft and light to the touch, it may as well be made of clouds. I pull it out of the box, standing up. It's the color of rich caramel.

"Try it on." His fingers tap on his knee as he watches me put on the coat.

I slip my arms into the sleeves, close the lapels around me. It's so warm and comfortable. I've never owned anything this nice or beautiful or warm. "It's beautiful. I love it, thank you. I don't know what to say."

"Glad you like it. Open the other one." His gaze never leaves me.

"Another gift? Gosh, you didn't have to. This is more than enough."

The coat feels so good and warm. I don't want to take it off, but do it. I fold it carefully and back in the box it goes.

Dylan picks up the small box from the table and gives it to me. I sit down next to him and remove the same red wrapping paper. When I open the velvet box, I find a silver necklace with a glass pendant. I pick it up. The pendant is a sphere and encased inside there's a dandelion seed. The delicate wisps forever frozen in time.

I look up, find his gaze on me. "You gave me wishes?"

His smile grows. "I guess I did. I didn't think of it that way. I know you like dandelions. I wanted to give you something you could wear all the time."

I close my hand around the pendant, bring it to my chest. "How did you know I like dandelions?"

"I saw you pick them and make wishes a few times."

"You did? When?"

He shrugs. "Around campus."

"This means a lot to me. Thank you." I give him the pendant, turn my back to him and move my hair to the top of my head.

Dylan holds the necklace over me, then lowers it and closes the clasp. His fingers linger on my neck. The tiny hairs on the back of my head stand in attention. His touch always affects me. I turn to face him. "Thank you, this is beautiful." My throat contracts, and I swallow down the butterflies trying to escape through my mouth.

"My turn. Open mine now." Tommy waves his gift at me, giving me a much-needed break from the well of emotions churning in my chest.

His wrapping is not as elaborate, but it's funny. Sponge Bob Square Pants wearing Santa's hat, dancing with … pickles? I laugh. "Where did you find this paper?"

"Same place I found the gift, now open it." He's like a little eager kid on … well, Christmas.

I open the package with the same care as before and pull back when Tommy threatens to rip the paper because I'm taking too long.

"He never could wait for anyone to open his gifts," Dylan says.

It's a book. A leather-bound hardcover copy of my favorite book, *Pride and Prejudice*. It's deep red with a beautiful gold inlay design on the cover and the spine.

"Wow, this is … amazing, thank you, Tommy." I look at Dylan. "This is the best Christmas I've ever had."

Dylan pulls me into him and drops a chaste kiss to my lips. I hold back and push away the need to chase his mouth as he sits back. "I have something for you guys too. I put it under the tree."

Tommy vaults over the loveseat and slides into the tree, stopping just short of crashing and knocking it over. Dylan's chest shakes with laughter. "He does that every time. I'm waiting for the day he'll go too fast and crash into that tree."

"This?" Tommy calls back to us, holding two bags for me to see.

"Yes. The green bag is yours."

Tommy vaults back over the loveseat and plops down on it, giving me the other bag with Dylan's gift. Tommy's diving into his bag and tossing tissue paper over his shoulders before I can prompt him to open it. He pulls out the T-shirts I got him and starts laughing. "No, you didn't."

"You said you'd wear them. Now you can." I smile.

Tommy holds up the T-shirts, showing them to Dylan. Three shirts, each with the enactment of a different knock-knock joke. They're so cheesy, one can't help but laugh when they see them. He opens Dylan's gift next. A new iPad to replace his old one with a cracked screen.

"Now, my gift to you. I hope you'll like it." I bite my bottom lip, clasp my hands together. My heart speeds up.

Dylan takes the bag from me and opens it. He removes the

tissue paper and the wrapped gift with far gentler hands than Tommy. He places the gift on his lap, looks at me and then removes the tape and unwraps it much the same way I did. With care and perhaps a little delayed gratification, which makes me even more nervous.

He removes the wrapping and opens the box. Goes still and looks at what I got him for a few seconds, then runs his hand over it before looking at me.

"This is beautiful." He opens it to the middle.

"What is it?" Tommy asks.

"It's a journal." Dylan holds it up for Tommy to see.

Dylan runs his hand over the leather-bound book, a rich whiskey color that reminded me of his eyes when I first saw it. I had his name engraved in gold on the cover and the spine.

He opens it to the first page, his gaze fleets to mine before going back to the journal. I debated long and hard if I should write something on it or not. Maybe add a card or a sticky note. Something less permanent. But defiance arose in me. I've lived my entire life as a passerby. Temporary. Transient.

No more.

I want to be a part of something. To be permanent. To have roots. The inscription in the journal, as short and as frail as it might be—the page can be ripped after all—is a first step at saying I want more.

Dylan,

Because once you told me, you had stories to tell.
Start now. Start here.
Bring to life the stories from the past.
Create new ones for the future.

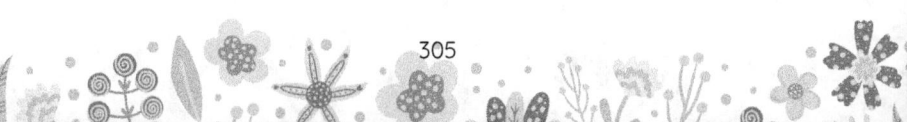

305

Perhaps even some with me in them.

Love,
Becca

He stares at the page, reading and re-reading. Seconds stretch into centuries. With each moment the weight in my chest grows heavier, the pressure unbearable. Did I misread him? Is my veiled confession of wanting more too much? Even Tommy is quiet. The silence hurts my ears.

His gaze lifts to mine in slow motion, a hand reaches to me and cups the back of my head, his lips are on mine a moment later. The kiss is sweet, brief, and intense. He pulls me into a hug, his face into my hair. His mouth brushes my ear. "Let's write those stories together."

Shivers dance on my skin.

CHAPTER FORTY-EIGHT

BECCA

It's Dylan's birthday, and we're hanging out at his house, dressed in green since it's also Saint Patrick's Day. The last four months have been the happiest of my life. It's just the three of us, but Tommy is leaving soon to meet his girlfriend. I'm looking forward to alone time with Dylan.

But for now, I take turns dancing with my two favorite boys to the soundtrack of P!nk.

Dylan steals me away from Tommy again. I giggle and laugh like the little girl I never had a chance to be. Tommy tries to cut in, but Dylan turns and spins me out of reach.

"Dylan Jameson Beckett!" Tommy's voice paralyzes me.

"J-Jameson?" I stutter.

Dylan tries to twirl me, but I'm frozen in place—my feet have grown roots.

"Yes." Dylan runs a hand through his hair. "Jameson is my middle name. It's a family name. After my father and grandfather—"

"And his father and grandfather and so on." Tommy finishes the sentence in a way that tells me this is something that was repeated often. "All the firstborn males get the middle name Jameson. We can trace it back to the eighteen hundreds." He tries to step around Dylan again, but gets blocked.

Everything comes rushing at me. Every word we exchanged. The tapping. Their voices so similar. Their voices! It all clicks into place like the pieces of a puzzle. How is this possible?

Oh my God. Oh my God. Oh my God. How could I have been so stupid?

"Becca? You look white as a ghost, are you okay?" Dylan's gentle hands on my waist are more than I can bear. I break his hold, step away. His hands drop to the side. Dylan and Tommy look at each other and back at me.

It's him!

Dylan is Therapist11. Therapist11 is Dylan.

My heart rages inside my chest like a trapped wild animal. "It's you ... It's you!"

"It's me what?" He takes a step closer, and I take two back.

"You're Therapist11. It was you all along."

The realization hits me like a tidal wave. I let my guard down. I wasn't ready. I didn't have a chance to prepare, to protect myself.

I'm caught in a riptide of emotions. I'm tumbling, going under, drowning. My lungs are robbed of air. Coldness closes in on me, climbing up my legs, numbing my fingers, creeping into my chest, constricting, squeezing my heart into a painful and erratic cadence.

Dylan tilts his head, blinks, opens and closes his mouth. "How do you know ..." He blinks again. His face rearranges from confused to knowing. He makes the connection.

And I helped him.

My hands reach into the space between us and cover my mouth, one hand over the other as if I could capture the words

and shove them back inside. If I had kept my mouth shut …
maybe he wouldn't know.

Stupid. Stupid. Stupid.

"Cougar22," he mouths.

Tommy gets between me and Dylan. "What's going on?"

I take another step back. My entire body shakes as if I'm
standing in my own personal earthquake. Everything is
crumbling. All my layers of lies and protection that were so
carefully built turn to dust. Rage and fear erupt, and I scream.
"Did you know? Did you know it was me? Has this been a
game all along? Did you get a good laugh at my expense?"

Dylan's arms come up, trying to reach me. "Becca, no!
Never. I had no idea. How could I?"

My face burns. The heat spreads to my chest. My entire
being is ice and fire and shame. Devastating shame, that *he* of
all people should know all the horrible and sordid things that
happened to me. And *I* was the one to tell him.

"Becca?" He tries to reach out to me again.

I stumble back. My eyes dart everywhere, searching for a
point to fix on so I can ride this down. But panic has a hold on
me, and there's no fight left. Fueled by adrenaline and fear, my
legs gain purchase and turn. There's not a rational thought left
in me. It's just the need to escape now.

I run.

I run like I could never run before.

I run from him.

From the ghosts of my past.

I run from myself.

I'm out of the house in seconds, bursting through the front
door with no idea of where I'm going. My feet pound the
ground, and I run—the street blurred by tears and the cover of
the night.

Dylan chases after me.

My chest hurts, my lungs burn with each inhale of the cold spring air, and yet sweat breaks on my skin. My legs carry me away, putting distance between me and what just happened.

I cross the street, and I'm blinded by lights followed by the sound of screeching tires and an angry car horn. My steps falter, and I lose speed.

"Becca!" Dylan calls to me.

He's a figure coming from the shadows. Streetlights sharpen his features as he moves into the glow of the light. I stumble backward and out of the street. I turn and gain purchase again, but flight has abandoned me, and my steps slow with each wheeze for air.

All my senses come back on full alert. The car that almost hit me drives on. Beyond my own loud breathing, lies the quiet of the night and the sound of someone else heaving.

I stagger backward, only to turn and fall on my hands and knees. Cold grass softens the fall. I squeezed my eyes shut and cover my ears with dew-wet hands. But the images I try so hard to forget flash in my mind, and I open my eyes to shut them down.

His shadow falls over me, and he kneels. He's close, within arm's reach, but he gives me space. The few inches between us— a wall of safety, a prison—the loneliest of spaces.

"Becca …" His voice is just above a whisper, my name dropping out of his lips in an exhale.

His hands come closer, but don't touch me. Is he repelled by me? Repelled by all those who touched my skin before him?

I crave his touch … and hate that I do.

His arms come around me and embrace me, I turn to stone at first, then my entire being folds into him.

I tremble. I'm cracking into a thousand pieces that can never be put back together.

His chest presses to my side, his arms circle me, He pulls me close, and the heat of his body envelops me, melting away the coldness, layer by layer until my skin burns from the inside out. I want to push away, to fight him off me, but I have no fight left.

His cheek presses to the top of my head, he tightens his arms around me—my entire universe goes askew. What is this? My mind races, trying to place the foreign feeling cuddling my heart. It takes me a couple of minutes to figure it out.

Refuge. Sanctuary. Heaven.

Dylan feels like home.

The notion is so unreal, so bizarre, that a bubble of laughter erupts out of me.

Then I'm laughing and laughing until the misplaced sounds of joy turn into sobs.

And I cry. I cry and cry. A deluge spilling out of me.

A waterfall of tears.

A broken dam.

My stomach clenches and heaves.

My body, my heart, my soul choosing this moment to spill all the pain, all the hurt, all the ugly out of me. I cry until I'm empty of everything.

And Dylan holds on to me.

CHAPTER FORTY-NINE

BECCA

THE SCENT OF COFFEE NEEDLES ME AWAKE. LIGHT SHINES through my closed eyelids. The faint chirps of a bird follow. My body aches, and my mouth tastes sour. I stay in place, comfortable and warm despite the aches. I'm slow to fully awaken as I figure out what my senses are trying to tell me. I have a headache, but I'm not hungover—that's good.

I nuzzle deeper into the covers.

Wait!

This is not my bed.

My eyes pop open. I sit up, brush the mess of hair out of my face.

I'm not in my dorm. The room is big, airy, clean.

Dylan.

I'm at Dylan's house. But this is not his bedroom.

Then the memories hit me.

Dancing with Dylan and Tommy.

Laughing.

Therapist11.

Dylan is Therapist11.

Me running. And him picking me up and carrying me back.

I scramble out of the bed. I need to get out. I can't face him again.

I find my purse and jacket on a chair. My shoes next to it. I'm moving now, putting my jacket and shoes on, my hands shake so much it takes me three tries to lace my sneakers. I check my bag for my cell and find my keys.

My heart is thundering. I take a deep breath trying to calm myself, but I know I won't be okay until I'm far away from here. I can't see him again. I can't look at him and know that he knows everything. Almost everything about me.

My hand pauses on the doorknob, and I wait—listen for movement outside the door. It's quiet. I open the door and make my way to the stairs, go down the steps like a ghost, cross the living room to the front door.

"Becca? Wait."

Dylan calls to me, but I don't stop. I don't look at him. I can't. I'm out the door and running to my car. He follows me. Stops me on the lawn a few feet away from my car. His hand is gentle on my wrist, he turns me to him.

"Please, stop. Don't run away from me again. Let's talk."

"There's nothing to talk about. I said too much already. You know everything." Almost everything.

"I had no idea it was you, please believe me. I would never do anything like that. I would have referred you to someone else if I ever thought this was possible."

I pull my hand from his grasp. "It's a fucking small world, isn't it?"

He runs both hands through his hair. "Becca, please! I swear, I had no idea. The program received over three thousand calls since it started. This changes nothing."

"It changes everything. Don't you understand? I can't be this person." I slap my chest with both hands. "There can't be an us when you know what happened to me. I can't leave her behind, she's here now, and she makes everything ugly."

"No, she doesn't. There's no her. There's only you, and nothing about you is ugly. Not a single thing. It makes no difference to me."

"It makes a difference to me." I hit my chest with a fist now. "You think I'm good. You think I won't drag you down with me. You don't know everything."

He takes a step closer. "I know everything you told me."

"Not everything. I—" I drop my voice. "I killed him. I watched him die, and I did nothing. I walked away and stayed away for hours. By the time I came back, my mother was screaming in hysterics, and the cops where wheeling Theodore out in a body bag."

Dylan watches me.

I punctuate each word with a thump to my chest. "I. Let. That. Happen."

"How?" Dylan asks.

"What?"

"How did he die?"

"An overdose. What difference does it make? He's dead." My head pounds in rhythm with my heart.

"You couldn't have killed him, then. Not unless you somehow shot him full of drugs. What did the police report say?"

"What does it matter?"

He leans closer. "What did the police report say?"

"It said he OD'd because of a combination of alcohol and drugs. They found Oxycontin, Vicodin and hydrocodone in his blood."

"And how is that your fault?"

"Did you miss the part in which I said I watched him dying and walked away?"

"Did you give him the alcohol and drugs?" He hisses the words.

"What? No! Of course not."

"Then, again, how is it your fault? You didn't hurt him or cause him to die. You walked away, which is a lot less than I would have done. His death is not on you. And good riddance."

I stand there and look at him. Now he knows everything. Why isn't he running as fast as he can? Why is he still standing here?

"I can't do this, Dylan. I can't."

"We can figure it out together."

I need to make him stop. I need to make him understand we can never be. I need to push him away. Now. Before I cave in. I heave in a breath and square my shoulders. Dig deep for the coil of anger inside me. Grab a hold of it. Let it spring.

"I'm not your pet project. I don't need your pity. I'm not your dead girlfriend. You can't redeem yourself through me." The words taste like venom on my tongue, and they bite me.

He flinches, his eyes dull, and he takes a step back, hands dropping to his side.

He looks smaller somehow. "No, you're not. You're not a pet or a project. And you're not Annelise. You're nothing like her." He closes his eyes, and when he opens them again, they're brimming with pain. "Annelise was weak, timid, afraid of life. Even before what happened to her. The world was always too much for her to take. But you? You are none of those things." He comes forward, cutting the space between us in half. "You're strong. Alive. A fire burns inside you. What happened—what that scumbag did to you may have molded your life, yes. It may have even broken you, but you didn't fall apart, and you didn't give up. You rose above, and made yourself better than them and your circumstances."

My head shakes in denial with each word he speaks. My body rejecting what my heart has been trying to tell me for months now. Muscle memory attempts to take over and fight him and everything he says. I cannot accept his kindness. The chaos inside my chest barely contained.

Fear is fighting hope.

Anger fighting trust.

And hate fighting … love?

Yes. Underneath it all, there's love. Fragile and tentative, like a candle flame in the breeze, it flickers and sways, not sure if it wants to grow or extinguish itself.

I don't know when it came to happen. I don't know when I started to care for this man standing in front of me. But I do. I care about Dylan, and I crave him as much as I despise myself for wanting him. I don't want to want him. I don't want to love him. I don't want my skin to anticipate his touch, and my stomach to clench when he's near me.

My heart thunders in my chest to the point of pain. Everything in me rebels against the feelings pouring out of me. I squeeze my eyes shut so I can keep him from seeing the storm raging inside. I want to feel numb again. I want dull and boring and nothingness. I grew comfortable in the absence of love. I don't know how to tame what I feel.

I understand anger. I understand bitterness and sadness. I understand revulsion and fear.

I don't understand this.

I don't understand what he wants to give me. And yet, I desperately want it. Need it. Hunger for it.

I hate feeling this way. Feeling like I'm at his mercy. Like I'm a little kid again, hoping for salvation.

Dylan steps closer. His fingers weave through my hair, and he nudges my chin up with a feathery touch. Our eyes meet, we're inches apart, so close his breath fans across my face, warm and coffee scented. "Becca?"

I bite my tongue to keep from saying what's churning in my chest. To keep from asking him to stop me from running, to keep from showing how vulnerable I feel, and how much I want him to want me, to love me, to need me.

He cradles my face, leans into me, his lips touch my forehead with a kiss so gentle it's barely there, and yet it touches me to the very depths of my soul.

"Let me in," he speaks against my skin. His lips brushing my temple send shivers down my spine. My entire body trembles with the need to give in and the need to run. I'm split in half. Adrenaline pools in my veins.

Fight or flight? I do neither. I freeze. I hide my emotions behind closed eyes. I dare not breathe for fear of what I might do. Of what I might say. He pulls me into his chest, his arms a welcome and warm cage around me. I'm so small inside his embrace I dread I might disappear, evaporate into thin air like I was never here, or that this hug I didn't even know I needed is nothing but a dream or a taunting nightmare. I don't want to want this. I don't want to find comfort in his arms or his touch. Hope is a weakness. A chink in my armor. I cannot allow myself to give in. I can't give him power over me.

His head drops to my shoulder, he molds himself around me, his much bigger body enclosing mine into his, like a shell around me, he envelops me. "Can you feel this?"

I don't move, my arms ache with the need to embrace him, but

I keep them at my side. I don't speak. I don't react. I'm frozen in a battle between agony and hope. I do nothing because I have no idea of what to do. And I don't trust myself to make the right choice.

"Becca?" he calls my name again. But I'm empty of words.

He disengages with just enough space between us so he can see my face. I can feel his gaze burning into my skin. I open my eyes, and I'm instantly lost in his. This is a mistake. This can't be real.

His thumbs caress my cheeks. "Say something! Tell me that what I think is happening between us is true."

I shake my head and step away from him, his hands linger, touching the air where I once stood, and then ever so slowly, they drop to his sides.

The weight of unspoken words hangs between us, like a darting butterfly. Flitting here and there and never landing to rest its wings. That weight settles in my chest and drops to my stomach, bringing me down with it as I fall back into my parked car behind me and lock my knees so as not to slide down to the ground. Not for a moment does his gaze leave my face, reading, learning, assimilating but never judging.

Something that looks a lot like resignation and understanding washes over him. It fills his lungs as he drags a deep breath in, expanding his chest. Then, without a word, he turns and walks away.

He doesn't see the first tear that runs down my face or the ones that follow.

CHAPTER FIFTY

BECCA

I'VE BURIED MYSELF UNDER BLANKETS AND SHUT THE world out since everything happened. Has it really been a week? It almost feels like years have passed. God, I never imagined this could hurt so much.

I have dozens of texts and calls from Tommy. I shut him out too. And a voice message from Dylan that I can't bring myself to listen to. I'm glad no one knows where I am. Lucas' apartment is my sanctuary right now. I'm sure Tommy has gone looking for me in the dorm.

But spring break is almost over, and I'll have to leave soon. Lucas will be back, and I don't belong here.

The only person I communicate with is River, and even then I haven't told her everything. But she's coming over today to talk. I drag myself from the bed and get into the shower. Make myself look human again.

A knock on the door makes me jump even though I'm expecting it. I open the door and step back, River comes in, and my tears start before I even close the door. What's wrong with me? How can I possibly have any more tears to cry?

River pushes the door closed and hugs me. No words are said. She holds me until I run dry again. I step back and walk to the sofa, wrap myself in a blanket.

River stands looking at me. "You look like a wiener in a blanket with just your head popping out."

Only River could make me laugh in a time like this. "You mean a pig in a blanket?"

"Nah, wiener in a blanket is so much more fun to say than pig in a blanket."

"Sit." I wave at a spot next to me.

She kicks her shoes off and sits, her legs crossed on the couch so she can face me. "Okay, friend. What happened?"

I heave in a breath. "Dylan and I are no more."

She nods. "I figured as much. But what exactly happened? You guys were so happy. Last time we talked you were spending Dylan's birthday with him, and everything was great."

"And I did. We were together on his birthday. And it was amazing until it wasn't." Even now it's hard to speak about it.

River listens, and I tell her everything. Leave nothing out. How happy I was. How I loved being with him. How I ran away that night and again the next morning.

She holds my hand through it all, and when I'm done, she grabs a tissue box from the coffee table and gives it to me.

"Do you love him?"

I didn't expect the question and stutter without answering.

"It's not a difficult question. Do you love him?"

"Yes. I do." My heart squeezes under the weight of how much love I feel for Dylan.

"Do you think he loves you?"

"I don't know." I'm afraid to hope he does.

"Think, Becca. How did he act? How did he talk to you? How did he behave?"

Dozens of images of us together play in my mind like the scenes of a romantic comedy. Moments filled with laughter and … loving gestures. "I know he likes me. I don't know if he loves me."

River drops one leg to the floor. "Fair enough. The question is, what do you want to do?"

"I don't know what I want. I want to go back in time and erase everything so I don't feel like this."

"Do you? Do you really want to erase all the times you spent with Dylan?" River challenges me.

I sigh. "No, I don't. I loved every minute. Even in the beginning when he annoyed me, I still enjoyed being close to him."

"Then what are you going to do about it?" Where is she going with this?

"What can I do? It's over!"

"Is it? Is it really over? Because it seems to me that as long as you two have feelings for each other, it's not over. Not by a long shot."

I grab my hair with both hands and tug with a growl. "I don't know what to do."

"If you were telling all of this to the therapist, what do you think he would tell you to do?"

"What?" I blink at her. "What do you mean?"

"You talked to him dozens of time, correct?"

I'm getting hot. I push the blanket off of my shoulders. "Yes."

"You know what he would tell you. What do you have to fix first? Which steps should you take next?"

"He would tell me to figure out why him finding out who I am upset me so much."

"And?" Her one-word question comes with the arching of

an eyebrow.

"I have to work on myself first. I have a shit-ton of crap to dig up."

"We all do. It won't be easy, but you don't have to dig alone. I'm here. I can help."

"Not in this, River. I've been thinking a lot. Heck, that's all I did for a week. Think and cry. Cry and think."

"So, what's next?"

"I have to go back to where it all started. I have to go see my mother first. I won't be able to deal with myself and Dylan until I face her. This has been a long time coming."

"If you want me to come with you—"

"No." I cut her off. "I need to do this alone. But fist I have a few text messages to respond to."

I start with Tommy.

> Becca: Hey. Sorry for ghosting you for a week. I'm OK.

Five seconds is all it took for my phone to ring. "Hi."

"What the hell, Becca. I've been worried sick. I didn't even know if you were alive or dead. Dylan won't tell me what happened. He spends the entire day locked in his office staring at his computer. He shut down and won't say a freaking word." Tommy's voice is both angry and sad.

"I'm sorry. You're right. I'm sorry for worrying you. I wasn't in a good place and needed some time away."

"What the hell happened?"

My eyes sting. "It's not something I want to talk about, but I'm okay, you don't have to worry."

"Did he do something? Did Dylan hurt you somehow?" His voice rises.

Hearing Dylan's name again makes my heart ache. "No. This has nothing to do with Dylan. It's on me. I had a panic attack. And I need time to figure some things out."

"Where are you? I've been to your dorm a dozen times. I even made them open your room. I thought … God. I thought you hurt yourself."

Jesus. I never imagined Tommy would be that worried about me. "I'm at a friend's house. I'm okay, Tommy. I swear. And I'll be back in a couple of days."

There's a long silence where all I can hear is him breathing.

"You sure you're okay?"

"I am. I promise …" I hesitate. "How is he?"

"Miserable, grouchy, running morning, noon, and night."

Running. That's what Dylan does when he can't sleep, or when he's stressed out. "Listen, I have to go. But I'll be back on campus next week. I have a few things I have to do first. But then I'll see you and … and maybe fix this mess I made."

"I want you and him to be happy. He's happiest when he's with you."

"I'm happiest when I'm with him too."

CHAPTER FIFTY-ONE

DYLAN

Becca: Give me time, please.

CHAPTER FIFTY-TWO

BECCA

I PAUSE ON THE SIDEWALK, MY FEET HESITATING TO TAKE that next step.

Everything is the same and yet so different. It's been nearly four years since I last stepped foot in the house. It has never been a home. Not in all the years I lived here. Time worked its unforgiving will over the building. It looks smaller than I remember. The walls, once white, are now the kind of muted gray only time and age can paint on.

My shoes step through mud and leaves where grass had once been. A sudden bang sounds from the house, making me jump. My gaze darts across the yard for the source. All the shutters are missing except for one that hangs by a single hinge, refusing to give in to the ravages of time and let go.

The air smells dry and dusty with a tinge of decay. The type of smell one finds in abandoned buildings.

I take reluctant steps toward the front door, raising my hand to knock when I'm close enough. So many layers of peeling paint, different colors fighting each other like a chaotic and uneven kaleidoscope.

I waver. Do I really want to do this? No. I don't. But I need to. I need to see her again. Speak my mind. Be heard. Maybe give my mother one last chance. See if there is anything that can be salvaged between us even if I don't believe there is.

The palms of my hands dampen, my heart flutters with an uneven tempo. What am I waiting for? I knock on the door. Wait. Knock again.

Thumping sounds come from inside, something crashes to the floor. The door yanks open, and she stands inside. My mother.

A multitude of images flash through my mind. A reverse timeline of my life—from the day I left without saying goodbye to my earliest memories. She's even thinner now, yellowed skin hangs on her bones. Bloodshot eyes look at me, unseeing at first. Then a glimmer of recognition. A smile filled with rotting teeth.

"Becca …" Bony hands reach to me, and she pulls me to her chest. She's frail to the touch. I both crave and am repulsed by the embrace. She steps to the side, making space for me to enter. I freeze at the door. Look around the room, strain to hear the sounds of someone else there with her.

Nothing has changed. The same dirty beige walls greet me. The same stained couch. Three empty soda cans and dirty dishes litter the old wooden table in the middle of the room. The old box TV is on with the sound turned off. A blanket hangs half on and half off the couch as if someone, she, was just lying on it, taking a nap, perhaps.

"Come in. It's only me here." She steps back. "All alone," she adds. A tinge of guilt threatens to surface. I shut it down. She was always good at that. At making me feel guilty with a single word.

I step in, close the door. It's stuffy and too hot inside. The air smells stale. It's a miracle she remembers to pay the utility bills. Maybe someone else does. She never stayed alone too long. But she's no longer the beautiful woman I grew up with. It's hard to imagine anyone being attracted to her sickly figure.

"How are you, Mom?"

"I'm better, much better." She sits on the couch and pats the spot next to her. The same couch Theodore attacked me on. Revulsion sends a shiver down my spine. She doesn't look better.

I move the cans into the trash bin, put the dirty dishes in the sink, and sit on the table instead.

She pulls the blanked over her legs. Tucks it around herself. "How are you? You look good. What have you been doing all this time?"

I swallow. She doesn't even know? "I'm doing well. I'm a senior in college, two more months until graduation."

"I guess all that hard work and studying paid off. God knows I wasn't any help."

Her confession stuns me. This is the first time I have ever heard my mother say or do anything that remotely looks like accountability.

She pulls at a thread in the blanket. "After you left, I was so mad. First Theodore died ..." Her eyes narrow, confused, and her gaze drifts, lost for a moment. She shakes it off. "Then you left. I didn't know you left until the bills piled up, and they cut the power."

Months. I was gone for months before she realized it?

"I thought you were in school still, or working, or hiding. I was in a terrible place. But I'm better now." She lifts a sleeve to scratch at her arm.

Track marks line the inside of her elbow. I can't stop staring at it. Venom bubbles up inside of me and spill out. "You don't look better."

"I knew then you weren't coming back." She continues as if I had said nothing. "I tried to get clean and failed. I failed more times than I can count. But I'm mostly clean now."

"The track marks on your arm say different."

"Ah, those? They're old. I haven't shot in almost a year. They itch like a mother though … but that might be a reaction to the meds too."

What meds? I look around at the mess, an ashtray holds a blunt. Legal as it may be. "And that?" I point at the ashtray.

"That's medicinal."

I snort.

She nods. "It helps me breathe better."

"Breathe better?"

"Ah, yeah. You don't know, do you? How could you know?"

"Know what?" What is she talking about?

"I'm sick. Lung cancer." She laughs. "After all the crap I did, all the drugs and alcohol, cancer is what will take me out. I always thought it would be an overdose."

I'm dizzy, all the blood has left my brain. Cancer? She's lying. She has to be. "Cancer?"

"You're white as a ghost, girl." She pulls the neck of her sweater down, shows me a chemoport before letting go of the shirt. Taps the port under the fabric. "All the shit I took for God knows how many years, and if the cancer don't take me, this poison will."

I'm trembling. I didn't prepare for this. I expected her to either behave as before, with hate and accusations or for her to be high and have another man living here. Or maybe for the house to be empty. But not this. Not her on the verge of death and not even forty yet.

I dig my nails into my thighs. "I don't know what to say."

"Eh, nothing to say. It is what it is. I made some very shitty choices in my life. I said and did some terrible things to you. I let horrible things happen to you. But you were never a mistake. No matter how many times I said it."

My throat closes, and I have to put a hand on it to push down the forming knot. Is this a confession? Is she finally admitting to what happened? A fire burns under me. Of this too I'm robbed. How can I rage? How can I be angry? How can I confront her when she just told me she's dying?

"All the mistakes were mine. I'm sorry. I'm so sorry I was such a horrible mother. I didn't know how to love you. I didn't know how to love myself."

My eyes burn. My chest is a ticking bomb ready to explode, and the pressure in my throat is so big I can't breathe. I open my mouth to speak, but I can't. A croak and a sob are the only things I'm capable of right now.

She goes on. "I got a lot of help at the hospital. Some social worker lady helped me get a small disability check. Not much, but enough to keep the lights on and the water and heat running. The church brings food every week, and the hospital is helping me too. I said that already, right? Sometimes I get confused. I forget things too."

She settles back into the couch. "I'm tired. I think I'll take a nap now." She lies down, closes her eyes and is asleep seconds later.

I'm frozen in place. I don't know what to do. Should I leave? Wait for her to wake up? I check my phone, and it's morning still. I look around again. The house is a mess. Stuff everywhere. I can clean up a little. I can't let her live like this. Not in her condition. I go to her room. The door is closed, and when I open it, I know why. It smells like vomit. She got sick in here. I open the windows, let the brisk March air in. Take all the bedding down. Bring it to the garage where the washer and dryer are. Put a load in.

I will need supplies if I'm to clean this house. I drive to the store, buy gloves, cleaning products, paper towels. And also get some packaged foods she can easily prepare.

Back at the house, she's still sleeping. A low rattling and wheezing sound, the only sign she's alive. I go to her room and clean it the best I can, throw away the trash, paper plates, piles of old magazines. None of this can be good for her, trying to breathe in this dirty and dusty room. It's frigid because of the open windows, but at least it no longer smells. I find clean sheets in an armoire and make the bed, but I'll have to wait for the blanket that's now in the dryer. I move to the bathroom and clean that next. Then the kitchen. I throw away old food I find in the fridge, and clean that too. Then put the fresh fruit I bought inside, along with bottles of Gatorade.

I do a few more loads of laundry, while she continues to sleep. I clean around her in the living room as quietly as I can. I've swept the floors and mopped. I don't think this house has been properly cleaned since I left. But being so small, it takes a little over two hours. My bedroom door stands closed. I haven't stepped in yet. I check on my mother again. Then open the door. It screeches with disuse. It's like stepping back in time. My bed is still made and set against a wall the same way I left it. There's a thin covering of undisturbed dust everywhere. The urge to close the door and run is overwhelming, but I fight it and stand my ground. I stay still, taking in everything again. This room is even smaller than my dorm room. Just big enough for the twin-sized bed. A small closet is to the left, and a desk and a kitchen chair are placed next to the door. I step in. Sun-faded curtains hang open. The magazine cutouts I taped to the walls are dulled gray by dust. I open the closet. Thin metal hangers dangle from the single rod across the top. I only left behind the clothes that no longer fit me or were too ratty to wear. Some magazines lie on the bottom. I'd grab them from people's garbage on recycling days. And sometimes I got lucky and found books too. I close the closet door and retrace my steps backward until I'm standing outside the room. Then close that door, too. No need to clean this room or revisit ghosts from the past.

It's past lunchtime, and my stomach grumbles. I go back to the kitchen and grab ingredients to make a sandwich. Check on my mother again. She stirs, mumbles something I can't make out. Opens her eyes. Blinks at me several times. That old familiar angry expression that I know so well twists her thin pale face, then she blinks again and relaxes. "You're here? I thought I had dreamed that."

"I'm here for a little longer, then I have to go. Are you hungry? I got food."

"Food? We don't have no food."

"I went to the store. Got a few things for lunch and dinner. Stuff you can prepare with no trouble. Some frozen meals, pasta, and fruit."

She stretches her arm to me. "Okay then. Help me up, please."

I take her frail hand. I can feel every bone under the dry, patchy skin. Help her up. She looks around and walks to the kitchen. "You cleaned?"

"A little, yes."

"Looks good, thank you."

"Sit down, Mom. I'll make you a sandwich."

I make the sandwiches in silence. She watches my every move. I set a plate in front of her and take a seat on the other side of the table. "What would you like to drink? I got milk and some Gatorade too."

"Gatorade, please." Her eyes light up in a way I can't remember ever seeing.

I give her a glass and open the bottle for her. Get myself water. "I cleaned your room too, did some laundry. You can sleep on your bed tonight. It will be more comfortable."

"Ah, thank you. I couldn't make myself go in there. Every time I tried to clean, I got sick again."

She's so polite, I'm not used to this. It's disarming. I came here ready for a fight, ready to confront her for everything she did to me and for everything she allowed to happen to me. But now? Now I can't. And I don't know if I'm mad that this too was taken from me or relieved that I don't have to bring up the past and all of its sordid details.

She eats with slow, measured bites, as if it hurts to swallow. "Where do you go to college?"

"Riggins."

"That's a good school. When is your graduation again?"

"Less than two months, May seventeen."

She's pensive. "May? I guess I won't make it, then."

"What do you mean?"

"The doctors gave me a month, maybe six weeks, if I'm lucky. I've never been lucky." She attempts a laugh, but it sounds like a cry and turns into a coughing fit. She covers her mouth with a napkin, her frail body convulsing with each attempt to draw breath.

I come around to her side, hesitate, step closer and rub her back, as gentle as I can. Tears blur my vision. Why? Why is this upsetting to me? This woman who I have not seen in four years. This woman who was never a mother to me. This woman who never loved me or cared for me. And yet I cry for her. Knowing that she'll die in a few weeks tears something in me.

After all this time, and after everything she did, I still love her. It surprises me, and it doesn't.

When the cough subsides, and she stops gasping for air, I go back to the other side of the table. "There's nothing else they can do?"

She takes a drink. "No. And even if they could, I don't know that I'd want it. I'm tired. So tired. I did enough living. Bad, horrible living. I'm done."

I reach for her hand across the table. "Mom ..." I don't know what to say, but in this moment I forgive her. "I guess we must make the most of that time."

She squeezes my hand. "I'd like that. And maybe I can be a good mother for you now."

I want to believe it. And I want to believe that a month or two will be enough to erase a lifetime of pain and neglect. Maybe there will be a miracle cure in the next few weeks. One can hope. But ...

Sometimes hope is a dragon.

Sometimes hope is a butterfly with broken wings.

CHAPTER FIFTY-THREE

BECCA

I SPOT MY FATHER CROSSING THE STREET TO GET TO MY building and meet him halfway.

"Thanks for meeting me. I needed to talk to someone, and you're the only one who can understand this."

"Sure. Is everything okay with you?" His gaze searches my face.

"Yeah, I'm fine. Let's get some coffee, then we can talk."

He falls into step next to me for the next couple of minutes until we get to the mostly empty cafeteria. We get our coffees and find a quiet place to sit against a wall.

I meet his eyes. "This is about Mom. I went to see her yesterday."

"How is she?"

I shake my head. "Not good. Not good at all."

He takes a sip of his coffee and waits for me to elaborate.

"This … this was the first time I went back since I left for college. Nearly four years." If my confession surprises him, he doesn't show it.

"Was she mean to you?"

"Not at all."

He leans in. "Was it drugs? Was she high?"

I shake my head again, dreading the word. Is there a more hated or vicious word in any language? "Cancer. She has cancer."

He falls back into his chair, his shoulders drop, his lips move silently, and his gaze shifts to the side as if trying to comprehend what I told him.

"Cancer?"

"Yes. Lung cancer. She ... she looked terrible. Sickly and emaciated."

"Is she getting help, getting any treatments?"

"She said she was, she showed me a chemoport on her chest. It's not good. Not at all. She doesn't have much more time."

"How long?" His voice trembles.

"A month, six weeks at the most."

"God." A hand covers his mouth, then drops. "Thank you for telling me. I would like to do something. What can I do?"

"I don't know. The house was a mess. She said she has a caseworker who helps, but I was in such a shock I forgot to ask about it. And she was so tired, she fell asleep after a few minutes of talking. I cleaned the house, bought some food. I'm not sure how much more I can do."

"I could get someone to help. Check on her, clean the house, make some food. You think she'd be okay with that?"

"I don't think she's in a position to reject any help. And I would like that. I'd feel better if I knew for sure someone was there."

"I'll take care of it. Don't worry. I'm glad you told me."

I'm glad too. It's nice being able to talk to someone who understands. "It's a four-hour round trip for me. With classes coming to a close and work, I can't be there every day. On some weekends, maybe. But I work a lot of weekends too."

He sits back. "I want to stop by and talk to her. Is that okay with you?"

"Yes, of course."

"Would you want to go together sometime, maybe?"

"Yes. She's different now. I think she would like to see us both together." I hope she would. I hope that seeing me with my father would make her feel better for all the crap she put me through. Maybe then she can forgive herself for keeping him out of my life. And I can forgive myself too.

"Okay. I'll go visit her tomorrow. I'll ask about the caseworker and get in touch with them, see what I can do to help."

"She said someone from a church was bringing food in. But the fridge was empty. I'm not sure if I believe her, or if they don't visit her enough."

"I'll check into that too and let you know."

"Thanks—" I hesitate, then go for it. "Thanks, Dad. I don't think I can do this alone."

His eyes fill with unshed tears, and he smiles. "You're not alone. You'll never be alone again. And thank you."

"What for?"

"For calling me Dad."

CHAPTER FIFTY-FOUR

DYLAN

It's been weeks since Becca's last text message. Time. She asked me for time, and if it's all I can give her, I will. But that doesn't mean I can't try to check on her through other means.

I ruffle Tommy's hair and pull a chair to sit next to him. He inhaled the breakfast I made for us.

"Want more?"

"No, thanks." He speaks around a mouth full of pancakes.

I wait until he swallows, finishes his orange juice and settles back into his chair. "How is she?"

His shoulders lift nearly to his ears. "Okay, I guess. She says she's okay, and she looks all right to me. But she won't tell me what happened, and *you* won't tell me what happened, so why am I the errand boy between the two of you?"

"Errand boy? What do you mean?"

"Every time I see her, she asks about you."

"She does?" Hope plays games with my heart, and it bounces around my chest tripping on itself.

"Yes." Tommy pushes his dish away. "I wish you two would

figure out whatever it is that's broken and fix it already. I like both of you better when you are with each other."

I cross my arms on the table, scratch at the stubble on my face. "I like myself better when I'm with her too."

"See what I'm talking about?" He gets up and pushes his chair back with more force than necessary. He's clearly annoyed. "She told me the exact same thing."

"She did?" My heart is doing somersaults now.

"I don't get it. You two are idiots. You know what? I'm going to her building right now and telling her that to her face. You're an idiot, and she's an idiot. And I'm the idiot in the middle."

"She asked me to give her time, Tommy. You know that."

"The thing about time, big brother, is that you can never get back the time you wasted."

CHAPTER FIFTY-FIVE

BECCA

I PACE MY ROOM, SHAKING MY HANDS AND KEEPING AN EYE on my laptop screen. Waiting for his link to go live. If I keep this pace much longer, I'll wear down a path on the floor.

The moment his name shows in bold, I jump on the bed. I nearly drop the laptop on the floor in my eagerness to get to him before someone else does. I hit the link to dial him and put my earbuds in. He answers on the first ring.

"Becca? Is that you?"

It's so strange to hear him say my name this way that I'm momentarily frozen.

"Becca, talk to me, please."

I swallow the lump taking residence in my throat. "Hi. Yes, it's me."

"God, Becca." The sound of a loud breath comes through the connection. "You asked me to give you time, and I have, but it's been weeks."

"I know. I'm sorry, I had—have a lot of crap to work on. I've been busy. But that's not the reason I ghosted you."

"No, it's not." He sounds sad.

"I had a lot to think about. That day—your birthday was both the best and worst day of my life. It was the highest high and the lowest low. I was so happy, and then everything came crashing down." I stop, breathe, blink away the tears. Dylan's rhythmic tapping tells me he's still listening. "You finding out everything was my worst nightmare. And then the stuff I told you about Theodore … I was sure you'd hate me or call the cops on me. God. I expected the police to come find me for a week."

"I would never. My only regret is not being able to kill him myself." There's such a contained rage in his voice it surprises me.

I never imagined Dylan as a violent man.

I lick my dry lips. "I want to thank you for everything you did for me. For listening and guiding and pushing me when I didn't want to see or do what I needed to do to free myself from the self-imposed prison I created."

"You don't have to thank me. How have you been? Tommy said you're okay, and you said you needed time. But not being able to see you and talk to you …"

"It's been hard for me too. But I needed this time to figure myself out."

"I miss you, Becca."

"I miss you too. And I miss our talks."

"Our talks? Is this what this call is about?" His voice goes cold.

"I need your advice."

"My advice?" His tone is incredulous and not professional at all.

I take a breath, dig deep for courage and push it out of my mouth. "Yes. You see, there's this guy I like, and I'm not sure how to tell him. We had a bit of a misunderstanding and a fight. I want to let him know how very attracted I am to him. I want to let him know how much I miss him, and how much I care about him. So, how should I do this?"

"Have you tried just saying the words?" His voice softens.

"I'm not that great at expressing myself. What if he's changed his mind and doesn't want to be with me anymore?" I hold my breath.

"He hasn't."

"I come with a lot of baggage. What if he tires of me?"

"He won't. He has baggage of his own too."

"Do you think there's a chance this guy cares for me as much as I care for him?"

"He loves you, Becca."

Oh my God. My heart stops for a second and then resumes beating so fast it's like a sonic boom inside my chest. "I love him too."

"You should invite him to come to commencement tomorrow to talk to you."

My entire body is trembling. "Do you want to come to commencement tomorrow and see me graduate?"

"I'd love to."

"Okay. I'll see you tomorrow."

"Tomorrow."

CHAPTER FIFTY-SIX

BECCA

THE WEATHER IS PERFECT FOR GRADUATION DAY. CLEAR blue skies. The sun is shining, and a balmy breeze ruffles the flowers and leaves on the trees that I can see through my dorm room window.

How long have I waited for this day? It's finally here.

I adjust my cap, grab the green stole and put it over my shoulders and look at myself in the mirror hanging on the back of my door. The stole makes my eyes look greener. I can't stop grinning. A knock on the door makes me jump.

"Come on down, it's showtime!" Tommy's voice calls from the other side.

I open the doors and get squished in a hug before I can even say a word.

He steps back, takes a bow. "My lady."

I grab my cell phone and keycard and put them in my pocket.

He gives me his arm. "Ready?"

"Yes." I take his arm and close the door behind us.

The ceremony is being held in the campus Green. The

biggest open area at Riggins. Hundreds, maybe thousands, of chairs have been set up in front of a large stage decorated in black and green. The same colors of my gown and stole.

Tommy walks me to the area where all the graduating students are gathering. Organized by major and last name.

He kisses me on the cheek. "I'll see you after. Break a leg."

"That's for theater," I say.

"And that"—he points a couple hundred yards away—"is a stage."

He got me there.

Tommy points at a willow tree. "Meet me back here, right by this tree, when it's over. Okay? I'll be waiting for you."

"Yes." I squeeze his hand and walk into the auditorium, finding my spot.

My stomach rolls in anticipation. Four years of hard work, studying, volunteering, busting my ass to get here. And beyond that, how hard I applied myself in high school to have a better chance—the only chance at escaping my life so I could become someone else, someone better than my circumstances afforded me.

And now it's finally here. Commencement. Graduation day.

"Becca Jones."

I walk on trembling legs when they call my name, blinking away the tears when the Riggins president gives me my diploma. My hand shakes in his when he congratulates me. A long and loud whistle pierces the air following my name and a low rumble of laughter rolls through the crowd. I search the crowd—a sea of black and green among the students. Family and guests sit behind them. Too many for me to see who whistled for me. I exit the stage and take back my place. I clap when they call River's and Skye's names.

Two hours go by and the ceremony is over with flying caps and shouts. Graduates and families mingle. There are people everywhere. I pick my way through the crowd to the tree Tommy asked me to meet him at.

I freeze in place, my feet rooted to the ground. I sway a little, mimicking the vines in the willow tree Tommy stands near. He's not alone.

I'm overcome with gratitude. I hoped he'd come, but I didn't expect this. The emotions I have been keeping at bay catch up with me. A sob escapes. I press my knuckles to my mouth, blink away the pesky tears.

Tommy stands with Hunter and Mara—my brother and sister—and their mom, Linda. My father pushes my mother in a wheelchair. She's gotten weaker and thinner since I saw her a week ago. A thick blanket covers her legs, a shawl sits around her frail shoulders and her bald head is covered by a knit cap. She's hooked to an oxygen machine. She defied the doctor's prediction of six weeks, but anyone looking at her knows she doesn't have much longer.

Mara and Hunter rush to me and hug my legs. I drop to my knees and embrace them back. I'm enveloped in a cocoon of little arms and giggles. I could get used to this.

"Congratulations, Becca." Linda pulls me into a hug.

My father comes to me with open arms, and I let myself be hugged by him with no restraints. "You came," I whisper into his shoulder.

"Of course, I did. I would never miss this. As long as I have breath in my lungs, I'll never miss another important day in your life again." He pulls back, holds my shoulders, making sure our gazes connect. "I'm so proud of you. I couldn't be more proud if I tried. I love you, remember that always."

I nod, too filled with emotion to say anything. Hug him again.

"Your mom," he whispers.

I step back from him and walk to my mom, kneel on the grass and hold her hands. "Thanks for coming, Mom. I know this is hard for you."

A smile cracks her thin lips. "You're strong. You're so much stronger than I ever was or could be." She pulls her hands from mine and cups my face, speaking with slow, labored breaths.

I cover her hands on my face with mine. Swallow down the knot in my throat. I have no idea what to say. But that's okay, she understands me. She knows I have forgiven her. Her hands drop to her lap, burrow under the blanket. She's dying before my eyes.

My father puts a hand on my shoulder, squeezes, then moves her wheelchair into a sunny spot. She closes her eyes and tilts her head up to the sun.

Tommy steps in and hugs me. It's a much-needed distraction. "Don't forget me."

"Nah, never. Thank you for being here. You're a good friend, Tommy."

He whispers in my ear, "I'm not alone."

I step back. "What do you mean?"

He nods toward the willow tree.

Dylan.

He's leaning on the tree, legs crossed at the ankles, hands in his jacket pocket, looking casual and absolutely perfect.

He pushes off of the tree and takes lazy steps my way. People call his name and wave. He acknowledges them and continues to walk in my direction. My heart takes a dive into my stomach when he stands in front of me. He hasn't shaved in a few days.

My hands ache to touch him, I cross my arms and grasp my elbows.

A lazy, sexy smile grazes his lips. "Hi."

I want to taste that smile. "Hi."

He flexes his fingers, steps closer, inches between us. "You did it."

"I did it." Everything and everyone fades away. It's just the two of us standing here.

He reaches for me, touches the tassel, letting it slide between his fingers. "You're all done now."

Shivers run down my spine, and it has nothing to do with the cool breeze ruffling my hair. "Not quite. I got accepted for a master's program. Starting all over again in September."

"Here?" He searches my face, a smile spreading on his lips.

"No."

His face falls, the smile gone. "Where?"

"UV."

"As in the University of Vermont?"

"That's the one."

His smile returns. "Not too far, then."

"No, thirty minutes away."

"Why? I thought you wanted to stay here and work with Magda."

"I did. I do. I'll still work with her. She's helping me with a job. But there was another little matter to deal with."

He tilts his head. "Which little matter?"

"You know, the matter of a grad student dating a professor."

His smile broadens. "You know there's no policy in the books against it, right?"

"I do. But still. I didn't want to call attention to it and have anyone talking. Especially when he's a professor of ethics."

"A professor of ethics, huh? Who's this lucky guy you plan on dating?"

I almost make a joke, come up with something clever or evasive. But decide the plain truth is best. "You."

"Oh my God, get a room already. The eye-fucking is killing me!"

River. Of course it had to be her. So much for not calling attention to us and having people talking. Everyone is looking for whom she's talking about. We take a step back from each other.

"Nothing to see here, move along, people. You graduated, now go away." She approaches us, followed by her new guy. She engulfs me in a tight hug, then play-hits Dylan in the shoulder. His reaction is comical. Brows pop up, he sidesteps and glances at me.

"I knew it." River goes on. "Called it almost a year ago. First week of classes."

She did.

"River," I whisper-shout.

"Whaaat?" she whisper-shouts back at me. "If he's going to be in the family, he better get used to me."

Dylan looks from her, to me, and to her boyfriend, Liam.

Liam shrugs. "Just go with it, dude. It's a lot easier. Trust me."

"Guys?" my dad calls. "I got reservations in thirty minutes. Everyone hungry?"

He looks at Dylan and Tommy. "Let's go, you two are coming too."

When I first walked into Riggins, I never imagined I'd leave with a best friend for life.

I never imagined I'd leave with a family.

I never imagined I'd leave with a man who loves me and whom I love just as much.

So much can happen in four years. So much can happen in a few months, in a single moment.

For so long I allowed myself and my life to be defined by what happened to me. Defined by the hurt, angry, and afraid girl I once was.

No more.

It's not as simple as that, I know. I have much to do. Loving myself, learning to heal and forgive is something I may have to work on for the rest of my life.

I have learned I can't change the past. But as my father said on that very first day we met, I can change the future.

The choices I make today, the people I keep in my life will set the path of my tomorrow. And I'll be damned if I don't make it a much better one than I ever thought possible.

EPILOGUE
BECCA

Two Years Later

"When are you guys going to make me an uncle?"

Tommy's question startles me so much I drop the cake pan I'm washing into the sink. The sound reverberates throughout the quiet kitchen.

"Jesus, Tommy. You scared the heck out of me." I grab the pan and finish rinsing it, ignoring his crazy question.

"I'm home. Smells so good in here—oh, hey, Tommy. Didn't know you were coming over today," Dylan says when he walks into the kitchen.

I smile. Looking at him always makes me smile. "I made you banana chocolate chunk cake."

Dylan slugs his brother's shoulder, then ruffles his hair before stopping behind me and holding me to him. My back to his front. He drops a kiss on my shoulder and a chaste peck on my lips when I look up at him.

"Yum." I don't know if Dylan is referring to me or the cake.

Tommy drags a chair and sits at the island. "Don't ignore me. When are you guys going to make me an uncle?"

Dylan stiffens behind me. "What?"

"You've been dating for two years, the last year of which you're living together. It's time, no?"

Dylan steps back from me. I turn around, grab a dish towel and dry my hands. Don't look at Dylan. We've never talked about the future or kids in any meaningful way. Dylan knows the idea scares me. We're taking it a day at a time.

Dylan crosses his arms, leans on the sink next to me. "What are you talking about, Tommy?"

"You two and this whole 'taking it slow, a day at a time' thing. Two years. That's like …" He pauses and looks up, his mouth moving silently. "Like seven hundred thirty days. That's enough thinking. I'm not getting any younger, and I want a nephew or niece to spoil."

Dylan's body shifts next to me, and I meet his gaze. One eyebrow raised. I don't know what to say either. I take a page out of Dylan's therapy book. "What makes you say that?"

"I thought it would be fun to have a baby in the house again. Bring some life back into it. Make some changes."

As far as I know, no changes have been made to the house since their parents died. A baby would definitely force Dylan to make some changes. He has kept it up and painted the house, but always the same colors.

Dylan is nodding. "You're right. The house could use a freshening up. But I don't think we need a baby for that."

"How about a dog instead?" Tommy says.

"A dog?" Dylan scratches his head.

"Yes." Tommy nods aggressively. "This house needs a dog for sure."

I shrug. "I've never had a dog before. I like dogs."

"And I'm moving back in. I'm tired of the dorms. So next semester, I'll be home, and I can take care of it. We can go to the shelter, and I'll have the entire summer to train her and—"

"Tommy! Is this your roundabout way of telling me you want to move back in? Because if so, you don't need a baby or a dog for that."

"I know."

"This is your home. This will always be your home. We"— Dylan points at the three of us—"are a family, and will always be."

"Can I still get a dog though?"

Dylan nudges me with his shoulder. "Guess we're getting a dog."

I smile. "Can we name it River?"

Dear reader:

The Riggins U series is finished—for now, anyway. Thank you for joining me in this journey along with these characters who are real to me and live on in their own universe.

I want to thank you for coming along on this ride. I hope you enjoyed reading Becca and Dylan's story.

I would love to read your thoughts on it. Please consider leaving a brief review in one or more of the following:

Amazon
GoodReads
BookBub

AFTERWORD

As promised, I highly recommend these books.
They have been an invaluable resource.

The Body Keeps the Score: Brain, Mind, and Body in the Healing of Trauma by Bessel van der Kolk MD.

It Wasn't Your Fault: Freeing Yourself from the Shame of Childhood Abuse with the Power of Self-Compassion by Beverly Engel.

Daring Greatly: How the Courage to Be Vulnerable Transforms the Way We Live, Love, Parent, and Lead by Brené Brown.

And also RAINN.org. You don't have to be silent.

BOOKS BY ERICA ALEXANDER

Stand Alone Books

Courage, Dear Heart

In Her Eyes

Seventeen Wishes (free)

Riggins U Series

Because of Logan

Because of Liam

Because of Dylan

Resources for Authors

500 Words and 500 More: Original

500 Words and 500 More: A Spooky Version

500 Words and 500 More: The romance version

Would you like a signed paperback?

Find them at:

authorericaalexander.com/store

Want a free book?

Join my newsletter and download One Wild Night.

ACKNOWLEDGMENTS

Writing is a solitary endeavor, but that does not mean that we are alone in this author journey. The book you hold in your hands, be it virtual words on a device or a paperback, is just the tip of an iceberg made up of many people. People who stand in the shadows and behind the curtains. But their support and presence is no less important. While I can't name every person who in one way or another guided and helped me in this journey, my heartfelt thanks travels across the universe to each of them, and each of you.

To my husband—my real life book boyfriend—I'll love you across space and time and multiple life times.

To my two boys, who taught me the meaning of unconditional love. You are as excited as I am about every book. But no, you can't read them.

Thank you Johana Vera for all the support, and for being my side-kick from the other side of the world. Can't wait to read your books.

Thank you Giseli Vargas for being an awesome book-buddy and friend, and sorry, Sophia—you can't read my books until you're at least 30. #Momrules.

Thanks Lisa Hall-Wilson, and also all the girls in the Deep POV workshop. You were the first to have eyes in this story and your feedback was invaluable.

To the dozens of mental health professionals who took the time to listen to my questions and answer them, I thank you again. I have learned much from you.

I also want to thank my fellow authors Mia Kayla, Lisa Suzanne and Erika Kelly. Your support makes all the difference.

And last, but not least, I want to say thanks to *you* reading these words right now.

Thank you for the kindness, for telling me the words I've written have touched you. You have no idea how meaningful it is to me that something I created has touched you. Because above all, as human beings, what we crave most is connection. And words are a beautiful bridge between us.

Much love,
Erica

Erica Alexander

RIP YOUR HEART OUT ROMANCE

Erica Alexander is known for crafting emotional stories filled with complex characters, a touch of angst, and just the right amount of humor. She loves taking her characters—and readers—on a journey that may be bumpy but always ends with a well-earned happily ever after.

Happily married to her husband for over 30 years, Erica is a proud mom to two amazing kids who inspire her every day. When she's not busy catering to the small feral cat colony she cares for—or tending to her two rescue cats and loyal pup—she's likely reading, baking something delicious, or binging Netflix and Prime marathons.

Erica lives in New Jersey with her family and her menagerie of furry friends.

You can find Erica at: